# BLOOD FROM A STONE

## DAVID M. SALKIN

D1319125

Blood from a Stone
ISBN # 978-1-83943-975-9
©Copyright David M. Salkin 2021
Cover Art by Louisa Maggio ©Copyright April 2021
Interior text design by Claire Siemaszkiewicz
Totally Bound Publishing

Published in 2021 by Totally Bound Publishing, United Kingdom.

# BLOOD FROM A STONE

# Dedication

Dear Readers,

It's been three years since you read my last story. This book is dedicated partly to you, with my thanks for reading my books. It's also dedicated to a few very special people who left this Earth since my last book hit the shelves.

My dad, my hero and my rock, left me on my birthday in 2018 after we watched the sun come up together. It was the proper ending to an amazing life. I miss him every day, and still reach for the phone to call him.

A week later, one of my best friends, Kristian Rex, joined Dad in the great beyond. Kristian left us way before his time and left a huge hole. His talent and larger-than-life persona are so greatly missed. The "two Martys", Marty Moore and Marty Strumpf, also left too soon. These were all great human beings. A solid reminder to have fun every day, because this trip is so damn short.

Thanks to my editor, Jamie Rose, for surgically repairing any issues in the manuscript, as well as Totally Bound Publishing, for believing in this novel. A few friends will find their names in these pages, and no, I never asked for permission. They usually don't resemble the real person, although Colonel Cantor is a sommelier, cook, great friend and somewhat Cory-like. If you see your name, it just means I love ya...even if I kill you on paper.

Last, and certainly not least, this book, like all others, is dedicated to my family, my friends, and the countless Americans who have worn the uniform of my beloved nation.

# Chapter One

Harkers Island, N.C.

Amanda was driving down from Twin Oaks. I had a bottle of Italian red, a Super Tuscan called *Le Volte* by Ornellaia, decanting in the kitchen. I'd made a puttanesca sauce, and the garlic, red peppers and crushed anchovies sautéing in olive oil had perfumed my new home. The sizzle was a magical noise. Into that, I'd added diced Kalamata olives, capers, tomato paste and crushed tomatoes.

The spaghetti alla puttanesca was just a little taste — a traditional Italian pasta before the main course. The *secondi* would be a huge bone-in rib-eye steak, grilled out back on the patio. I had dry-rubbed the steak with my list of secret ingredients. It's a secret because I never make anything the same way twice, so it's a secret to me, too. A little sautéed broccoli rabe and *badda-bing*, dinner would be served. It would be our first meal together in the new house. I was trying to cook my way into her staying with me forever.

In my other life, I had eaten MREs on a regular basis — government-supplied packets of food designed to make you angry enough to kill people. 'MRE' — *Meals Rejected by Ethiopians, Meals Rarely Edible, Meals Requiring Enemas, Massive Rectal Expulsions*. You get the idea. They weren't very good. As a result, I learned to cook — foraging and becoming a creative genius to turn the rancid packets into something my comrades and I might actually eat.

Amanda arrived right on time, and with her, a breath of fresh air and an aura of positive energy and bright light that I'd been missing all my life. Her mere presence made me smile. I was hoping my cooking skills would make up for whatever other shortcomings I have. It seemed to be working. I have two great skills — cooking and killing people, and I planned to leave the death and destruction part in my former life. I was determined to be a kinder, gentler version of myself going forward. I would gourmet my way into Amanda's heart.

Dinner was a smashing success, with conversation that covered a hundred topics and had us both smiling like lovestruck teenagers as we caught up on each other's weeks. It was pretty darn perfect. After dinner, we finished that great bottle of Ornellaia, opened a bottle of port and decided to take a walk to the beach.

It was the kind of peaceful night that reminds one of how amazing life can be when everything falls into place. We ended up in the warm, flat ocean up to our knees and I asked her yet again about moving in. This time she didn't say 'no'. Instead, she talked about maybe trying to find a physical therapy job down here, closer to the island.

We walked home and sat outside in the back garden, looking at the stars. The moon lit the white marble faces of the two angels who resided in my yard. The pair had stood sentinel there for years before I'd purchased the house. They came alive softly in the moonlight, and with them, their sad story hung in the still air. The house had a history—one that the folks on Harkers Island wanted to forget.

On Sunday, after a late, leisurely brunch, Amanda left. It was like the air had been sucked out of the house. Loneliness snuck back into my soul and once again I had to fight off the ghosts of those last days in Afghanistan.

I needed a mission to focus on. And this time, it would be for *me*. A wine cellar... It would be a surprise for Amanda when she came back down in two weeks.

When I had purchased the house, I had been surprised to find it had a basement. The island is only a few feet above sea level. When this house had been built, the foundation had been set on a man-made hill, making the house one of the tallest on the island. It made the stately home regal, perched slightly above the rest of the houses like a castle above the serfs. It had an attitude—and I probably had one of the only basements on the island. There were plenty of newer and fancier homes, several worth seven figures, but this house had character—along with that dark history.

The basement was cool, the perfect temperature for wine. I'd sketched out a design and purchased lumber and some tools. The first thing I did was put in some overhead fluorescent lights. Then I scrubbed the poured concrete floor. The walls were cinderblock, with a few open crawlspaces.

Channeling my energy into something positive, I was going to finish making a rack system against one of the walls. Nothing too fancy. I would have the shelves slightly pitched forward. That way I could see the labels and keep the corks angled to the floor. It was a great way to design a wine cellar, but I couldn't take credit for inventing it. Back in my days with Special Forces, a buddy and I used to kill time talking about our dream houses, and all of them included a great wine cellar. He would have built it someday—I'm sure of it—if some fanatic wearing a bomb vest hadn't run into his tent one morning in Kabul and killed him and a few other great guys I knew. I'd build it for him. And that first bottle would be used to toast my friend.

I was cleaning off the cinderblock wall, getting ready to nail in the studs, when the beam of my flashlight caught the edge of something inside the crawlspace. That was when my dream house turned into a nightmare and ancient history became my new reality.

Sitting on the sand behind the top of the cinderblock wall was a small leather-covered book. Old and worn... I picked it up and looked at the cover. It must have been covered with doodles and cartoon flowers years ago, but the ink had faded, and insects and moisture had damaged it. When I opened the front cover, it cracked slightly at the binding.

*Casey A. Stone 1991.*

It took me a moment to realize what it was—a diary.

The paper was stiff and crinkly in my hands. The penmanship was neat and feminine...

My brain started playing catch-up, making the hair on the back of my neck stand.

*Casey Stone.*

She was one of the angels in my yard.

# Chapter Two

Afghanistan — Back in the Day

A million miles away and maybe three centuries back in time before that day I found the diary, I was with the 75th Ranger Regiment in Afghanistan.

Near Khost.

In August.

With a hundred pounds on my back and a hundred degrees blasting in my face.

I served in the 75th Ranger Regiment for nine years before being selected for 1st Special Forces Operational Detachment-Delta. Delta operators simply referred to our organization as 'the unit' and we filled a variety of counter-terrorism roles, all of which relied on speed, surprise and extreme violence. Because of our specialized missions and covert activities, we were given a lot of latitude when it came to weapons, uniforms and haircuts while in the field. That was a nice way of saying we didn't look like American soldiers. We looked more like a bunch of terrifying, long-haired, bearded mercenaries from Hell. Or Afghan locals.

We started out early to take advantage of the darkness and avoid the heat. The day went longer than planned because this was the Army, and nothing *ever* went according to plan. A quick recon and raid to take out a few high-value targets ended up being a full-scale battle against superior numbers high in the mountains.

We came under withering fire from the mouth of a cave above us. I grabbed my guys and a half-dozen Rangers and started heading up the steep slope toward the cave to eliminate the machine guns and RPGs.

I was in command of my three-man Delta team. Sanchez and Watters, outstanding NCOs, were both staff sergeants. Sanchez reminded me through his shooting why I was glad he was on our side. We led the Rangers quickly and silently up the steep left flank, following a goat trail, weaving through the rocks, while the bulk of our Ranger force kept up fire support to our right.

It took twenty minutes to get close to the cave.

I carried an MK-16 SCAR assault rifle and a Sig Sauer P226 pistol, but it was my compact shotgun that I wanted in my hands when I was going to be up close and personal. Ice, a Mossberg Compact Cruiser. While a sawed-off shotgun isn't exactly sexy in a world of fancy automatic weapons, I *loved* that shotgun. And its vicious firepower had saved me too many times to count. I wore it across my back on a strap when not in use, like a samurai warrior, and could have it in firing position from my back to forward-fire in one second.

As we picked our way through the boulders and got closer, the enemy soldiers in the cave spotted us and readjusted their fire. The tracer rounds looked like spears of light coming out of the hot sun. Incoming rounds were bouncing around us.

"Watters! With me! Sanchez, kill that motherfucker on the PK! *Cover fire!*"

Watters was bigger and faster than me. I'm no slouch, but Watters should have been making ten million a year playing linebacker in the NFL. The two of us started sprinting while Sanchez used his sniper rifle on the targets around the cave. The Rangers were laying down suppressing fire as they followed us up through the rocks.

When we got closer to the mouth of the cave, the goat trail ended. Moving forward exposed to enemy fire required some trickier climbing. Sanchez was popping off targets near the cave, but that damn PK machine gun was raining down holy hell. The Ranger closest to me, one of the newer guys in his platoon, decided to be a hero. He ran to my right and cooked off a grenade to toss up into the cave.

I could see the wire from twenty feet away. How the hell did he miss it? I shouted as loud as I could. And that was the last thing I remember.

Sanchez told me later, as we were waiting for the PJs—Para Rescue Jumpers, crazy-ass Air Force medics—to come haul my bleeding ass out, that the kid had tripped the wire and taken out the whole front of the cave. The Hajis hadn't thought it out so well, because the detonation had been so damn big that it had killed most of them, too. They made their own bombs—Improvised Explosive Devices. IEDs—full of pieces of chain-link fence, scrap metal, ball bearings, spent shell casings and whatever the fuck else they could find on the ground. It was a good thing I'd had my tetanus shots.

Watters had caught a few scratches, but not enough to take him out of the fight. My vest saved my life, but it didn't cover everything. I almost had my right arm blown out of its socket. A big piece of hot metal went straight through my shoulder and removed my AC joint. This is a procedure best left to surgeons while under general anesthesia. Having it done with dirty hot metal while getting shot at is not recommended.

Sanchez told me he saw me get blown about twenty feet, which I don't remember. A piece of my clavicle was sticking out. Watters was kind enough to push it back in and duct-tape it, but it killed that young Ranger. The poor kid who tripped the wire would never be fit for a viewing at home.

The Hajis who were still alive began pouring fire at us, but without the PK, it wasn't as effective. For who might be offended at my use of the word 'Haji', keep in mind that we never knew the actual name of the locals trying to kill us. Some were Taliban. Some were Al Qaeda. Some were probably just local tribesmen who still thought they were fighting the Russians. *No shit.* Sometimes, when we were far out in the Kush, the guys trying to kill us were firing bolt action rifles from World War I.

They picked me up and carried me down the mountain. I would have done the same for them, but it didn't make me feel any less guilty about having my guys expose themselves to save my lame ass.

By the bottom of the mountain, I was awake, but I had bled out pretty good and was wondering if I was going to make it. I was sort of in and out of consciousness, bleeding from a dozen holes in my arms, neck and the big one in my shoulder. A medic came running with pressure bandages.

When the helicopter roared in with an Apache gunship escort, I saw Watters' big white smile against his dark skin. "Your ugly ass is gonna make it. Send me cookies when you get back to the world." Then the big homo kissed me and told me he loved me. And because he really did love me, he shoved Ice into my hand, hidden under my thigh. If my bird went down and I lived, at least I'd have Ice with me. It was just the Delta mindset—never go down without a fight. That would remain with me for the rest of my life.

A few PJs came running and popped a morphine syringe into me, and that was that. Last thing I remember was the sound of the mountain coming apart under the fire of that Apache.

# Chapter Three

Home?

Coming 'home' from Afghanistan was a bit of a blur. I'd had multiple surgeries at Walter Reed Medical Center to repair my shoulder and remove a few dozen pieces of shrapnel. Turned out that the shoulder was just the obvious wound. The piece of metal in my neck missed my carotid artery by only a couple of millimeters and would have ended this story on page one had not fate decided I needed to play detective.

After a few weeks at Walter Reed, I was 'officially retired' with an honorable discharge and a few extra ribbons for my uniform, should I ever have reason to wear it again. *Poof.* I was a civilian.

Not knowing where else to go, I went back to North Carolina. Twin Oaks was where I'd graduated high school and where my parents are buried, but the truth was, I could have picked any place in the country and been just as much 'at home'.

I had lived all over the world, changing girlfriends as often as I changed locations. I didn't mean that in some macho-bullshit way. It would have been great to meet someone, fall in love and all that mushy stuff, but in my chosen profession that didn't really work too well. I'd met some women here and there, managed to get laid often enough not to go insane, but hadn't pondered my future with anyone. I really *was* a good soldier. I *'had my shit wired tight,'* as we liked to say. Retraining my mind from 'combat situational awareness' to 'relax mode' was proving extremely difficult...and so was sleeping through the night. I ended up being the vampire of Twin Oaks for my first two months, taking long walks in the dark, hoping to get sleepy. PTSD? I don't know. I just couldn't calm the fuck down.

Every time I walked anywhere, I was looking for a field of fire or some object that didn't belong that might be an IED. After two months in my rented apartment, I still hadn't bought any furniture. I slept with Ice next to me on a futon on the floor, usually in three- or four-hour intervals, without anyone to relieve me for guard duty.

Living like a Neanderthal.

Trying to figure out what I was going to do for the next fifty years.

My shoulder hurt like hell and wouldn't move the way it was supposed to. The VA was an hour away. The Army surgeons had been great, but the follow-up was a pain in the ass. A local doctor recommended a nearby physical therapy place. I opted to be tortured at the local PT.

It was a life-changing decision. Actually, it was almost a life-*ending* decision.

# Chapter Four

## PT and Amanda

Physical therapy was definitely invented by Al Qaeda. The pain even a petite female physical therapist could inflict on the human body was immeasurable. My first few visits had me in tears — and I *don't* cry.

Delta had beaten the tears out of me years ago. But *sonofabitch*. When they started moving my shoulder to places it didn't want to go, I'm pretty sure I would have divulged national secrets. I always heard this little voice in my head laughing at me when I groaned or broke a sweat, taunting me with, *"You got beat up by a girl?"*

After the third visit, one of them finally clued me in — take a pain killer before I went.

*Good advice.*

There were eight therapists working at that place. Several days in, it occurred to me that a therapist named Amanda wouldn't leave my brain. The woman was kind of *perfect*. I'm thirty-one now but was thirty at the time. She was twenty-five. She was tall, dark and handsome — which is to say she was maybe five-foot-seven, with long dark-brown hair and green eyes that smiled when she did…and great teeth. I pointed out her great teeth, because if I'd said she had great tits, someone would think me shallow.

By the end of the first month, I refused to let anyone touch me but her. I spent an hour a day, three days a week, getting to know her in little snippets while she tortured me. She had the cutest Southern accent I'd ever heard, with a crystal-clear voice that I could listen to all day. I couldn't stop thinking about her. When it got to the point where I couldn't take it anymore, I asked her out.

She said no.

Remember what I said about Ranger school and Delta? We were trained to *never* give up. Die first, period.

So after my asking politely for another week, then begging her for several more, she finally agreed to go out with me. I was hoping she had been waiting until my shoulder had improved enough so as not to impinge on any physically challenging plans she had in store for me. In real life, she said she wouldn't date a patient, but my PT was coming to an end, and my begging was finally wearing her down.

We made a date.

Figuring she knew my military background and had still agreed to go out with me, I decided to wear my dress uniform. It was the first time I'd put it on since I'd come home, and I really was *not* supposed to be wearing it, since I was now out of the unit and this wasn't a parade or anything. But what the heck. I was trying to impress a beautiful woman, and that called for special tactics.

The truth was, I looked way better in my uniform than in street clothes. With multiple dings and dents in my face from jagged pieces of hot metal, rocks and a few fists, I had a face meant for a Green Beret or a brown bag. And, after nine years in the Rangers then Special Forces then with Delta, I had acquired quite a chest full of ribbons. While I'd made SFC – in almost record time, I would proudly add – I'd also received quite a few medals, including a Silver Star, which is how the government says, "Wow, you didn't get killed?", and two Bronze Stars with V devices for valor. I'd also recently received my second Purple Heart, which was the reason I was no longer in the Special Forces.

So anyway, I picked up my date, who was obviously impressed with my uniform and chest full of ribbons – or maybe it was the flowers. I don't know. Who can ever figure women? We were going to dinner out near her house, which was about thirty minutes from me, so she picked the restaurant. The place was just right – dark and cozy, but not outrageously expensive. *My kind of woman.*

It was a three-hour dinner and seemed like five minutes. By the time we finished dinner, we had also finished two bottles of good wine and had both concluded that this was going pretty well. We decided to go out for a drink. *Bad idea.* More on that in a second.

Amanda wasn't much of a partier. She'd had a boyfriend for several years, and they'd broken up recently. While she did know of great restaurants, she was at a loss for a cool bar, so we just strolled around downtown and picked one…hence the problem. A guy in uniform can walk into several types of bars. One kind is where they see your uniform and a chest full of ribbons and you don't pay for a drink all night. I *love* those bars. Another type of bar is full of mostly men who look like they arrived via swamp-boat instead of car and have never served in the military. We had walked into *that* kind of bar.

Amanda took a quick look around and said, "Maybe we should go somewhere else." *Smart lady.* But *I* was thinking, *Yeah, like one beer here then to your place.* So, being in uniform, which always increased the amount of testosterone in the bloodstream, I said, "We'll stay for one beer. It'll be fine." *Big mistake.*

We walked over to the ancient wooden bar, which was fairly abused-looking—some might say it had character—and I ordered us two Sam Adams. This was not being cheap. This was because beer came in bottles that were freshly opened, and there was no way I was drinking from mugs in *that* place. This coming from a guy who once drank blood from the neck of a goat to get some liquid while trying to avoid dying of thirst. So I ordered the beers, gave the bartender a bigger-than-normal tip just to prove I wasn't an asshole and leaned with my back against the bar to face my gorgeous date.

We might have had just one beer and been out of there. We might have ended up back at her place making passionate love until the sun came up. There were all kinds of possibilities. But that was not what actually happened. We were standing there, totally minding our own business, when things went south.

Getting injured and spending a few months home doing rehab had *just* about turned me back into a human being, and being on a date with Amanda had managed to help me turn off my constant 'battle-space, head-on-a-swivel, fully amped' mode. Then this guy showed up. This character looked like something out of a B horror movie.

He stepped *right* between me and Amanda and leaned over real close to her. "When GI Joe goes back overseas, why don't you give me a call?"

I could have lived with that. Really. I was cool with being called 'GI Joe'. But then several loud laughs encouraged him. He put his arm around her, dangled his hand over her breast and smiled, showing the nastiest set of choppers I'd seen since Afghanistan. I mean, seriously, even the Muj would brush their teeth if they had a toothbrush.

Amanda's face showed absolute horror.

"You should go back to your friends now," I said calmly.

"What are you gonna do about it, soldier boy?" he sneered then squeezed her breast. I reached for the man's throat and squeezed his trachea hard enough to cause him to immediately release Amanda. His eyes bulged. His face went red, then a nice shade of purple as he automatically went to his tippy toes. He started doing what we in Ranger School called 'the happy dance'. That's when your arms and legs start moving around searching for oxygen and you look a lot like the cartoons of Snoopy dancing.

Amanda put her hands over her mouth and managed not to scream. I whispered in the dirt-bag's ear that we would be leaving now and he'd better just find a seat somewhere. That actually *was* my plan—to choke him out and leave, and by the time he came to, we'd be in the car heading to her house for a seven-hour kiss goodnight.

Now...in the movies, when a guy in a bar hits *another* guy in a bar over the head with a bottle, the bottle breaks harmlessly and no one gets cut. That's Hollywood. In *real* life, when this guy's buddy hit me, the bottom of the bottle felt like a baseball bat and it did *not* break. The only thing that broke was my head. I saw little stars and the world started going black.

Fortunately for me, the floor broke my fall. Equally fortunate was that two guys quickly jumped on me and pulled me over on my back to make sure I would stay awake for the beating of my life. I had just about nodded out when they started punching me back awake. The punches to my face woke me back up—or maybe it was the sound of my nose breaking. The chokehold on the guy at the bar had been well thought out and carefully executed so as not to inflict lethal force. When the two guys on top of me began trying their best to break my face open, a little switch inside my brain flipped, and I no longer had to think about *anything*. First Sergeant Walker had arrived.

I remember Amanda screaming. I couldn't see her, but I hoped she wasn't being raped or killed. She was really screaming bloody murder, as they say. I think it was *my* bloody murder she was screaming about. I remembered the sound of the first goon's neck snapping. I had managed to work my arms around his head and I broke it on autopilot.

The second guy? I remembered using the blade side of my hand to hit his throat as many times as I could. I still had Grizzly Adams lying across my legs and couldn't move. It's funny the stuff a person thinks of at the weirdest times. Chopping away at this guy's throat, I was thinking, '*All these motherfuckers are wearing flannel.*' I know, bizarre. But this bar was right out of *Deliverance*.

About the time I was pushing Grizzly off my legs, and Flannel Boy was gurgling and dying next to him, the original asshole who had started this whole disaster pulled out a big old hunting knife. That was really lucky.

He moved toward me across the bar room as I was getting to my feet. I could only see out of my right eye, my left having been closed by Grizzly before I'd sent him to the happy hunting lodge in the sky. The guy with the knife was holding it blade pointing down in his fist, meaning he was going to have to raise his arm and go for an overhand strike. If I had a dollar for every time I'd had to defend myself against the rubber version of a knife during hand-to-hand combat schools in Delta, I'd have that fishing boat.

So this wild-man came across the bar with his knife—and I knew it sounded stupid, but I was thinking, *Holy shit, he's wearing flannel, too.* And he came at me and raised the knife like I knew he would, and I kicked him in the you-know-what, and with a quick wrist-lock, took the knife and sent it up into his solar plexus right into his heart.

We both went tumbling to the floor at that point, *me* out of complete exhaustion and a serious ass-whooping, and *him* out of, well...being dead. It was at *this* moment, when I was flat on my back trying really hard to stay conscious, that I saw every cop in town flying into the bar.

I figured one beat-down was enough for the day, so I feigned death. I didn't have to act very much. I felt fairly dead. Then I heard screaming and remembered I had other responsibilities, so I tried to get up. That action was met with a nightstick being pushed into my chest and a stern, "Don't you fucking move!" from a very tall policeman.

I collapsed back on to the floor and tried to wink at Amanda. She was being comforted by a female police officer who was slowly leading her in my direction at Amanda's agitated insistence.

At that point, I vomited blood all over myself. My nose had been broken and lots of blood had run down from my throat into my stomach. My stomach apparently didn't want it there. That was enough for the cop who had been ready to thump me to call for an ambulance. He told me he would cuff me in front instead of behind if I promised not to cause any trouble. I politely passed out.

# Chapter Five

## Ouch

I woke up in the hospital. That is to say, handcuffed to a gurney. A young doctor was standing over me.

"How are we doing, Sergeant?"

*That's right.* I'd had my uniform on when I went out that night. I had forgotten that somewhere along the beating, and now wore a silly hospital gown. I wondered if Amanda had taken off my clothes and seduced me when I was unconscious. *Nah. Probably some giant male orderly.*

I started to answer the doc, but it didn't come out so well. What I wanted to say was, "What's this 'we' shit? I didn't see *you* there getting your ass whooped." But my jaw had been bruised pretty good, along with a broken cheekbone and a broken nose, and my face felt like a large purple ball. In fact, I remembered watching the Afghans play a game like polo on horseback, where they used mallets to knock this dead goat around. I felt a lot like the goat. My headache was beyond migraine, and my right shoulder, which Amanda had helped heal almost back to normal, was lit up like a Christmas tree.

Instead of my wise-ass answer, I said something that sounded like, "Vuvuvuvv."

"Yeah, you took a pretty a good beating there, soldier. I understand from your lady friend that you were assaulted while trying to protect her." He leaned real close to my ear and whispered, "Don't say a fucking word to anyone until you get a lawyer."

That doc was all right. He not only saved my face, but he probably saved my ass, too.

Not long after he stepped away from my bed, two detectives introduced themselves.

They explained that Amanda Jensen had given them a full statement, but they needed mine. They would prefer to have mine now, if I could. What they *really* wanted to say was, "Before you can get a chance to check your story with your date," but they were polite about that.

I tried my best to ask where and how Amanda was. I honestly didn't know what had happened to her after the fight had started, and my brain was still super foggy. One detective said, "She's outside and wants to see you. We just need to go over a few things."

"I need to speak to my lawyer first," I mumbled. I'm not sure what it sounded like to them, but they apparently didn't hear the word 'lawyer'.

"We're trying to get an idea of exactly what happened. Can you tell us what you saw?"

I decided to be vague but helpful. I spoke slowly through the drug-induced haze, attempting to enunciate so they could understand me. My lips were swollen and split, and my tongue felt so thick that I could barely speak. "A guy grabbed my date. I tried to stop him and another guy hit me in the head with something. Two other guys jumped in, and one had a knife. I don't remember much more. If I remember, I'll tell it to my lawyer."

This time, they got it. The detective looked around to make sure no one was looking at him other than his partner, and he pulled up his sleeve. He had a USMC tattoo on his forearm. "As far as I'm concerned, you did a community service. Don't say anything else until your lawyer shows up."

And that was that. They left.

I had now been lucky twice in a row. First a cool doc, then a cool cop. The third thing that happened that was lucky was that asshole number one had pulled a knife on me. Without the knife, I was maybe looking at triple manslaughter charges. *With* the knife, it was a much better case for self-defense. The *fourth* lucky thing — yes, there was a lot of luck involved in this whole thing, trust me, I know — was that the newspaper wrote a headline that totally saved my ass. Now, as a soldier, I'm not a big fan of the liberal anti-war press, but in this case, a reporter named Kim Predham really did come through for me, big time.

If they had printed "*Trained Killer Slaughters Three in Local Bar*," I might have gotten a cold needle in the arm or something. "*Wounded War Hero Kills Three Defending Woman*." *No shit*. That was the headline. Amanda's interview had really helped. She had been such a sympathetic victim, terrorized by a group of groping animals that might have raped her and killed her *boyfriend* — she said it, not me — had I not saved her and taken on three men, one of whom had a knife.

By the time I came out of the hospital a few days later, I had given no fewer than half a dozen interviews to reporters and been on the national news, with my left eye still being half closed and golf-ball-like. At the advice of the lawyer Amanda had found for me, who happened to be a retired JAG lawyer, I played the wounded warrior card and gave the interviews.

The day of my release, Amanda wheeled me out of the front of the hospital to a cheering crowd. I know — surreal. The cool part was that the police had gone from treating me like a suspect to treating me like a good guy, and they 'escorted' us back to Amanda's house.

Amanda drove. It was a little awkward. My face was changing colors and I still had a wicked headache. In fact, *everything* hurt.

"Some date, huh?" I finally managed. It even hurt to talk.

"One I will never forget. How are you doing over there?" she asked. She really was about the sweetest person on the planet at that particular moment.

"I'm okay. You?"

"I'm good." She paused. "I took a few days off. You know, I *am* a physical therapist. I'll take very good care of you for the next couple of days, okay?"

"You didn't have to do that. Look... You don't owe me anything, right?"

I really didn't want her feeling guilty — unless it would get me laid, I mean. Maybe I only half-meant that. I really didn't want her feeling like it was her fault, and I told her.

"I can't believe I picked that bar," she said quietly. "I'm so sorry. I didn't know."

"Oh, stop. How could you know? And besides, I was the one who wanted to stay. Wasn't your fault. Wasn't mine, either. Shit happens."

She started crying. *That* caught me off guard. She had really been so great about everything. The only time I remembered her being upset was when she was screaming at the top of her lungs in the bar. She had been totally together with all the reporters, with the police, with the attorney that she'd found for me. Seriously, she'd been running the operation and taking care of everything. I guess it caught up with her in the car when it was over.

I reached out and held her right hand, and she said something about them almost killing me.

"*Lots* of people have almost killed me. That's how we met in the first place. Remember?" We pulled into the parking lot in front of her townhouse and our police escort left us.

Then it hit me. We were at *her* place. "Um, Amanda? This is your place…?"

"You just noticed *now*?" she said, and looked at me with an evil grin. "I *told* you I was going to nurse you back to health."

"I don't have anything here," I protested.

She reached into her bag and pulled out the key to my apartment. "When I went to get your clothes to leave the hospital, I picked up a few extra things for you. And I confess, I was very relieved when I let myself in and didn't find a wife and four small children."

"So you're pretty much kidnapping me back to your house to take advantage of me in my weakened condition?" I asked with my usual sense of humor that's only funny to me.

She cocked her head and made a serious face. "I *have* a spare bedroom."

"The newspapers said I was your boyfriend," I teased her.

"Don't believe everything you read in the papers," she retorted. Sarcastic little thing.

I liked that.

# Chapter Six

## Healing

So one might think, "Isn't this all a little fast? You went from your first date to staying at her place?" I know. It sounds nuts. But here was the thing... By the time we'd had our first date, I felt like I had known Amanda for years, and the date itself, prior to being almost killed, had been the most fun I'd ever had. Truth be told, she had been enjoying herself as much as I had. That was not me being cocky. She'd actually told me that. That was, right up to the part where Dental-Boy grabbed her boob and started the small riot. In any event, she took me back to her place to make sure I didn't die or something. And I couldn't have been happier.

The first day was spent with her running around making icepacks and freezing my head. It helped. By early evening, it almost looked like a human's again, albeit in Technicolor. My black eyes looked nice against my purple forehead with red blotches, along with a black, blue and purple cheek. I looked worse than I felt, but I sure as hell wasn't going to tell *her* that. She was actually starting to dig me, which was bizarre, considering that I was so scary-looking I could haunt houses.

I feigned extreme pain and enjoyed every second of her nursing skills. I refused the painkillers because I am extremely macho and because it didn't really hurt too badly. *And* because I would have rather be able to drink. Amanda gave up trying to give me Percocet and instead, at my urging, she opened a bottle of red wine. It was an exquisite Italian brunello di Montalcino. And no one should make fun. Even macho Army types can enjoy wine. I'd taken several of my leaves in Italy and France, where I had acquired a taste for wine and never looked back. It was only out of lack of options that I would drink beer – or anything else.

Amanda was surprised and impressed at my knowledge of wine, but the truth was, when a person is in the service, they have hours of boredom interrupted by moments of terror. A buddy of mine, a colonel, was a sommelier. Who could even believe that? A combat hardened bad-ass, who, when he retired from the service, could work at any top restaurant in the world. Col. Cantor and I had become friendly, which was a little unusual for an NCO and brass, but our love of wine surpassed our strict observation of formality. One month I was killing people and blowing things up, the next I was sipping wine in a stunning vineyard, discussing *terroir* and *tannins* with the colonel. His passion was contagious, and pretty soon I was on my own path toward wine snobbery.

We'd used our time off to travel to vineyards and taste wines from all over the world. The wine region in Tuscany where the hilltop town of Montalcino is located might be one of the most beautiful places on

Earth. The fact that Amanda owned a bottle of brunello di Montalcino, such amazing wine, gave her extra brownie points.

We split the bottle, which was a good idea, because I could 'sip' much better than I could drink, since my face was still rather alien-like. She ended up getting slightly buzzed and very philosophical, then downright mushy.

When she leaned over and kissed me, I knew I had a real special woman. *I* wouldn't have kissed me, *that* was for sure. I'm not sure how she was even *looking* at me, never mind touching me, but she was, and I kissed her back as best as my busted lips would allow.

Well, I guess she had a pretty good buzz on, because she kept making out with me, even though I looked like roadkill. We're talking Scaryville. But she was evidently much less shallow than I am.

One thing led to another—maybe it was called guilt—and she undressed me then undressed herself. And oh my. Unlike *me*, she hadn't gotten her ass kicked, and *her* ass was *perfect*. So were her teeth. I think I might have mentioned them earlier. So there I was, naked on her couch, watching her undress until she was naked and just standing there wearing only a smile. My heart skipped a beat, probably because of all the blood had been rerouted somewhere else. I think I decided to marry her at that particular second. She then began doing things that I hadn't experienced in several years. *Years...* Believe that?

"Your heart is beating pretty fast," she said softly, putting her head on my chest when it was finished.

"I am pretty sure I just had a minor heart attack," I explained.

"I think you'll live. You're pretty tough."

"Was that a physical therapy technique?" I asked.

"Yes," she replied, and although I couldn't see her face, I could feel her smiling.

"How come I didn't get that when I was going for PT at the rehab center?"

"Your healthcare coverage was lousy. This is an out-of-office visit and it's treated differently." She laughed. "By the way, you owe me twenty bucks for the co-pay."

"Twenty bucks? Hell, let's plan for two hundred a week."

"Nice try," she said.

We remained cuddled up naked on the couch, just enjoying each other for a while, until Amanda decided it was time for round two. Even in my weakened, battered condition, I was enthusiastic about trying again.

She climbed on top of me, straddling my hips, and began moving slowly. I'm not sure how long it had been for her, but it had been forever for me, and I didn't last very long. Luckily, she didn't either.

I think I was in a deep sleep in about thirty seconds. It was the best nap I'd ever had. Because I am a gentleman, I have spared the details of the rest of that day — and evening and next morning. But suffice it to say I was hooked and so was she. Things seemed like they were going perfectly.

# Chapter Seven

## Now What?

After three solids days of bedroom antics that were designed to either cure me or kill me, Amanda had to go back to work. She gave me keys and told me she would be home around six. Home. I loved the sound of that.

When she left for work that morning, it felt like we had been married for ten years — except I'm guessing that couples who were married for ten years didn't try to do it in every room of the house, on every piece of furniture and on the floor and in the shower. My right shoulder occasionally reminded me that three swamp rats had tried to kill me and my face was still sore and bruised, but Amanda made me forget about anything that hurt every time she took off her clothes. I'm not bragging. In fact, I'd come right out and say that she was definitely better at the whole screwing thing than I was. That woman was amazing. I was already madly in love with her, even though, admittedly, I hardly even knew her. Oh well…I had taken a lot more risks than that.

After she left, I showered, dressed and decided to go walk around the neighborhood and grab some coffee. It still felt strange to me to be a civilian. I had spent my entire adult life in the military and had always been sure I would retire a sergeant major after twenty-five or thirty years. It was all I'd ever wanted to do. Now, because of the injury, I was out of the military forever and had zero idea what I was going to do with my life.

Amanda had made enough of an impact that I was pretty sure I could stay in Twin Oaks, North Carolina for the rest of my life, assuming she would keep me around. But I had no idea what I would do for a job. The types of things I was trained for and good at were not things that had much use in civilian life. Unless, maybe, I'd lived in a *really* bad neighborhood—like Kandahar or Fallujah.

I found a trendy coffee shop and ordered a cup of coffee. When I went *into* the Army, I could go into a coffee shop in the morning, still half asleep, and grunt "coffee...regular," and somebody would hand me a cup of joe with milk and sugar in it. It cost less than a buck and took less than twenty seconds. Somewhere over the past ten years or so, somebody changed the English language and how we dealt with a cup of joe.

As I stood listening to the people in front of me in line ordering, I began to tense up. I had no idea what anyone was talking about. I spoke English, Pashtun, Farsi and a smattering of some other tribal dialects. In Afghanistan, I could simply say *qahwa* in Pashto and some guy would hand me coffee.

When the guy in front of me ordered a *'vente skim caramel macchiato, extra foamy with an extra shot,'* I froze in panic. He walked away to another part of the coffee counter where people apparently picked up their orders and left me standing there facing a very young woman with a nose piercing. The nose thing had me as weirded out as the coffee. *When did American girls start emulating Calcutta?* Man, was I out of touch with the new, improved America.

She welcomed me, gave me a huge fake smile and asked me what I would like. Not knowing what else to say, I said, "Coffee." It took a while and I pissed off the people behind me, big time. In the end, I paid a couple of dollars for a black coffee and was guided to the 'fixings bar' like I was going to make a cheeseburger or something. *Holy shit.* I'd just wanted a cup of java.

I bought a paper and sat at a very small table in cramped quarters. I was reading about the fighting going on in the Middle East when I felt eyes on me. I looked up and realized a cop had sat down at the table next to me.

I gave him a polite chin nod and a grunted, "Morning," and went back to reading, but he was still looking at me. My face was no longer Elephant-Man-like, but I was still black and blue and swollen in a few spots, with some fine tape on my cheek over the purple part. I had also opted for a very high and tight military flat-top before donning my dress uniform on date-night, so it wasn't like I exactly melted into the landscape.

Recognizing my busted face, he asked, "You the soldier I was reading about last week?"

"Yeah. That would be me." I stuck out my hand and said, "Cory Walker." As we shook hands, pain shot from his grip up to my bad shoulder. My smile probably looked like a grimace.

"Nice to meet you, Cory. John McBride. I followed your story for a few days. I was a ground-pounder myself back in the first Gulf War. Glad you made it through okay."

"Thanks. For a few days, I thought I was going to end up in jail. Actually, I should back that up. I *originally* thought I was going to end up in the *morgue* but landed in the hospital instead."

We bonded over my cup of coffee and his grande soy mocha bullshit. I asked him about being a cop. I really didn't know what I wanted to do. Maybe law enforcement would be interesting enough to keep me from getting bored. As a 'disabled vet', I would get bumped up on any civil service list, which meant my chances of getting hired were very good.

After twenty minutes of listening to his career, I decided I would rather work at a car wash. It wasn't that he didn't have an interesting job that was personally rewarding or anything like that. It was just the amount of bureaucratic bullshit and paper shuffling that seemed unacceptable. Where I came from, we had a specific mission, we hit our target and we split. After I listened to him explaining the limitations placed on law enforcement personnel, I had to wonder if the American judges were Al Qaeda. Hell, the cops couldn't even search a car without *asking* for permission. It would be *way* too frustrating for me, and I told him so.

We talked about working for the FBI, CIA, DEA, or NSA — even Border Patrol, which was currently hiring lots of former military. By the time he left to go back to work, I had decided I couldn't be a cop, but maybe I could use my years of military experience in some other branch of government service. The biggest question would be whether I could stay in Twin Oaks if I signed on with one of those outfits. Amanda probably wouldn't want to move for a guy she'd just met, and I didn't like the idea of leaving her behind. I left the coffee shop to walk and ponder the universe and my place in it.

# Chapter Eight

## My Crazy New Idea

After what seemed like a twenty-mile walk, I'd come to several conclusions. I was in love with a woman I had just met, I couldn't sleep most nights because I was still in combat-mode most of the time and I couldn't help but feel guilty and worried about my guys back in the sand box. There was a lot to ponder. One thing I did know for sure. I needed to spend as much time as I could with Amanda and preferably some place very quiet, where I could allow my brain to return to whatever was considered 'normal'. And *that*, I knew, would take some effort.

The other thing that kept coming back to me was my uncertainty about what I would do for a career. I had saved a boatload of money, not having had time to spend it on anything other than wine, so I could take my time and sort things out. It's a little hard to explain to a civilian, but as a Special Forces soldier, the constant sense of mission and preparation for the next operation kept us all extremely focused. For my entire military life, I had been surrounded by warriors I'd kill and die for and they for me. And now, here I was, without a mission or my men, feeling lost.

It didn't feel good.

I read the papers. I saw how many of my brethren committed suicide every day after they left the service. I was starting to understand it better now. While I wasn't clinically depressed, I was lonely and out of place. My guys were still out there, and I couldn't help them. Hell, I didn't even have any clue where they were or what they were doing. And even if I could have called them, they couldn't tell me shit anyway. Almost everything we had ever done had been classified. Now, I was just another civilian trying to figure out what I wanted to be when I grew up.

I went back to Amanda's. She came in from work wearing her khakis and polo shirt with the words 'Physical Therapy' and a logo embroidered on it. I was staring at the name on the shirt only because it covered her perfect left boob. Then it dawned on me about how many other guys at her work probably took their time reading the name. *Men are such pigs.*

She came in, kissed me hello and commented about how I was almost looking like someone she would be seen in public with.

"Good," I replied, "because I think you should be seen with me in public on a great vacation for a couple of weeks."

She laughed.

"I'm serious. Let's go down to the shore somewhere and rent a beach house for a few weeks. I want to spend *whole* days with you — several in a row, in fact."

She cocked her head. "Are you serious? Just like that? We take off for the beach?"

"Just like that. You and me — on the beach — bottle of wine, a picnic, a sunrise over the water… What do you say?"

"I say you're crazy," she said, but kissed me anyway. "A beach house might be hard to get so late in the summer. And even if we could, it would be a fortune."

"I'm not asking *you* to help pay for it. I just want you to say yes, drive away with me to the beach and keep going until we find a place to spend some time."

"No reservations? Just drive east until we hit water and try to get a place? You *are* crazy. We'll end up driving for hours and have to turn around and come home."

"Man, I had no idea you were so negative! Call work and tell them you won't be in for a few weeks. We'll leave in the morning."

She laughed in my face. "Oh yeah — that'll go over really big! 'Hi, boss, I'm taking off for the beach for a few weeks. *See ya!*' He'll fire me."

"So let him fire you. Come away with me."

We went around for a while, and in the end, I just sort of blurted everything out — how wound up I was, how lost I was. She listened and agreed to try to get time off. It turned out her boss was a good egg, knew who I was and the whole story of how I'd almost gotten turned into chopped meat at that bar. He told her he had enough staff to cover for her for two weeks if she could work for two more days before we split.

I spent those two days online searching for places on the Outer Banks. There was Kitty Hawk…and Nag's Head. There were so many cool places to choose from. I decided we would head east and just see what happened.

# Chapter Nine

## Road Trip

We stayed at a few different B&B-type places that were ridiculously overpriced but cozy and right near the ocean. We relaxed in the sun, played in the ocean, went for long walks — all the mushy stuff couples do in the movies.

I kept thinking I'd say or do something really stupid that would screw everything up. Or maybe I'd discover that she had some horrible secret. I wasn't used to things going so well for so long. Back in Ass-Crackistan, any time things were going well for more than a day or two, we knew some seriously bad shit was coming. Being happy made me paranoid.

We ate and drank like pigs, had lots of laughs and made goo-goo eyes at each other. Happiness. That was the only way I could describe it — *happiness*. I had never felt so good in my life, and with Amanda's patience and off-beat sense of humor, I was learning how to relax again. There were spans of hours at a time when I was totally calm and at peace. I think my soul was smiling.

The vacation turned into days that were something out of a chick-flick. We talked about all kinds of stuff — including emotional subjects that were pretty foreign to me. I'd spent ten-plus years killing bad guys, not watching Oprah, and spilling my guts about 'how I felt' was *not* something I'd ever done before Amanda. I have to say, though, talking to her was just so easy. Not only was she a good listener, but she also had ideas and suggestions. Our conversations seemed to go on effortlessly for hours. I had never known anyone like her. I was totally smitten.

I'd known Amanda was intelligent the moment I'd met her. She'd rattled off human anatomy and her therapy procedures at a hundred miles an hour. But it hadn't been just that. When we talked about any subject, she knew something about it. The only things I considered myself expert in were killing and wine. This wonderful woman could talk about anything. And she was thoughtful enough not to dump her problems on me — if she had any. Her interests were varied and exciting, and I loved the way her face brightened when we hit on a subject she found fascinating, like old black-and-white movies or rescued dogs that had saved their families.

Turns out Amanda had graduated magna cum laude from East Carolina State on an academic scholarship. I had definitely done that wrong. She had basically been paid to attend college while I was being paid to get shot at. While her major was kinesiology, in preparation for training as a physical therapist, she had also taken lots of classes in art and literature. Not a conversation took place where I wasn't amazed by something she knew. She was the kind of person I could talk to for another fifty years and not get bored. I just hoped I was the kind of person *she* could talk to for the next fifty years. That fact bounced around my head every day.

We were lying on a beach blanket enjoying the sun and I just came right out and asked her, "How is it you're not already married with kids? You're the smartest, nicest, funniest, sexiest woman I've ever met. What defect are you hiding?"

She rolled up on one elbow and looked down at me with a funny expression. "You haven't figured it out yet?"

"Not yet."

"I'm a sucker for lost causes."

I laughed and grabbed her then tried to kiss her, but she just squealed and bit me. We laughed and enjoyed a long kiss, then I pulled her sunglasses off so I could see those green eyes. "Come on. Cough it up. You're a psycho, and I haven't figured it out yet."

"I was wondering the same thing about you."

"Yeah, well, I did just kill three guys in a bar." I was making a joke, but it didn't come off as funny to either of us. We just stared at each other, now both of us obviously feeling a little awkward.

"That was the single worst and best day of my life," she said.

It hit me hard. "Really? I mean...I get the *worst* day part."

"You're fishing? Okay..." She sat up, escaping my arms, and sat cross-legged and very straight-backed in front of me. She had her serious face on—one I hadn't seen much these two weeks. "You asked me out like ten times before I said yes."

"Yeah, no kidding."

"Look... I get hit on a lot, even at work...maybe especially at work. I'd never said yes to anyone before. I've had my share of long-term boyfriends, so that was always an easy out, but even when I didn't, I'd never date a patient."

"How did I win the prize?"

"There was something about you, Cory. Something different." She shrugged. "When we would talk during your appointments..."

"When you tortured me and made me cry..."

"Yes. When you cried, big baby. Our conversations were just so—I don't know—*easy*. It wasn't like I ever had to make small talk. Almost every session every day is the same. '*How was your weekend? Do anything fun? Any improvement?*' Yadda yadda. It's routine, you know? But with you, we just seemed to really connect."

"I couldn't agree with you more. But I give you a lot of credit for not letting me know."

"Then, a perfect date," she teased me. "The best dinner date of my life. And that fight in the bar... That was the single most violent, God-awful thing I'd ever witnessed. Part of me wanted to never see you again after that. I mean, you were *scary*."

I started to speak, but she held up her finger for me to shut up, which I did.

"Then I remembered you'd been trained to defend yourself. You were defending *me*. And in that moment, instead of feeling horrified I just felt *safe*."

I sat up across from her, not sure what to say.

"But it's not just that you were brave. You're also gentle...and thoughtful...and funny. I love your sarcastic sense of humor. And you can talk to me about anything. The other guys I dated... I don't know. Don't take this the wrong way, like I'm stuck up or something, but they just weren't interesting. And under that sarcastic wise-ass exterior, you're a sensitive, caring person."

"Funny," I said, "that's exactly what I thought about you."

I moved in for a kiss, which got me a little peck.

She leaned back. "So...*are* you...okay?"

I knew what she was asking. It was my turn to be serious. "Amanda, I've seen and done some crazy stuff. I've killed a lot of people and seen a lot of killing—and not like the three guys in the bar. Nothing at all like that. You think that was horrible? That was *nothing*. The aftermath of combat is the bloodiest, messiest, most gruesome thing imaginable. In fact, it's *not* imaginable. Until you see someone you've served with for years blown to pieces, you *can't* imagine it. That's probably a good thing. And the enemy? It's our job to kill them. It changes everyone who's ever been a part of it. But I'm out. I'm done. I've tried really hard for the past couple of months to turn off the auto-pilot. It's not as easy as people think."

"I know it's not easy, Cory. Do you have PTSD? Nightmares?"

I was a little surprised by the question. It was more than personal. It was a glimpse inside my head, but it was a fair one to ask. I always pictured civilians looking at vets with PTSD as though we are some kind of crazy people about to snap at any moment. Amanda was different, though. I knew she cared and wasn't judging me.

"I don't know if I'd say it was full-blown PTSD. I mean, I think every combat vet has *some*. But it's more like just trying to unwind. You're in your car looking down the street in town, and *you* see traffic. I look at the same street and *I* see a three-dimensional battle space. Is there an IED in that trash can? Is the trunk of that car sagging too low? Did someone move in that window? Is that a booby trap or a piece of garbage? Where's my best field of fire? It's tough to turn off the stuff that kept me alive all those years but I'm trying. And the nightmares are coming less and less."

She was nodding as she listened and I knew she understood.

"More than that," I continued, "I miss my team. The bonds forged in combat are more than just friendships. These guys are my brothers. I miss them. But I'm out and they're in, and once you're out, you're out. We won't have much to talk about until they're out, too, then we can pick up where we left off. But for now, they're in the shit and I'm back in the world. Prior to meeting you, I was just kind of lost."

"I'm glad you asked me out," she said.

"Me, too."

We sat in silence, listening to the waves lapping the shore.

Finally, Amanda announced she had a hidden agenda—a bucket list item. "I've always wanted to go see this place called Harkers Island. It's like going back in time. It's funny because you'd think it has an apostrophe, but it doesn't. I think it might be around here somewhere."

"Then let's go find it."

Neither of us knew at the time how that bucket list item would change our lives.

# Chapter Ten

## Welcome to Harkers Island

We drove south, following the Outer Banks as it became more and more remote — smaller town after smaller town. Amanda explained the history of Harkers Island to me as we drove, and, in typical fashion, impressed me with her total recall of otherwise useless information.

"The whole island is only two and half square miles, with a total population of less than two thousand. Most of the islanders are fisherman or local merchants — people who rely on tourists who are *also* there to fish or hunt birds. The decoy carving industry is a local specialty. There is supposedly even a little museum dedicated to wooden ducks. For the tourists, of course," she added, laughing. "Most of the waterfront has docks for fishing boats or trawlers. The rest is grass-covered dunes that are protected by law."

Much of the island's beauty, she said, was in its simplicity — unspoiled and unchanged for the last few thousand years. "Nothing ever happens there."

"That's about what I need right now."

She told me the island didn't get phone service until 1948, nine years after it got electricity. Separated from the mainland, the islanders still had a dialect reminiscent of Elizabethan English. "It's called 'High Tider' and I'm dying to hear it. It hasn't been spoken anywhere else in two hundred and fifty years. Can you imagine? And I guarantee you that there's no way we'll be able to understand a word!"

"Bet?"

"Bet!"

We followed Route 12 until we ran out of road. There are only two ways onto the island — the bridge or the ferry — unless a person is rich and has their own boat. Or should I say *yacht*? We chose the ferry. The bridge would have required a four-hour detour through farm country.

The ferry ride was a first for both of us. Neither of us had done a lot of the things we were doing on this trip, but that was what happened when one gets silly in love. After a short trip across the sound, the ferry docked, we drove off and began a slow tour of the island.

We drove by some fancy estate homes and a few summer beach houses of the rich and famous, but, for the most part, Harkers remained below the radar, known only to duck hunters and avid anglers who didn't mind a long trip. The island was for islanders, same as it had been for a few hundred years — and that was seemingly just how they wanted it to stay.

We ended up stopping at a little restaurant overlooking the dunes for the world's best soft-shell crab sandwiches, then went for a walk down a quiet beach road, narrow without sidewalks, and into a postcard neighborhood. Turning a corner, we found ourselves staring at a Victorian house, perched slightly on a mounded yard that could only be described as perfect, with a big ole' 'For Sale' sign out front.

Lots of the homes we had walked past had patchy front lawns because of the sandy soil, with very limited landscaping. *This* place was out of a magazine. As beautiful as the house was, what was most impressive were the grounds. There were perfectly manicured beds, outlined by tiny hedges, contained magnificent flowers of every color, and butterflies seemed to dance in celebration over them.

The large lot was surrounded by pine trees and shrubs, like a frame around a painting. The wooded border offered privacy and a feeling that we were the only people on the island. It left me speechless.

The Victorian architecture was stately and grand in its own way, with a raised wrap-around porch and fluted columns in front of the house. The attention to detail in the woodworking made every square inch of the exterior worthy of inspection. The coffered panels and geometric paneled friezes were painted in different colors to highlight the details, with various blues and grays making the exterior warm and soft. White fish-scale shingles seemed to belong on the island, and although they were slightly weather-beaten from the hot Carolina sun and the salt air, the wood was in perfect shape. There was one rounded corner tower which presumably held the master bedroom upstairs, and it had windows all around it, which would afford a magnificent view of the sound.

We just stood there for what seemed like a long time, admiring the house and its landscaping. Then, as if in a trance, we both started walking up the curving driveway to explore.

I know how totally insane it sounds that Amanda and I could be 'house hunting' after only knowing each other for a few months and only dating for a few weeks. And we weren't—but we were feeling nosy, or curious, or both, so there we were, walking down a slate path, through a rose garden and into the backyard of this beautiful, old home. An immense but graceful statue of two angels caught my immediate attention just as I realized two women were standing there. We felt like we had just been 'busted' sneaking around on someone's property.

The younger woman smiled, which took the pressure off, and she walked over to greet us.

"Well, hello, y'all!" She extended her hand like she had been expecting us. She had a thick Southern accent, even compared to Amanda. She told us her name was Belle and explained we were still in time for the Open House.

"Excellent!" I looked at Amanda, winked, and said, "I'm Cory Walker and this is my friend, Amanda Jensen."

Belle said, "And this is our *de-ah* Agatha, who lives right next door." Agatha smiled sweetly, sizing us up. Belle offered to show us inside, and Agatha stepped through an opening in a hedge and disappeared into her own backyard.

As Belle led us toward the back porch, I asked, "Who lives here?"

"At the moment, no one." She stopped, cocking her head. "You are *fah-miliar* with the history of this house, Mr. *Wal-kah*?"

I told her we were not.

"Well, I do have to tell you that this house *does* have a history—and not all of it is happy, I'm afraid. It had a famous owner. You *do* know who Congressman Stone is, I presume?"

Someone would have had to have lived on the moon not to know his name. He was being mentioned repeatedly as a Presidential hopeful.

"Well," she said — and her 'well' sounded more like 'whale' — "Congressman Stone lived here with his first wife and daughter many years ago, before he was a congressman. He was a judge back then. Quite a local celebrity. His daughter died when she was sixteen — murdered, to be truthful, and —"

"*Murdered?*" Amanda gasped. "In this house?"

"Oh no, my *de-ah*," Belle said, "Not *he-ah*. Over *they-ah*." She gestured vaguely. "The strain was too much for his wife. The poor woman hung herself. It's the most terrible thing that's *ev-ah* happened on Harkers Island. Of course he sold the house immediately. He moved to Raleigh. That was twenty years ago."

We let that sink in. I was having visions of walking into the house and finding the mother in the kitchen, still swinging.

Belle headed for the back porch. "There have been two owners since then, and they have both kept up the house and the grounds."

She opened the back door and we found ourselves in a mud room, which continued into a hallway. "I just hate taking you in from the rear of the house," she said. "The front foyer is magnificent."

I started singing *Back Door Man* by The Doors. That went over Belle's head, but Amanda elbowed me — at least she appreciated my sense of humor.

Amanda and I walked through the house, mostly in silence as we listened to Belle drawl on about the many features of the place. She wasn't pushy, just overly charming. By the time we ended up at the front of the house, Amanda and I found ourselves shaking our heads repeatedly, amazed at how much we both just loved the place. It had that Old-World feel found in homes built with hardwood floors and tons of wood moldings that cost a fortune nowadays.

As we walked through the front doors and out onto the wide veranda, Belle announced, "Well, that's about it. What do y'all think of the place?"

"It's gorgeous," Amanda said.

"How much are they asking?" I queried matter-of-factly.

"Well, the sellers are motivated and the market *is* a bit soft," she said, now changing to her selling voice. "They are asking five hundred." She then leaned closer and whispered, as if anyone else was within a mile, "But I think they'd take four-eighty."

"Find out if they'll take four-fifty," I whispered back. My whispering went over her head. When I looked at Amanda, her mouth was wide open and her eyes looked like they would pop out of her head.

"They are leaving all the furniture, you see, all included in the asking price," Belle said, sweetening the pot. "They have already moved to Florida to be near their grandchildren."

Before Amanda could speak, I shushed *her* for a change, and gave Belle my cell number. I thanked her and told her to call me if they took my offer. We said our goodbyes.

As Amanda and I walked down the wide front steps, she asked me just what I thought I was doing.

"I think I'm buying us a house," I said, somewhat surprised to hear myself say it.

# Chapter Eleven

## The Stone House

Amanda's reaction was a little different from what I'd expected. Actually, I'm not sure *what* I expected, because I hadn't really planned anything, especially making an offer on a house. She looked, well, kind of pissed off. We walked down the driveway in silence until she just stopped short, turned to me and blurted out, "Cory, what the hell do you think you're doing?"

I didn't really have an answer for that. I shrugged. "I dunno. It's a perfect house. This spot is beautiful. I thought you liked it, too."

"It's gorgeous. What's not to like? Besides somebody getting murdered here."

"Not in the house," I pointed out.

"Did you really think we'd just buy a house and move in after dating for less than a month?" She shook her head, said something under her breath that sounded a lot like "Idiot!" and stomped off down the road.

*Holy crap. I wasn't prepared for* that.

I followed her in silence as she walked back in the direction of the car. After about five minutes of me walking behind her like a squaw trailing ten feet behind the chief, she stopped and turned around. She had tears on her face.

"And what would I do for *work*?"

I smiled. So she *had* been thinking about it.

With that, she turned and started walking again, fast. I followed her in silence until she spun around again. "And we're an *hour* from *any*place! This house is in the middle of nowhere! What would *you* do for work?" She smacked her hands against her thighs and stared at me, shook her head in disgust and marched off again, only to stop a fourth time and scream at me, "And how the hell are we going to buy a four-hundred-and-fifty-thousand-dollar house?"

I *had* her. She had said 'we'. I'd heard it.

"Can I answer these in any order?" I asked as I approached her with great caution, the way I would approach a tripwire. Even mad, she looked so cute.

She squinted and jutted her chin out at me. *A tough gal. I love that.*

"I have a lot of money in the bank. I've been saving for over ten years. My parents also left me and my brother a little bit of money. I can put more than half down, cash, and *still* have money. As far as work goes, well, I have no idea. I don't know a damned thing about Harkers Island. Pretty nice house, though, huh?"

She looked away, and I think she was still fighting off tears. *Women. Who knows what they're thinking half the time?*

"And I'm just supposed to leave everything in Twin Oaks and move in with you?" I shrugged.

"Um, yeah," was the best thing I could come up with.

"You're a complete lunatic," she said, and turned back toward the direction of the car.

It was a little embarrassing. I mean, what if a future neighbor had been watching this whole scene? After some time had passed, I noticed she had slowed her pace so I would catch up. I slowed mine as well 'to keep my interval', as we called it up on the goat trails of Afghanistan.

She eventually stopped and turned around with what I can only describe as a 'moo-moo face', and asked me if I was going to walk next to her.

So I did.

# Chapter Twelve

Homeowner?

We walked back toward the car, mostly in silence, but at least we were holding hands, so I figured we were temporarily okay. Finally, I guess the silence was too much for her.

"You know we can't buy that house and move in together, right?"

I shrugged but didn't say anything. She stopped walking and gave me a surprise kiss, albeit on the cheek. "I'm pretty sure I'm in love with you, Cory, which is totally insane after knowing you all of a few weeks, but I'm not ready to move from Twin Oaks to the middle of nowhere and buy a house."

"First of all," I responded very calmly, "we have known each other for *months* —"

She cut me off. "I'm not talking about *rehab*."

"*I* am. I was already crazy about you back then."

"You didn't even know me."

"Say what you want. I'm counting office visits as knowing you — or at least *getting* to know you. Second, we aren't in the middle of nowhere. I have *been* in the middle of nowhere, and trust me. It doesn't look anything like this. And besides, you can hop in your car and be anyplace you need to be in a little while."

"We don't know one person out here, Cory."

"Good. The only person I want to talk to is right in front of me."

"I'm serious. We'd go nuts out here. It's beautiful, but you are totally out of control. You don't just buy a house like you're buying a pair of shoes."

"Tell you what... How about *I* buy the house, and you can come visit me any time you want. I'll even give you your own key."

We got to the car and I opened her door for her, gentleman that I am. She got in without looking at me — a serious puss back on her face. I closed the door and let out a very long sigh. *Now what?* My cell phone rang. It was the Realtor. I let it go to voicemail and hopped into the driver's seat.

"Where to?" I asked.

"Just drive," she said quietly.

*Man.* We'd been having such a phenomenal trip. I guessed I'd totally screwed that up. I was waiting for her to say, "Take me home," but she just sat in deep thought and I drove around the island to the bridge that connected Harkers to the mainland.

When we were just about to cross the bridge, Amanda looked out of her side window and said, "I think it's almost time for your next feeding."

I saw the same sign, showing a blue-claw crab. "Joe's Crab House?"

"Done," she replied.

Well, at least she was *almost* speaking to me again. And if she weren't, at least I'd have some spicy crabs and a few cold beers. How bad could that be?

We pulled into the gravel parking lot. When I reached for the key to cut the engine, Amanda took my arm. Before I knew what happened, we were making out in the front seat. Quite honestly, it was already pretty warm outside, but I think we had the inside temperature of the car up to about a hundred and fifty. A car pulled in next to us. Amanda looked over and saw two little kids with their parents.

"Busted."

"Does this mean you're speaking to me again?"

"No," she replied. "I was just horny and you were the only one here."

Did I mention I love this woman? She's as sarcastic as I am—and that's saying something. I got out of the car and laughed when I saw that she didn't move a muscle. I walked around and opened the door for her. As she stood, she casually grabbed my dick and gave it a squeeze, then walked toward the restaurant like nothing had happened. She waited at the door for me to open it for her. Quite hilarious.

We walked in and were greeted by a kid who sat us at a window looking out at the bridge.

"I hope the food's great," I said, "so when we live here we can come back all the time." I waited for her to raise her eyebrow. She very politely showed me her middle finger at the edge of the table so no one else could see it, but I saw her smile.

We ordered a dozen 'jumbos' and a pitcher of beer, and the waitress laid out a big sheet of brown paper. I love spicy hard shells with enough Old Bay and garlic to make me sweat. Amanda told me she did as well. It was yet another reason to hope she would keep me around.

I waited until we were halfway through the pile of crabs, and more importantly, on our second pitcher of beer, before I broached the subject again. "The Realtor called," I said matter-of-factly as I sucked out some delicious crab meat. I am pretty sure my face was as messy as hers was.

She looked at me from behind the claw she was sucking on. "When? What did she say?"

"I dunno. I didn't listen to the message."

We just kept eating for a while, drinking cold beer to put out the fires in our mouths. Finally, she said, "Well? Are you going to listen to it or what?"

"What if they meet our offer?"

"*Your* offer. Then I guess you buy a house in East Bumblefuck and I come visit you whenever I feel like it, until we decide we either *really* like each other or until I stop showing up."

I sat back and let that sink in a bit. "Seriously, Amanda, I know this is totally nuts. We hardly know each other. But that house— I don't know. It's just so perfect. The whole area is gorgeous. It's *peaceful*. I *need* peace."

A moment passed as I tried to form the next sentence correctly. "Readjusting to civilian life back here in 'the world' has been harder than I thought it would be. The last couple of days here with you it's been... I can *feel* myself calming down. Being hyper-alert has kept me alive for my adult life. But turning that off and becoming a regular human has been tough. PTSD—or whatever you wanna call it. It's hard to just be a civilian. But this place is quiet and naturally beautiful, like the woman across the table. I can see myself here. I can see myself here with *you*."

For some reason, I had a lump in my throat. "I'm not sure what I'd do for work here, but I'm not sure what I'd do for work back in Twin Oaks, either. I honestly have no idea what I want to do, except spend time with you."

She started getting watery-eyed. I had no idea she was so mushy. Not tough like me. I wiped my eye. *Must be allergies.*

"This *is* nuts," she said.

"It wouldn't be the craziest thing I ever did," I said, almost to myself.

"Yeah? What's the craziest thing you ever did?" she said, obviously trying to change the subject.

"I'm pretty sure it's totally classified. Let's just say I have *not* had a normal life in any way, shape or form."

"I can get your secrets out of you..." she said in her sexy voice, then proceeded to slowly suck out a crab claw. *Man, she kills me.* And yes, she could probably get all my state secrets out of me.

I pulled my phone out, pressed the speaker icon and listened to the voicemail message. The nice Realtor with the Southern drawl was going on in her sing-song voice.

"Mr. *Wal-kah*...I spoke to the owners of that lovely estate home you fell in love with..."

Oh, man, she was laying it on thick. *When did it become an estate?*

"They *ah-hr* motivated to sell, as they have already purchased *anotha* home. It took some doing, but they have agreed to your *offah*, if you are willing to close quickly. Please give me a call back at your earliest convenience..."

And that was how I bought a house on Harkers Island that had once belonged to a judge who was now Congressman Earl Stone, Presidential hopeful.

# Chapter Thirteen

## My New Home

A week after I bought the house on Harkers Island, I moved in and started cleaning. I asked Amanda to move in with me no more than forty or fifty times, but she wasn't quite ready for that. I figured another hundred or so times and she would say yes. Maybe. I didn't blame her for being cautious. She'd had her share of bad relationships.

She was back at work, and we spoke on the phone a few times every day. I had activated the landline and put it in my name, at Belle's suggestion. She reminded me that this area was famous for hurricanes. If the power went out for days and I couldn't charge my cell phone, at least the landline would probably work. It was always nice to find the blinking light on the machine and hearing Amanda's beautiful Southern twang talking to me. I *missed* that woman.

The previous owners had left quite a bit of furniture, so I'd inherited a baby grand piano, great patio furniture, all the office furniture, what they called 'the library' and the huge old kitchen table, which I absolutely *loved*. It was made out of rescued barn wood and looked like it was two hundred years old. Maybe Robert E. Lee had eaten on it or something.

Belle stopped by and brought me a houseplant and a bottle of six-dollar wine. She didn't know I was a wine snob, and I faked being impressed with her bottle of cabernet, but what the heck. It was the thought that counted. I'd use it for making sauce.

When Amanda came down, she was surprised at how nice things looked.

"Nice, Mr. *Wal-kah*..." Amanda said, doing a perfect impersonation of Belle.

Amanda had a little twang anyway, and now, she sounded so much like the Realtor.

I burst out laughing and bowed very low. "Mr. *Wal-kah* will be along presently. I am just Mr. *Wal-kah's* butler, but I'd be happy to show you out to the back veranda..."

"Ohhh! A *back* veranda?" she feigned with great drama.

"Well, the rear patio, anyway... Follow me, miss..." I dropped the Southern accent and laughed as I led her out of the back door.

"I think this whole mess started out here in the backyard, if I remember correctly," she said. "They left you the table and chairs?"

"Yes, ma'am," I said with a grin.

"Are you going to give me a proper kiss hello or am I driving back to Twin Oaks?" she asked with her hands on her hips.

I snatched her up and gave her a proper welcome to my humble abode. After a long liplock, we sat down at the wrought-iron table. I had cut some flowers from the garden and put one of my favorite chardonnays into an antique silver ice bucket on the table. Robert Mondavi ages it in bourbon barrels for a couple of months, and for less than twenty-five bucks, it will knock anyone's socks off.

I may have to take a trip to Monterrey County one of these days. Anyway, the bottle of white was a starter.

"Impressive," she said, eyeing the wine and flowers.

"Just wait until you see the bedroom," I said with my oh-too-sly face.

"I intend to," she retorted. "Seriously, Cory, I want to see everything! I can tell you did a lot of work."

We talked a hundred miles an hour for a few minutes while I poured us each a glass of wine to take while I showed her the house. My tour was designed to end in the master bedroom, where my new mattress and box spring had been delivered but had not been officially broken in yet. Notice I didn't say bedroom set—because there wasn't a stick of furniture in the master bedroom, just the mattress and box spring. As planned, we broke that in shortly after entering the room.

While we were lying in bed recovering from almost two weeks of abstinence, she asked me about bedroom furniture.

"I thought after I got married, my new wife would want to pick it all out."

"Oh yeah? Is your fiancée going to be upset when she finds out I'm part of the deal?" We looked at each other, and she 'shushed' me the way she usually did, and just curled up with me. We dozed for a bit, and it felt perfect just having her next to me again.

When we woke, we went for round two then took our first shower together in the new house. The master bathroom was awesome. Everything had been upgraded—tiled with Italian marble—all earth-tones and warm colors, with a rainmaker shower. We could have stayed in there for an hour.

In anticipation of her visit, I had stocked the fridge and pantry. I didn't tell Amanda that to get the grocery shopping accomplished, I'd had to drive almost forty-five minutes to the mainland, which was going to be a pain in the ass for the next fifty years—but would be worth it. Besides being a wine snob, I like to cook and have become decent at it because I also love to eat. If my bedroom antics wouldn't totally win her over, my cooking would.

We talked in the kitchen as we made a salad for the dinner.

I had two lamb shanks cooking low and slow in the heavy Dutch oven. The brown bubbling broth of wine—the Realtor's gift—root vegetables, tomato sauce, garlic and herbs filled the house with a delightful aroma that would make anyone want to eat immediately.

"There's something else I have to show you," I said. I took her hand and led her to the basement door. Amanda followed me down the stairs and saw my pile of lumber and tools in the middle of the floor.

"What on earth are you doing down here?"

"Making a wine cellar!" I announced proudly.

"You don't even have a *bedroom* set yet but you are building a *wine* cellar?"

"Priorities, ma'am. I've always dreamed of having my own house with a great wine cellar. I'm halfway there."

She laughed at me, as usual, but I talked to her about my ideas as we walked around the basement. Racks here... A table there... An archway here...

# Chapter Fourteen

Casey's Diary

After she'd left, that was when I found the diary. Congressman Stone's daughter had been murdered. His wife had committed suicide. In *this* house. Casey Stone.

*April 2*
*I can't believe it! He found my other diary and* burned *it!*
*He's* such *an A-Hole. I* hate *him!*
*I am hiding this where he's* never *going to find it!*

And he apparently never had. I found myself plunged inside the head of this young girl. It felt like I was betraying a trust, but I couldn't stop reading. I was mesmerized. My first thought was that I had to give the journal to her father, but the more I read, the more I realized this was not 'daddy's girl', at least not in her mind. I read farther, now sitting on the pile of lumber that I'd temporarily forgotten about.

*Saturday*
*Tonight was* so *awesome! Until I got home. Dad flipped out again. He's totally out of his mind. All we did was hang*

*out on the beach. Mike and Pete built a bonfire. And it's not like Ben and I were there alone. And Darla and Lynn were there, too. If they only knew! I can't do anything without him calling me a 'little whore'. All we did was make out. Dad calls Ben every name in the book just because he isn't rich...and because he lives with his nana. That is so lame. And you know what? Ben would never hit me.*

The congressman was whacking the kid? But was he right about Ben?

*Dad said to be home by ten. I got home on time, and he still started screaming at me. Mom stuck up for me and he gave her the 'I'll talk to you about this later' routine. I know he hits her too. He doesn't think I know, but I hear everything. And he lies about it! Last time he hit me I got so mad I yelled at him about hitting Mom, too, and he had a hissy fit and threw stuff all over my room. I know he was hitting Mom later. Mom should divorce him. We'd both be better off without him. I don't know why she won't. I hate him!*

I stopped reading. Words from a murdered kid, who had a father who'd smacked her around. Sixteen and getting hit? That was just wrong. But what do I know? I loved my parents, and they loved me back. In my whole life, neither one of them had ever hit me or my brother. Not once. Maybe *we* were abnormal.

I decided to read the rest of this piece of history that maybe no eyes but mine — and *hers* — had ever seen, but that it would require one of the bottles for which I was building this cellar in the first place.

I thought about calling Amanda right then but I didn't, because she was driving back to Twin Oaks and I didn't want her to freak out. And I wasn't sure I should share its Pandora's Box of horrors with her. She might never come back. Or maybe somehow, just for now, I wanted this between us — me and this kid. I've seen death and destruction. I've seen dead kids, too. But for whatever reason — maybe because this was *my* house — it just seemed to instantly get under my skin. I thought I'd left death overseas, but sonofabitch, it had followed me home — and I felt violated.

I found a bottle of Joseph Phelps Cabernet that was deserving of a steak or special occasion, but I opened it anyway. I had resigned myself to the fact that this would take a while to read. At least I would have a great bottle of wine to drink while I got depressed.

I picked up the journal and went upstairs to the kitchen to grab a large wine glass. It was sunny outside, something I hadn't thought about in the dark cellar. I opted for reading outside at the patio table. Perhaps the flowers and marble angels would chase away the gloom. Maybe the gloom was just inside me.

*Sunday, April 12*
*I hate, hate, hate this house! I heard them last night. Mom was crying. I put my pillow over my head and cried and prayed he would stop. It went on for a long time. When I came downstairs for breakfast, they were just sitting there. Dad was reading the paper, drinking coffee, and Mom was sitting like a zombie. Her face looked bruised, but I didn't dare ask about it. Dad would go batshit on me. He grounded me for the whole week last night and wouldn't even say why. When he goes to work, I am going to make Mom talk to me. I can't take this anymore! Everyone is going to the beach tonight and I know Ben will be there — and that Jessica Smith will be there drooling all over him! And I won't be there to tell her to get lost. He'll end up going out with her and breaking my heart, all because Dad is such an idiot.*

I sipped my wine and read for almost half an hour. Most of what she wrote was typical kid stuff, I guess. Girls are mini-women — tough to figure out. Boys just want to get laid — or least touch a boob or something — when they are that age. They certainly don't keep journals 'to express their feelings'. Hell, by nineteen I was jumping out of airplanes.

A few things were becoming clear, though, if I could believe everything she wrote, which I wasn't sure about. I mean, would a kid lie to her own journal? Why? I *assumed* she was telling the truth, but I also had to remember that it was *her* perception of what was going on in the house. A sixteen-year-old girl can't know everything going on between Mom and Dad.

If I could take everything at face value — I mean, bruises are not something a person would imagine...or maybe they were — there were a few themes that seemed to run through the diary. First, the congressman was physically and mentally abusive to his daughter and probably to his wife. Maybe this wouldn't be so unusual in the world of twenty years ago, and there are lots of crazy people out there, but *this* particular person was now a well-known United States Congressman whose name was being tossed around as a Presidential hopeful. Now re-married, with a young son, the guy presented a model of great husband and father.

*An act? Who knows?* The other theme was this kid named Ben, who Casey seemingly had a crush on. She seemed slightly goofy about him, but that's called being sixteen.

The more I read, the more I got the sense that Casey Stone was a smart kid but a little troubled, maybe. The phone ringing snapped me out of my stupor. I was just sitting there staring at the pages. I wasn't reading. I was just in la-la land, shocked at what I had read. I finally looked at my cell phone on the wrought-iron table and saw Amanda's number. I grabbed it.

"Hey, I just got home. Miss you already."

I said hi, but Amanda knew something was up.

"What's wrong, handsome?" she asked, not sounding as cheerful as usual.

"Why?"

"Your voice sounds a little funny."

I couldn't see myself reading a hundred pages out loud over the phone, which was what she'd want me to do. I lied and said nothing was wrong and that I was just concentrating on my wine cellar. Never mind that the lumber hadn't been touched since I'd found the diary.

She got the sense I was busy working on the house and said she'd call me later. I hung up and looked down at the diary, the faded flowers on the cover now seemed so much sadder.

I went back into the kitchen and poured another glass of cab, praying my good friend Joseph Phelps would help me feel better, then returned to the patio. It had started like such a nice day. A *normal* day. Now I was one of two people left on the planet who knew Congressman Earl Stone's sickening secret.

By the time I had finished the glass of wine and walked through the flower beds, pulling weeds as I went, I had calmed down a bit. I went to the patio, where Casey's journal still sat on the table. When my day had started, I'd thought I should call the congressman.

Now I was thinking I should call the police.

I went back to the diary but I couldn't read any more. I skipped to the last entry she'd made.

*He did it again. He said it was going to be a spanking because I was* 'acting like a whore with Ben again, even after I warned you.' *Same speech as last time.* 'If you want to be a whore, I'll treat you like one.' *He made me take my underwear off. He unzipped his pants and made me touch it. I hate him. I told him I would tell mom if he didn't stop. That just made him madder. Then he got it all over me. I cried my eyes out and I couldn't stop. I hate him I hate him I hate him.*

I sat there, numb, a sick feeling in my stomach. Was it possible that this guy who wanted to be President of my country could have sexually assaulted his own daughter? I felt so disgusted that I wanted to take a shower. I would have expected I would feel anger and rage—but I didn't. I just felt sick and heartbroken for this little kid. *'He did it again,'* she had written. How many times *before* had this guy abused her? Did her mom know? What was he *doing* to her?

I decided to put the diary away and give myself a break. I hid it in the back of a drawer in a roll-top desk in the library. I'm not sure if I was hiding it to protect it or just protecting *myself* from the disgusting images it contained. I stormed down to the cellar to saw lumber and pound nails until I felt better.

I worked nonstop until the phone rang. Amanda would be the only one calling me, so I put the hammer down, grabbed the phone, looked at my watch and saw how late it was. I was surprised.

"Hey, baby, how's Mr. Fix-It doing?"

I looked over at the wall of the cellar and saw that I had done three days' work in one afternoon. My right shoulder ached from hammering nails. "Pretty good. I should be finished with the woodwork tomorrow, then I'll stain everything and I'll be done."

"Wow…impressive," she said. She sounded like she was smiling. "That was fast."

"Yeah," I mumbled. "I guess I just got going and cranked it out. What's up with you?"

"I have some news, actually."

"Pregnant?" I said, trying to be funny but not feeling particularly comical. As soon as I said it, I thought about Casey being abused by her father—a gross image.

"Very funny…and no. I spoke to my boss. Told him I might be moving…" She let that hang out there for a second. "And guess what! He knows a therapist in Morehead City who would hire me."

She was waiting for my reaction. I was happy to hear the news but just still felt sick. I tried my best. "That's huge news, honey. When are you coming?"

She was quiet. *Damn. Women have radar or something.* "You don't sound as I happy as I thought you would."

"I'm exhausted, Amanda, but trust me, I'm very happy. I can't wait until you move in." And I meant it.

"Well, I don't know exactly when, but I'm thinking maybe two weeks, if that's okay with you. I mean, if you really want me to move down."

"Of course I want you to move down! I've been begging you for weeks." I guess she was mulling over my sincerity.

"Well, I still need to get out of my lease and do a million things over here. Then I have to talk to this guy Frank down in Morehead City. Then I have to see how this will work out because there's no bridge to Morehead City from the island. I'd have to take the ferry. That might be a total nightmare getting back and forth to work. If I drive, it'll take me way out of the way."

"Well, just get down here and we'll worry about that when you get here," I said.

*Mr. Sensitivity.*

"Easy for you to say. And what about you? Did you decide what you are going to do for work?"

That was when I said it by accident. "Yeah, I was thinking about becoming a private detective." It just came out. I was still thinking about the kid, I guessed.

"A *private detective*? And when did you decide *that*?"

"I dunno. What else do ex-soldiers do? We become cops half the time...except I can't do the 'by the book' thing anymore, so I'll just work for myself."

"Don't you have to go to school or something? What do *you* know about being a detective?" She was laughing.

"Well...I know how to track people down and kill them," I said. That stopped the laughing.

"You can't kill people anymore."

"Too bad," I said. And I meant it. At that particular moment, I wanted a hug. "Listen... It's only been four hours and I miss you already. When are you coming back?"

"Friday night after work. You know, that *work* thing? Remember?"

"Right. That work thing. Okay. Well, call the guy in Morehead City and tell me when to be at your place with a moving truck." We talked a while longer, said our goodnights and I immediately went to my computer.

# Chapter Fifteen

Playing Detective

I sat down and started searching for any references I could find on the murder of Casey Stone. Sometimes a person should be careful what they wish for. I'd thought I wanted information. I'd thought I wanted details. Then I got them and I couldn't *un*-get them. I just *have* them...and they were burning a hole in my brain.

As I started researching, I remembered back to my Army days. I'd been looking into the case of a staff sergeant who'd 'lost it' on a patrol in Iraq. Over the course of one month, four Humvees had been hit by improvised explosive devices. The roadside bombs had killed six men and permanently injured four. One was a best friend of the sergeant, and the unfortunate soldier had lost both legs in the explosion. When the sergeant had come upon an insurgent running from his latest 'roadside project' some days later, the sergeant had run after him into his stone house. The sergeant had thrown two grenades into the house after the insurgent, then had hosed the house with his M4. When he went inside, he'd realized the insurgent had run into a house full of kids. It hadn't even been his house, just a place to hide. The kids had been in the wrong place at the wrong time. Such was life in a war zone.

I'd ended up having to investigate the wrongful deaths of the civilians, since the staff sergeant was in my outfit at the time. I'd had to look at the pictures of the inside of that house.

Point is, I couldn't *un*-look at it. *Ever*. And now I was about to start delving deeper into this girl who'd been abused by her own father, only to be murdered. *By him? And he got away with it? By someone else? Was he involved?* I think *she* was in a war zone, too. She just didn't know it.

I found an old article in the *Carolina Banks*, one of the bigger papers in that part of the state.

*Judge's Daughter Found Dead*

*The body of Casey Stone, sixteen, daughter of Judge Earl Stone, has been recovered. State police announced the body was found floating in the water behind the Woods' commercial fishing dock on Harkers Island at five-forty-seven a.m. Saturday by local fisherman Thomas Woods, forty-seven. Casey's mother, Anne Stone, forty-one, was found dead at nine-thirty a.m. in the basement of the Stone home by her husband. The cause of Casey's death has not been announced, pending an autopsy. Anyone with information is asked to contact the Carteret County tip line at 888-TIP-LINE.*

There was her picture, looking at me from my computer screen, staring right through me. Her green eyes stood out from straight, strawberry-blonde hair that fell to her shoulders.

She was *real* now—a pretty teenager, full of life, seemingly on her way to becoming a valued member of society, murdered on this quiet little island. The article was dated August third, 1991.

Her distraught mother had killed herself a few hours after Casey's body had been found. All of it was a tragedy.

I searched for other articles. August fourth had the next big headline, and reading it made my heart pound in my chest.

*Benjamin McComb arrested in the Murder of Congressman's Daughter*

*Benjamin McComb, seventeen, a local teen, has been arrested in the death of Casey Stone.*

*According to the autopsy report released by the medical examiner, Michael Greller, Casey was raped then strangled and her body was dumped in the ocean near a commercial fishing dock.*

I sat there stunned. She had been *raped*, then murdered. I wanted to kill somebody. It took a few minutes before I could read the rest of the article.

*Police arrested McComb at his grandmother's house on Harkers Island this morning. He will be tried as an adult. Judge Stone could not be reached for comment. His spokesperson, Barbara Ellis, expressed the congressman's gratitude for the many flowers and notes of sympathy the congressman has received.*

I read that and thought, *my* home. They left those flowers and cards at the end of *my* driveway. Then the light bulb went off—Benjamin McComb! Ben. Casey's crush. I sat back and let that soak in. The kid she'd had a crush on had raped then murdered her? And poor dad was home grieving? *Bullshit.* I kept reading. Article after article about the arrest, about the girl and her family, about how Harkers Island hadn't had a murder in a hundred years…and about the trial.

I stared at a picture of Ben at the top of the story. His booking photo. It was the first time I was laying eyes on the kid mentioned in Casey's diary. He had skinny features and long brown hair. He looked like a terrified kid, not a sociopathic killer. Not that anyone could know who was guilty or innocent by looking at a picture, but Ben McComb just didn't strike me as a rapist or a murderer. Casey had a little-kid crush on him. In another photo halfway down the page, he looked like a kid, too, nothing short of heart-broken.

There hadn't been any DNA evidence to link Ben to the rape. The body showed signs of forced sexual assault, but the saltwater had removed any DNA. Of course, DNA technology twenty years ago wasn't as good as it is today, either, so maybe not having any DNA evidence wouldn't have been unusual back then. This was Harkers Island twenty years ago—not last week in New York City.

Ben was linked to Casey by his own statement, given to police—they had been secretly dating—as well as the accounts of friends. Ben was the last person to be seen with Casey. Everyone placed him with the girl right before she was reported missing by her parents that Friday night.

She was found on Saturday morning, floating near the dock, not far from where the kids had said they had all been partying on the beach. Ben admitted under questioning that he and Casey had been secretly seeing each other but he denied having sexual intercourse with her. The prosecutor was quoted as saying, "Of course he would deny it. She said no, he forced himself on her, she threatened to tell her father and he killed her to keep her quiet."

The jury bought it. The jurors were from the surrounding area and Stone was an area judge. Before that, he had been a successful lawyer who had been politically active with the county and state party. The suspect, Benjamin McComb, had been represented by the state. His attorney should have requested a change of venue but he didn't. According to the newspaper, Ben had been raised by a grandmother. He had never known his father, and his mother had died young from breast cancer. Ben's grandmother had testified. Her testimony about what time Ben had arrived home had been shot to pieces by the prosecutor.

At the end of the trial, Ben was charged with second-degree murder and sentenced to thirty years to life. He was sent to the Maury Correctional Institute in Greene County, North Carolina.

I read a few more articles, looked at Casey's face a few more times and decided I needed to go for a walk on the beach.

I walked down the driveway of my house and realized that in another twenty minutes, it would be so dark I'd never find my way home. Where were my night-vision goggles when I needed them? In my gear, with Ice, but I didn't bother to get them. My great plans for a walk dashed, I decided to try my Jacuzzi instead. Definitely a sound move on my part. After a long, hot soak, I hit my mattress and was asleep and drooling in two minutes.

# Chapter Sixteen

## Making Plans

I woke up to the phone ringing on Monday morning. I was totally out of it when I picked up and grumbled hello.

"Were you still sleeping?" Amanda was laughing. "Do you know it's almost nine-thirty?"

I blinked a few times and looked around the room, trying to figure out where I was. I still felt like a visitor in my own house. "Hey...sorry. Yeah, I guess so."

"All that manual labor knocked you out?" she teased.

"Yeah," I said, then thought to myself, *That, and a whole bottle of really great cab.* I marveled at the fact that I had slept soundly a few times in my new house. Maybe my combat readiness was finally subsiding enough to let me start being a civilian.

She told me she was calling between patients. We chatted for a few more minutes until I was more awake, said our goodbyes when her patient arrived and I hit the shower. As I brushed my teeth, I decided that I would be launching my own investigation into a twenty-year-old murder case, which was already considered solved.

I threw on a pair of old shorts and an old T-shirt from Bravo Company, 3rd Ranger Battalion. It proudly boasted 'Rangers Lead the Way' across the chest. What the hell... I figured I was getting ready for *something*. When I'd left the Rangers for Delta, we hadn't gotten T-shirts. In fact, sometimes we hadn't even gotten uniforms with patches on them.

I made coffee, the lifeblood of any true military man, and a quick bowl of cereal, then I was off to the computer for more digging. I decided on several projects for that morning. First, I would meet my neighbors—preferably older neighbors who had lived on the island when Casey had been murdered—and second, I would try to track down Benjamin McComb, starting with where they had sent him. If he was still there—and still alive—he would be pushing forty. *Not so old and still a lifetime in prison ahead of him.*

Maybe I could find a local cop to talk to. Somebody *somewhere* had to know *something*. I'll admit it. I *am* a stubborn sumbitch. Once I make up my mind to do something, I *will* find a way.

I left my house and walked down the narrow road to see who might be out and about.

On a weekday morning, most folks would be at work, unless they were here on vacation.

They would not know anything about the subject.

At first, I didn't find anyone. When I got to the end of my road, it led to a dock. I walked out to where several boats were moored and found a few old-timers working on the inboard diesel engine of a large fishing boat. The hull was wood and painted red. I smiled and waved, and they waved back but kept with their work.

I ambled over to the three men and caught their island accents. *Holy crap.* I'd thought the Realtor had a thick accent until I heard *these* three. As Amanda had warned me, the islanders, especially the old timers, spoke High Tider, which sounded like *Hoi Toider* when they said it, and they might as well have been speaking Greek. It might be English, but it was nothing like I'd ever heard before. I think it was easier speaking to the tribes in the Northwest Frontier of Pakistan.

I walked over and listened as closely as I could. I'm pretty sure they were bitching about the engine, but maybe they were bitching about me. It was hard to say. I did catch the word 'dingbatter', which I came to find out later referred to new folks to the island.

I decided to try my best to make friends. Back in the day, I would give a kid a chocolate bar and he'd tell me where the IEDs were buried. These guys would be a tougher nut to crack.

"Nice-looking boat," I lied. It might have been nice forty years ago.

The three of them gave me a look that said it all and went back to working on the diesel inboard.

"Y'all commercial fishermen or you run day trips for the tourists?" I asked, as I walked closer. Obviously, I didn't know shit about fishing.

One of the fishermen couldn't contain himself. He stood and said something that sounded like, "Oh yeah, we take the tourists out to *feesh*. Always *bettah* with a net."

I glanced up at the huge nets suspended from the outriggers. The trawler was definitely a commercial boat, which anyone with half a brain could see. *Yup. I'm an idiot.* "Just kidding, fellas. Y'all sound like natives. I just bought the old Stone House." I realized after I'd said it that they were probably confused. "As in *Earl* Stone, not made out of stone."

They looked at me in silence. Finally, one of them stood and walked over. He looked to be in his sixties, maybe. It was hard to tell. He was weather-beaten, with skin that had probably been tan his entire life. He reminded me of some of the Afghans I had met, with wrinkled faces and deep-set eyes that looked wary. His dark hair, streaked with gray, was slicked back with sweat. He wiped his greasy hands on his overalls then on a greasy rag that was hanging from his pocket. He looked at his hand again. It was still black.

I figured this was my chance to make friends, so I grabbed his hand and shook it firmly. "Cory Walker. Nice to meet you."

"Caleb Jackson. The Stone place, eh?" He looked over at his friends and probably said something about me buying the house, but quite frankly, I don't know *what* the hell he was saying.

One of the other guys got up and walked over. He was a tall, lanky fellow, with slightly stooped shoulders and a slow, relaxed manner. If he had told me he was a flight mechanic in the Second World War, I would have believed him. He also gave me a black greasy handshake and told me his name was Thomas — not Tom, no last name, just Thomas. He looked to be about a hundred years old.

I missed everything Thomas said. He used the phrase 'dit-dot' a few times with his buddies, which I later learned was a reference to me needing Morse code. Evidently another jab at the 'off islander' who needed a translator. Listening to these guys made my head hurt, but I needed to learn whatever I could from them, *if* they'd talk to an outsider.

"Did you know the Stones?" I asked Thomas.

He just laughed and walked back to the engine he was working on. The third guy went back to work on the engine with him, never having introduced himself.

Caleb looked at me in a way that made me *feel* like an outsider. "We *all* knew the Stones. They was royalty, so to speak. Had a real nice place. Used to come out here from the county every summer."

He was referring to Carteret County — the mainland. I was surprised to learn that the Stones weren't here full time. I had just assumed, wrongly, that this was their only house. *Super detective work.* "How many years did they come out here?"

Caleb rubbed his chin, which was now black with grease. "They been gone a long time now. I reckon the girl was a baby when they first come out."

"Sad story about the girl," I said softly.

"No one talks about it." He gave me a firm look. "Not good for business."

"Yeah, I guess not. Although they got the killer, right?" I asked, trying to read his answer.

"Local kid. 'Bout her age." He yelled over to one of his buddies and they barked back and forth so fast I missed almost all of it. He turned back to me and said, "Ben. Ben McComb. Kid's name. His nana was an old islander. A good woman. That whole business broke her heart. She died right after he went to jail. Bess...that was her name. Bess McComb. Ain't said that name in many years," he mumbled to himself.

"Did you know the kid? Her grandson who went to jail."

"Last I heard, he'll die there."

"Think he did it?"

Caleb crossed his arms and looked at me real hard, the way I do when I'm trying to look into someone's brain. "You bought the Stone estate, and now you think you're gonna to write a book about it?"

I smiled. "No, sir. I'm not a writer. I'm a retired soldier. I just heard some things, that's all. Made me start wondering."

Caleb grunted. "Don't wonder too much. Most folks here just as soon forget about the whole yethy business."

"Yethy?" I asked.

He shook his head and mumbled about me being a dit-dot again. "Yethy... The damn thing stank to the heavens. Now ya folla?"

"Uh-huh," I lied. I learned later that 'yethy' was High Tider for an unpleasant odor.

"Best let that poor girl rest in peace. Her momma, too."

*That's right.* I hadn't thought much about her mother's death, but that was certainly a part of this whole mess. Caleb told me he needed to get back to his boat and said a 'welcome to the island' of sorts. I watched the old man walk away and wondered what all the locals must think about what had happened.

# Chapter Seventeen

## Mr. Detective

I went back to my 'estate'. After a morning of walking around the local houses, I realized just how special my house was compared to the rest of the ones on the island. My house had a definite Southern Gentry style architecture. Many of the other houses, except for a handful of new ones, were old wooden bungalows. Very few had the ornate wood workings of my veranda. Basically, I had the rich guy's house in a neighborhood of fisherman. My immediate neighbors also had nicer homes and I guess we were considered the local aristocracy. I figured I'd find out how we were viewed as I came to know more of the locals.

I called the prosecutor's office, which I was supposed to have done the previous week but had forgotten about. The assistant prosecutor I spoke to was obviously pissed that I was late checking in.

"You were advised to keep us informed of any address or phone number changes, Mr. Walker. We were ready to issue a warrant for your arrest."

"A *warrant*? I was told that your office didn't anticipate any formal charges. The man I spoke to over there, Grant Williams, said this was a self-defense case that most likely wouldn't go farther than a few more questions and I could forget the whole thing."

"Please hold for Mr. Williams," grumbled Mr. Personality.

"Hi, Cory," came his familiar voice. "You moved. You were supposed to notify us. We thought maybe you got scared and flew the coop."

"Not at all. I just sort of made a spontaneous decision on a house. Got a little caught up and forgot to call. Is there a problem?"

"Nah. Don't sweat it. I don't expect anything to happen 'til the end of the summer, at the soonest. Most likely it'll all be officially dismissed. Where are you?"

"Harkers Island."

"You bought a house on *Harkers Island?*" he exclaimed.

"Yeah. What's the big deal?"

He laughed. "No big deal. I guess you just like it *real* quiet. Damn, Cory, they didn't get electricity and phones until a few decades ago. You buying a boat?"

"Thinking about it," I said. "I'm an excellent fisherman." I was thinking back to the trawler catching mullet in nets for sport fishing. "Okay…not so much." My sarcasm was wasted on him.

He asked how I was feeling and how Amanda was. He was a good guy. I was dying to ask him about the Stone case but changed my mind and didn't. I'd wait until I had more, then ask him if it seemed like it was cool. I thought about calling Amanda and telling her about the diary but decided that was a bad idea. Maybe I'd wait until she moved in.

I went back to the library, dug Casey's notebook out of the desk and started reading where I'd left off. The entries had apparently stopped for several weeks. I guess the kid had been traumatized after the last episode with that sick-o she called her father.

*I keep wondering if I should talk to Mom. Dad says that if I say anything, I'll be sorry, and he means it. God, what if she knows and she doesn't care? He hasn't been as mean, but he keeps making me take my underwear off like he's gonna spank me. If I'm quiet, he just gets off on me and leaves without hitting me. It's better to just be quiet. I want to ask Mom what I did to deserve this?*

I sat back and exhaled. Now *there* was a thought. What if her mother had known and hadn't stopped it? How could a mother have allowed this? Had *she* been scared of him? Had she just been in denial? Or had she really not know what was going on? I could feel myself getting angry. *That* made me angrier—that I would allow myself to get so caught up in something that happened nearly twenty years ago and get angry and upset. This was all ancient history? *Bullshit.* Two of the four people were still alive—Ben, in prison until he rotted, and the congressman going to run for President. I decided to get back on the computer and start tracking down Benjamin McComb.

After a few phone calls and some lying, I confirmed that Ben was now in his later thirties and still an inmate at the Maury Correctional Institute in Greene County, where he had spent the last nearly twenty years. I decided I would be taking a drive to go visit him. The idea didn't seem any crazier than buying a house on

Harkers Island and asking—begging—Amanda to move in with me. Obviously, I am certifiably mad.

My next call was to the Carteret County Sheriff's Department. After about three transfers and some bullshitting on my part, I finally got someone to speak to me. The deputy I spoke with, a Bill Peace, didn't know about the Stone case, but when I asked about an officer named Arthur McDade—I'd read his name in a few articles—he was helpful. Arthur had left the department many years before, but they were still in touch occasionally. He wouldn't give me his number but promised he would give mine to Arthur.

When he asked what it was in reference to, I simply said I was an old friend of Casey Stone.

# Chapter Eighteen

Maury

After a couple of days of phone calls, I finally got Benjamin McComb on the phone. He agreed to allow me to visit him and told me I would be his first visitor in the whole time he'd been there. That was a pretty depressing thought. I decided to bring him a few foil packets of tuna. Prisons didn't allow smoking these days, and I wanted to bring him *something*. I know a care package with anything other than MREs always made me smile when I was deployed. Maybe a few packages of tuna would make his day, too. They *had* to be better than whatever crap they served in a prison.

I spoke with prison security and arranged for the visit. Maury was a medium security facility, but they were damned strict about visitation. One hour max, without contact, under supervision.

I 'sort of' lied to Amanda and told her I was going fishing. I mean, I *was* going fishing — just not for fish. Or 'feesh', as I was now calling them, to sound like a Hoi Toider.

The drive to Greene County was pleasant enough. I got to the prison in a little over an hour and a half. I'm not sure what I was expecting, but the place looked pretty darned prison-like. It was a large unpainted concrete expanse of non-descript buildings surrounded by huge barbed-wire fencing with razor wire on top. There were guard towers along the fence and large light towers, which I assumed lit the place up like a Christmas tree every night. It was no place anyone would ever want to visit unless they had to.

I went through several layers of security, working deeper and deeper into the bowels of the very sterile, unpleasant place. The guards were polite but also very specific about what was expected, what was not allowed, etc. At one point, the other visitors and I, maybe a dozen of us, were taken to a hallway where we were told what would happen to us if we were caught bringing drugs into the prison. The guard then opened a garbage can, told us this was our last chance to discard any drugs anonymously and said he'd be back in three minutes, at which time the drug dogs would be brought in.

He left us alone. I watched two young women engage in animated conversation. Finally, one of them took a book she was carrying and quickly threw it into the trashcan, then got back in line. The guard walked back in a moment later and led us into the next hallway through yet another series of locked doors.

True to his word, another guard arrived with an intimidating-looking Malinois, which worked his way through the line. I had seen them work in Ass-Crackistan and other shitholes of the world and had a tremendous respect for both those beautiful animals and their K-9 handlers.

The dog got to the friend of the woman who had tossed the book and started barking. She was pulled from the line, her friend acting like she had no idea who the woman was, as a female officer was brought in to take the woman to another room — for strip searching, I would assume. I never knew what they'd found, if anything, but I never saw her again. The rest of us were led through a myriad of hallways until we were walked into a large room filled with stainless-steel tables that were bolted to the floor. Guards walked around stone-faced, their eyes scanning every inch of the room.

As I glanced around, it occurred to me that I had no idea who I was looking for. He would look nothing like the kid who had been arrested, tried and found guilty twenty years ago.

All the other visitors went quickly to their inmate relations and sat right down. I stood and looked around the room like an idiot. A guard was kind enough to ask me if I was looking for someone, and I told him Benjamin McComb. He pointed to a man sitting alone at a table in yet another orange jumpsuit.

I walked over, sat down and looked into the eyes of a ghost. Ben had long, greasy-looking hair, tied in a ponytail. His face was clean-shaven, revealing a few nasty-looking scars over his eyes and chin. He was skinny and vacant-looking. I couldn't help but wonder if they had him drugged.

"Hello, Ben," I said in as soothing a voice as I could muster. "I'm Cory Walker." Out of habit, I extended my hand.

He shot a glance at a nearby guard and said, "Sorry, no contact."

"Right. Sorry. Thanks for agreeing to see me."

"You said you think you can help me get another trial?" His accent hinted at the Harkers Island sound that he hadn't heard in twenty years.

"Maybe. I want you to know that I'm not a reporter or a cop or a lawyer or anything like that. I'm just a regular guy who happened to buy the old Stone house on Harkers Island."

If he was surprised, his face didn't show much. In fact, he looked fairly catatonic.

"You were convicted of raping and killing Casey Stone. Did you do it?"

That got his attention. He stared at me for a full minute. He looked at me like he wanted to hit me.

"You drive all the way here to ask me that?"

"Pretty much," I said.

"No, Mr. Walker. Casey and me? We were boyfriend and girlfriend, sort of. Her father hated my guts. We were just kids. She'd sneak out to the dunes and we'd hang out with our friends. We'd make out sometimes, sometimes a little more, but it was *kid* stuff. We never had sex." His eyes welled up. He spoke softly, trying not to get choked up. "I'm getting close to forty years old, sir. And I ain't *never* had sex. Convicted of rape and I'm gonna die a virgin in here."

His eyes were watering over. It was pretty hard to watch. Of course, I could be speaking with a rapist murdering liar — which was the other possibility.

"Why did they arrest you?"

"'Cause they didn't have nobody *else* to arrest. You're living in that house now. You see how small Harkers is. Everyone knows everyone. And everyone knew that Casey and I were sneaking around together. Her father had a lot of juice back in those days."

"He has a lot more now. You watch the news?"

"We don't get much TV time. Assholes make us watch cartoons when they have the TV on. I think they're trying to make us all nuts."

"Yeah, well, Earl Stone is now *Congressman* Stone."

It was like I'd told him Santa wasn't real. His mouth opened and he just stared.

"*Congressman*? Like in *Washington*?"

"That's the place, yeah. He wants to be President of the United States."

Ben slumped back in his chair, destroyed, and stared at the ceiling lights. "You can't help me," he said, his voice flat. He looked like he was ready to stand up.

"Wait! Maybe I can, but I'll need your help if anyone is going to listen to me. I need to know exactly what happened that night. And anything you can tell me about Earl Stone? Or Casey's mom?"

He looked totally shot and spoke very softly. "It was a long time ago. But for nearly twenty years all I've had to think about is the good days with Casey. She was so smart and funny and beautiful. She was also pretty fucked up."

That didn't surprise me, after what I'd been reading. "What do you mean? How?"

"Shit was going on at home. I think her daddy was beating on her and her momma."

"Yethy," I said, trying to be cool. It had the desired effect. A long, slow grin crossed his face, showing me prison dental work.

"Yethy? God, Mr. Walker, I haven't heard toidy in twenty years. You been on Harkers long?"

"No. Just trying to catch on."

"Yeah, well...yethy is right. Something stunk *bad*. Once I asked her about her dad, and she got real upset, so I never did again. Then, another time, right before she was killed, we were messing around, ya know? We had gone farther than we ever had before, and it was getting kind of hot and heavy, ya know? Anyway...you know...well...she freaked out."

"I'm not sure I follow you," I said. I wanted him to be as clear as possible.

"I unzipped her jeans, okay?" He wiped his face awkwardly with his hands and took a moment, trying to find the right words, then leaned in real close, almost whispering. "We'd been humpin' and grinding on the sand, ya know? She was really pushing herself against me and moaning and I was thinkin' 'tonight's the night'. At first, she was totally into it. Then I unzipped her jeans and she freaked out and screamed that she wasn't a whore. It was weird, man...like I *made* her do it or something. But I swear on my grandma's grave that I wasn't forcing her to do *anything*. She was totally into it, the same as me. Then she just totally *freaked out*."

"What did she say about her father?"

"Like I said, it was babbling nonsense, but I know he hated my guts. I think he was crazy or something. She was scared of him."

"You were both young—"

"*No*, man. You don't get it. I ain't saying it right. When she was freaking out, she started babbling like a *crazy* girl and said some weird shit about her daddy. I didn't get it. She just wanted to get home, and she left. That was the second-to-last time I saw her."

"The *second*-to-last time?" That was stunning. "What happened the last time you saw her?"

A guard announced, "Two minutes!"

"Damn. We don't have much time, Ben. Tell me about the last time you saw her."

"We were down on the beach. Three couples. We made a bonfire. We drank some beers. Last beer I ever had." He wiped his nose with the back of his hand. Recounting all this was getting to him. "It was the best night of my life. I wouldn't ever have hurt that girl. I loved Casey. She told me she loved me that night. She *told* me!"

He was now getting fairly agitated, and the nearby guard walked over. "Okay, that's enough. Stand up, McComb."

Ben stood at attention like a conditioned robot.

"I'll come back, Ben. We need to talk more. I'll try to help you. I promise."

"*Time!*" announced the guard.

Ben didn't speak at all. He just turned and shuffled toward the door.

# Chapter Nineteen

Recap

When I got back to the car, I turned on my cell phone and found two messages from Amanda. I guessed it was time to tell her what was up, but I didn't want to do it on the phone.

"Hey, you," she said when she picked up. "Where the heck are you? I was worried when you didn't pick up. Are you okay?'

"Hey back. I'm fine. Where are *you*?"

"Driving home from work. I've been calling the house all day, and I tried your cell twice. Are you avoiding me? Afraid I'll really show up Friday night?"

"Actually, I am on my way to Twin Oaks to see the love of my life." That was kind of mushy. Maybe thinking about the kid's story made me corny.

She saw right through me. "You trying to butter me up for a conjugal visit?"

"Funny choice of words," I replied.

"What do you mean?"

"I'll explain when I see you. You *are* free for dinner, aren't you?"

"Well, I'll have to call my other boyfriend and tell him to change our plans, but yes, I think I can squeeze you in."

"Literally?"

"That, too." I heard her giggle.

I really did love that woman. I drove as fast as possible to Twin Oaks and was very happily surprised to find Amanda waiting for me in an outfit from Victoria's Secret. Did I mention that I loved that woman? Anyway, we were late for the dinner reservations she'd made. That was what happens when dessert is first.

We went to an amazing Italian place in Twin Oaks and ordered dinner and a bottle of red. Remembering the great bottle of red at her house when she had first kidnapped me, I selected their best brunello...Franci, which was perhaps one of the best examples that came from brunello di Montalcino that I'd ever tasted.

"So how's it going, Mr. Fix-It? Build an addition to the house yet?"

"Actually, I got sidetracked. Let me tell you what happened when I started working on the basement. This is going to take a while."

Then I spilled the beans. She sat wide-eyed with her mouth hanging open. I ended with the prison visit. When I was finished, I waited for her to say something.

She just stared at me.

Finally, she asked, "So what are you going to do?"

"I don't know. Practice being a detective, I guess. The guy I talked to in Maury may be a rapist and a murderer, for all I know. Twelve people on a jury thought so, anyway. But I just get the gut feeling he got railroaded. And I need to finish reading this girl's diary."

"I'm surprised you haven't already."

"Yeah, well…I can only take it in little doses. If the girl is being truthful, it was a horrible way to live."

"What do you mean *if*? It was her *diary*."

"You ever have one?"

"Actually, yes. Lots of girls keep journals at that age. Sometimes it helps to get stuff out on paper. I had lots of little secrets in mine…and they were all true."

"I guess boys are smart enough not to incriminate themselves on paper," I said with a smile.

"Yeah, well, maybe that's true, too. But me and my girlfriends, we all kept diaries. Sometimes we would show each other a page here or there. It was easier than telling each other some of the stuff we were doing or thinking."

"Would you want to read hers?"

"Maybe."

"I'll warn you now. I have taken to referring to Congressman Stone simply as 'That Sick Fuck'. That's his new name."

The wine arrived with great ceremony and was decanted tableside. The cork was presented to me like I had won an Oscar. We stopped our conversation and watched our server, who poured me a taste, which made my eyes close in sheer joy. Then he poured Amanda a glass.

She tasted hers with equal relish. "Wow."

"Yeah, pretty amazing, right?"

Our server filled my glass and smiled. "I'm glad you like it. Franci is the best brunello on the list. For dessert, I'll show you a Sauternes if you care for an after-dinner drink. Château d'Yquem. We have an impressive wine list here."

The server disappeared after our glasses were filled, and Amanda shook her head slowly and spoke quietly. "You hear stories like this all the time in the papers. I've never known anyone who was abused by their parents. You?"

"No. Only by my drill sergeant."

Dinner came and thankfully, we changed topics for a while. I was pretty fried thinking about Ben the whole ride from Maury. What if he were innocent? Twenty *years* in that place? I owed it to him as much as to Casey to find out what had happened. To try, anyway.

After an amazing dinner, with Amanda regaling me with amusing anecdotes about her new patients, then a half-bottle of that château d'Yquem, which cost almost as much as the whole dinner, we went back to Amanda's place and enjoyed a very romantic night. The next morning, I woke up to coffee in bed.

"God, Amanda. I loved you already, but the coffee in bed definitely seals the deal," I told her as she handed me my morning java. She sat on the bed and brushed her long hair out of her face. *Damn.* Even in the morning, she looked good.

"So what are you going to do, detective?"

"Keep digging, I guess."

"Going to call the police? I think you should. That diary is evidence. It might free an innocent man who just wasted twenty years of his life."

"*If* he's innocent. I have a call out to a sheriff's deputy who worked the case twenty years ago. I'll know more in a few days, I guess. For now, I am holding my cards close to the vest. Earl Stone is not someone I want to screw with before I have all my facts straight. Ben's already done twenty years. Another couple of days won't kill him."

# Chapter Twenty

## McDade

Amanda went to work, and I drove back to Harkers Island. It was about a ninety-minute drive through stunning farm country, but my mind was racing the whole time. I had a lot fewer answers than questions, but the idea of reading more of Casey's journal made me cringe.

I've seen some pretty messed up shit in my day, but I was having a hard time getting my head around this. I kept thinking about the last line I had read. *'What if Mom knows and she doesn't care?'* I mean, was that humanly *possible*?

When I got back to Harkers, I have to say I felt like I was coming home. I hadn't felt like that since buying the house, maybe because I hadn't been away overnight since being down there. Even *living* there, I still felt like an outsider, which I would probably be to them for the next two or three hundred years. But returning now, I really did feel like I was *home*. It was a warm feeling. I hadn't had a real home since I was a kid living under my parents' roof. I still missed them sometimes…like right now.

Anyway, when I walked in, I found the answering machine blinking. The first message was from Agatha. She had left me a present on the back porch. The second message was from a gruff-sounding man with a smoker's rasp who seemed half in the bag. It was the call I had been waiting for — Arthur McDade, Carteret Sheriff's Deputy, retired. The message had a strange tone, and I ended up playing it three times.

*"Mr. Walker, this is Arthur McDade. I hear you been asking about me. I always wondered if anybody would look at the Stone case again. You can call me on my cell…"*

It was like he had been expecting the call. But for twenty years? Was it so obvious that Benjamin McComb hadn't done the crime, and everyone had just let him rot in jail anyway? I walked to the rear door and opened it to find a jar of homemade apple butter and two Mason jars of spiced peaches. There was a handwritten note from Agatha Miles inviting me to tea. Her handwriting was neat but shaky. She hadn't looked that old when I'd met her briefly with the Realtor that day. Now I wondered how old she really was.

I picked up my goodies, went back inside and called McDade on the landline, which had better reception than my cell phone. I didn't want to miss anything he said.

*The wonders of caller ID…* He said, "Hello, Mr. Walker," like he had been sitting there for two days waiting for me to call back.

"Hello, Deputy McDade. Thanks for calling."

"It's Arthur. Ain't been a deputy for a very long time. You told my pal Bill you were an old friend of Casey Stone's. That right?"

"That's what I told him. It's a bit more complicated, though. I bought the old Stone house. There's something I need to talk to you about. Maybe we could meet tomorrow? Or the next day? How far from Harkers Island are you?"

"I ain't far *enough*. And I won't meet you. I'm ten hours away by car. That's as close as I'll ever get to Carteret County, and I don't take visitors."

I sat back and pondered his attitude. He *had* called me. He must want to talk about something.

"Okay, Arthur. But can I ask you a few questions?"

"You a lawyer?"

"No, sir. Not a lawyer, not a cop, nothing like that at all. I just own the Stone house, now…and I found something."

There was a long silence.

"Arthur, you were the first on the scene that morning, right?"

"First *deputy*, but not the first person. Earl Stone was already there with a few other locals. The man who found her, Tom Wood, he recognized the girl. He'd called the girl's folks. He'd pulled her out of the water next to his boat. Shook him up pretty good, as I recall. Anyway, the girl was dead. Looked like she had been in the water all night. Her mom hanged herself when she got the news."

"Do you think Benjamin McComb killed her, Arthur?" Another very long silence.

"I don't know, Mr. Walker," he said thoughtfully.

"He's been sitting in Maury for twenty years. Don't you think you should be *sure*?"

"Don't put that on *me*. I tried to broaden the investigation. I was taken off the case. When I went back and spoke to the detectives assigned to it, I was reprimanded for interfering. When I asked about it a few weeks later and tried to talk to the sheriff, I was moved to another station halfway across the county and given *bullshit* to do until I had to quit. They forced me out, Walker."

"Because of this case?"

"I never had anything below an outstanding review. And I wasn't the only one."

I felt my heart pounding in my chest. "Who else?"

"The medical examiner who did the autopsy...Greller. They got rid of him, too. He was good guy. He did the autopsy on Mrs. Stone."

"*Mrs*. Stone?" I had been giving all my brain power to Casey and Ben. I had sort of forgotten about her poor mother who'd hanged herself. My brain kicked into overdrive. *Did she kill herself out of sorrow or guilt for ignoring what was going on in that house of horrors?*

"Yeah. Anne Stone. Dr. Greller had a few too many questions. Rattled a few cages, I guess."

"Like whose?"

"Not sure. Maybe *Mr*. Stone."

So it was out there again. Stone. That Sick Fuck. I guess I wasn't the only one looking at him. "You think Congressman Stone had anything to do with her death, Arthur?"

"The daughter? You'd have to ask Greller....if you can find him."

"I'm asking *you*. Do you think Stone had anything to do with his daughter's death?"

"You *do* know that Stone is most likely going to be the next President of these United States, right? You sure you want to go digging into his life, Mr. Walker? They got rid of me twenty years ago when he was still a *nobody*. I don't think you want to fuck with Earl Stone."

I've been in plenty of scary places all over the world and I didn't consider Harkers Island one of them. "I'm not afraid of him, Arthur."

"Maybe you should be."

"What did the medical examiner say about Mrs. Stone, Arthur?"

"Like I said, you'd have to ask him. Greller left Carteret County right after that case. What a coincidence, huh? I have no idea where he is now."

"Okay, I'll just have to find him and ask him myself."

"Let me ask *you* something, Walker. What made you start diggin' so hard? You know how powerful Earl Stone is? Why are you going after him? Is this political?"

"No."

"You told Bill Peace you *knew* Casey. Did ya?"

"Casey Stone kept a diary, Arthur. I found it. She *told* me some things. I want to know the truth."

I could hear Arthur exhale, long and slow. "You *have* a diary? Or somebody told you about it? If you have an old piece of evidence that could incriminate Congressman Stone, you might just consider moving someplace safe—say...like Afghanistan."

"I just got *back* from there, Arthur, and I have no intention of going anywhere. If anyone needs to hide, it's the congressman."

*My next project? Find Dr. Michael Greller.*

# Chapter Twenty-One

Agatha

*I love Google.* I could find almost anything. It turns out that Michael Greller was not such a common name for doctors. It only took four phone calls to locate him, working at a hospital in Goldsboro.

I popped open the canned peaches, which I have to say were a little slice of heaven, and remembered to call Mrs. Miles. I promised I would stop by to thank her in person. She was a sweet lady, but she had the Toider accent, which made my head hurt. She also had lived in the same house for sixty years. She would know the Stone history. I'd be speaking to *her* real soon, too.

First things first... I devoured a few more spiced peaches, which were so delicious that they made me close my eyes and take a pause, then I called Wayne Hospital in Goldsboro, put in GRE and got Greller's office extension. Whoever answered told me the doctor was busy and asked for my number. I asked her to give the good doctor a message, that I was calling regarding Anne Stone. She put me on hold so I could listen to some really bad music.

"This is Dr. Greller. Who am I speaking to?"

"Hello, doctor. My name is Cory Walker. I'm sorry to bother you at work, but this is very important. I am looking into a twenty-year-old case and — "

He cut me off. "Are you with the Prosecutor's Office?"

"No, sir. I am not a law enforcement officer of any kind. I'm just trying to figure out why Ben McComb has been sitting in jail for almost twenty years when everyone I talk to thinks Earl Stone killed Casey." *Why not throw that out there and see what happens?*

"Who said *that*?"

"Some folks who know more than me. What about *Mrs.* Stone, Dr. Greller? You did the autopsy then you got canned? That right?"

"Medical examiner in North Carolina was strictly a volunteer business, so nobody canned me." *Click.* Just like that. I had a feeling I had really fucked up his day.

After Greller hung up on me, I decided to walk over and thank Agatha Miles. I walked up the pebble pathway to her house, crunching through tiny stones and seashells, and lo and behold, she was on her hands and knees weeding a beautiful little flower garden. I was impressed. It was hot as hell, and this lady looked to be about a hundred and fifty years old, give or take a year. She had on a straw hat and a denim dress and looked like a Norman Rockwell painting.

"Good afternoon, Mrs. Miles," I said in my most charming voice.

"Well, hello there," she replied with a yellow-toothed smile.

"I'm your neighbor," I said, still beaming like an idiot. "I'm Cory Walker."

"I know, Mr. *Wal-kah*," she said. "We met that first day Miss Belle showed you the house."

"So we did. I just want to tell you that those were the best peaches I ever had in my life!" And I wasn't lying.

I watched as the little old lady pushed herself up off the ground. My bones hurt watching her. *Definitely old school.* I liked that. Do a job, no bitchin' about what hurts. I knew guys like that in the Rangers and Delta, the ones who were always good to go, no excuses. She could hang with me anytime.

She pulled off a gardening glove and shook my hand. I was careful not to squeeze too hard, but she had a good grip with her bony hand.

"Call me Cory. You have a beautiful garden."

"Why, thank you," she replied proudly. "Nothing as grand as *yours*, Mr. *Wal-kah*, but I do try and keep up."

"Yeah, well, I guess I'll need to start weeding myself pretty soon. The gardens were one of the reasons I bought the house. I forgot the part about all the work that goes with them. I guess the original owner was big into flowers." I was *feeshing* again.

"Oh, *yes*," she said with genuine admiration.

She brushed a strand of her white hair out of her face. Her blue eyes were still clear and bright under the million wrinkles and age spots. *Getting old sucks. I'll catch up soon enough.*

"Mrs. Stone… I stole some of my best ideas from her. Well, they were not the original owners, Earl and Anne Stone, but they put in all the gardens. Now *your* gardens."

"Oh, you knew Mrs. Stone? Nice lady? I heard a horrible story about her and her daughter…" God, I loved 'feeshing' more than real fishing.

Her face turned gloomy. "Ahh, so you heard about the Stone tragedy, then?"

"Not really. I found out a little more after I bought the house. Looked some up on the Internet — just being nosey, you know, in case I see any ghosts."

She failed to see the humor in my joke. "Anne Stone was a sweet woman."

"I'm sure she was," I said, trying to backpedal from my faux pas. "So you two were friends?"

"She was one of my *best* friends. It broke my heart, that whole business."

"I'm sure. Well, I didn't come over here to make you miserable. At least the garden is cheerful."

"Yes. Anne and I spent many hours talking about flowers. She was a master gardener. I'm just a copycat. Have you seen the angels in your rear yard?"

*Yup, I know this one already*, I thought to myself, but I let her tell me her version anyway. "Yes. They're beautiful."

"Mr. Stone had them made after Anne and Casey passed. His little angels. I can see them from my kitchen window. So tragic. Well, time marches on, doesn't it?"

She picked up her basket of weeds, which I took from her. She thanked me and we walked around the rear yard, where she had a compost pile. I dumped them into the bin for her.

"Did you know Casey?" I finally asked.

"Well, I knew her as a little girl. As she got older, she became very quiet. She always looked so melancholy to me. I guess some folks are meant for the big city. Maybe Harkers Island just wasn't for her."

"But you watched her grow up, I guess," I said, still trying to 'feesh'.

"Oh yes. She was an adorable toddler. Then, as she got older, I tried to help Anne deal with her growing pains. I have three daughters myself, you know, all quite a bit older than Casey. All grown up, now, of course. Nine grandchildren and two great-grandchildren. I lost Henry four years, ago, bless his heart."

"Sorry to hear that, Agatha. So you must have been a big help to Anne, an advisor when it came to her only child, then, I guess?"

"Oh my, yes. Little girls can be a handful. Do you have children?"

"Not yet."

"Well, if the good Lord blesses you with children, you'll understand. Little girls become little women pretty fast."

*That* comment knifed my heart. Apparently that sick fuck of a father had thought so, too.

"Was she close with her parents? Daddy's little girl?" I was looking into her eyes as I asked, trying to see into her brain. Her face only revealed sorrow.

"Oh, I don't know. She was at a difficult age. So sad. I'm sure they would have gotten closer as she got older—if she had been given the chance, I mean."

She looked very upset, and now I felt bad for agitating a little old lady who'd made me peaches. I put my hand on her bony shoulder. "I'm sorry," I said. "It must have been very difficult."

She walked toward her house, which was another lovely old Victorian, albeit weather-beaten, like her. "Old memories, Mr. *Wal-kah*. Come in and I'll show you my family."

I couldn't say no and spent the rest of the afternoon looking at pictures and faking smiles until my face hurt. It was way easier interrogating Taliban insurgents.

# Chapter Twenty-Two

Dr. Greller

By the time I got home, it was near dusk. I was exhausted. My very nice neighbor could talk the horns off a steer. I needed a drink. I walked into the kitchen and saw my machine blinking. If Amanda was calling to rescue me, it was too late.

I hit the Play Message button. It was Dr. Michael Greller. Apparently, he had caller ID. I *had* really fucked up his day. The message sounded like he was about to have an aneurism. I smiled and called him back, using my most *soothing* voice. My greeting was met with a very pissed-off response.

"Who the hell do you think you are, calling me at work to bring up that bullshit? I am *done* with Carteret County. Do you hear me?"

"I'm sorry, Dr. Greller. If you would let me —".

"Who put you up to this?" He sounded out of control.

"A girl named Casey Stone," I said harshly.

That hit the mark and he stopped yelling. "What do you mean? Who are you?"

"I purchased the Stone residence on Harkers Island. I'm just a regular guy, Dr. Greller. This isn't political, and I'm not a writer or a cop. I'm just trying to comprehend what the girl is trying to tell me."

"*Telling* you? What the fuck are you talking about? And *please* don't tell me you are a psychic or some bullshit. I don't have time for that crap."

"I'm *not* a psychic, although that would make this all a lot easier. The truth is, I found something in the house, and it has led me to start asking questions..."

"Oh yeah? Well, here's some advice— You better watch who you start asking questions about."

"So I hear. And I want to know what *you* think, Dr. Greller. You autopsied Casey and her mother, right? The bottom line is, I don't think Casey Stone was killed by Benjamin McComb."

"Did you say McComb? *Sonofabitch!*"

I heard him throw something across the room. Whatever it was, it was heavy and made a tremendous racket as it crashed and broke. "Son of a bitch!" he repeated.

"You want to clue me in, doc?"

"He's on my autopsy table!"

My stomach did a little flip. I felt my mouth go dry. "Benjamin McComb is on your *autopsy* table?"

"Listen, Walker, I'll call you back in twenty minutes, then you and I are finished with this conversation. You are *not* to call this number again."

He hung up.

I just stood there in the kitchen, staring at my phone. Ben was dead? I felt sick. How was that even possible? I had *just* seen him—just talked to him in person. And Stone had gotten to him in prison and had him killed? Could that be? Was the same Benjamin McComb who

I'd *just* spoken to at Maury Prison *dead*? It was surreal and my head was spinning.

I paced around my house, hoping Greller would call back. The next twenty minutes seemed to take forever. When my phone rang, the caller ID read 'Unknown'.

My heart was pounding in my chest as I answered.

"Goddamn it!" It was Greller, just as pissed-off-sounding as he had been twenty minutes before. Wherever he was calling me from, it was dead quiet. I had the impression he was sitting in his parked car. He continued speaking loudly. "The name seemed familiar, but I just didn't put it together. He was a *kid* when I saw him at the trial. I didn't recognize McComb's name. My group volunteers for Maury, Wayne, Eastern and Green correctional facilities. I see prisoners in here all the time. They have a bad habit of killing each other."

*Coincidence?* I felt totally deflated. "What happened to him?"

"He got worked over pretty good. I don't think it was one-on-one. Looks like he had the shit kicked out of him before someone slit his throat. Lots of bruising, internal injuries, including a ruptured spleen and broken bones in his face and hands. I usually see guys with shank wounds, you know, deep punctures from homemade knives. Somebody opened McComb's throat with a *real* blade, went all the way through his trachea and esophagus — right to his spine. Almost decapitated him. They made sure he wasn't getting up from this one."

"*Jesus.*"

"You said you *spoke* to him in Maury?" he asked, his light bulb finally clicking on.

"Yeah," I answered quietly, feeling like I'd killed him myself.

"Walker, is it?"

"Yeah, Cory Walker."

"Okay, Cory Walker, listen carefully. My guess is, based on what I saw of his injuries, a few guys got together and interviewed your friend Benjamin before they slit his throat. If *he* knew your name, then so does anyone who spoke to him. You made a big mistake digging up this case."

"God, they fucking killed him. I knew this was bullshit. They railroaded him and shoved him in that shithole forever. And now they fuckin' *killed* him. Just for talking to me..."

"That's exactly right...just for talking to you. So what do you think they're going to do to *you* when they find out *you're* the one digging up all this ancient history? You can't bring them back. You should have let it go."

"Is that what *you* did, doc? You let someone rape and kill that girl? Let an innocent man go to prison...and you just *let it go*?"

Silence. I had to ask, "You there?"

"Yeah." Another long pause. Then finally, he spoke very slowly. "I'm going to talk to you this one time and one time only. If you get an indictment and something solid on Earl Stone, I'll testify in court. But until then, this is the only time I will ever speak to you. You got that, Mr. Walker?"

"I hear you loud and clear."

"Here it is — the whole story, near as I can remember it. I did the autopsy on the mother only, but I was an assistant on the daughter. Sewell Booth did the girl's autopsy just before he retired. His work was sloppy. I had asked him about sexual assault in this case. He did the internal himself, alone in the room. I was told it was 'at the family's request, out of respect to their daughter'. They didn't want anyone in there who didn't absolutely have to be. That's the only time I've ever heard that in my entire career—just to be clear."

I grunted an acknowledgement, wishing I had a damn tape recorder.

"So he finished the post by himself. He said the girl was most likely a virgin until she was raped during the attack. I wish I could remember exactly what he said word for word, but it was a strange comment, like he was playing to the parents. How would he know if she was a virgin prior to that? You follow me? It wasn't a scientific comment, more like he was making a point on behalf of the parents. Girls on Harkers Island aren't typically having sexual intercourse at her age—at least, not twenty years ago. Anyway, he finds the cause of death to be manual strangulation. The hyoid bone was broken, with bruise patterns to indicate hands, not a belt or rope. Basically, in layman's terms, someone squeezed her throat, broke the little bone in her neck that is attached to the vagus nerve. The hyoid breaks when someone *chokes* the victim. Great force is exerted and the bone snaps and the nerve tells the brain you're dead. Then the heart stops. That takes four or five minutes. It isn't quick. Everything I just explained to you is consistent with what you'd expect in this type of physical attack."

"What about the rape?" I asked. "Was DNA collected?"

"No. The girl had been in the ocean overnight, as I recall. There was no evidence that could be collected, only a visual examination, which I was precluded from seeing. And remember, this was twenty years ago. This isn't some *CSI* episode where everything gets solved in a TV hour."

"And you asked about it and were pushed out?"

"Not because of the girl…because of the mother."

I ran that through my brain again, not comprehending. "The *mother*?"

"*Her* exam."

"What happened there?"

"Police found her hanging in her home. Her husband had called it in. Except I did a quick exam with Doctor Booth. In the case of the mother, her hyoid was broken, the tell-tale V-marks from hanging on a rope were *not* present in typical fashion and there were no signs of petechial hemorrhaging. There were no inflamed edges on the skin from a rope."

"Doc, you gotta slow down. Remember I'm only understanding about half of what you're talking about."

He sighed and attempted to slow down for me. "Listen… When a person is hanging from a rope choking to death, they die due to lack of air and suffocation, or, if someone was good at tying a real noose, they snap their neck at the bottom of the rope. Her neck wasn't broken. *Her* injuries were obviously from being strangled, *then* hung *post*-mortem. You understand that? The rope never cut into her skin and she wasn't flailing around at the bottom of the noose, choking to death. She was hanged *after* she was already dead."

"And the other doctor, Booth, didn't see it that way?"

"The Stone's *family* doctor did a report that Dr. Booth signed off on. It was total bullshit. I *saw* that report. It was all wrong. I went over the long list of mistakes with Dr. Booth, and he just kept telling me that *'the family has been through a lot.'* No shit. Someone killed that woman *then* hanged her. And when I tried to explain that, I was told to stay out of it. Then I went to try to re-examine the daughter's report and I had people so high up the chain of command screaming at me that you would have thought *I'd* committed the damn murder. They threatened to pull my medical license!"

"Why didn't you tell the police?"

"Oh, *sure*... I could just call over to the sheriff and interrupt his golf game with Earl Stone..."

"Stone had ins with the department over in Carteret County?"

"What planet are you living on, Walker? Earl Stone may be the next President of the United States!"

"Yeah, well, I'm thinking, not so much. I'm thinking more like a cell in Maury. I hear they've got a vacancy now." My sarcasm didn't do anything to diffuse my rising anger.

"It'll never happen. Anyway, that's all I can really tell you. The autopsy on Anne Stone was a sham, and no one would dare cross Stone on it. Not one doctor, not one administrator, *nobody* would talk to me about this. Wait. I take that back, there was one cop. I think he got shafted, too."

"Yeah. Arthur McDade. Sheriff's deputy."

"That's him. McDade. Get in touch with him. Look, Walker... If any of this helped, great. I never believed Ben McComb killed that girl or that Anne Stone hanged herself. That's the opinion of one medical examiner who was never given all of the evidence to examine. Thinking back on it now, it would never happen in today's world. The state office of the chief medical examiner is set up differently nowadays, but some twenty years ago, it was just a network of local docs who volunteered. There wasn't much oversight, and if someone like Stone wanted a certain doc to issue a report? Trust me, he could make it happen. Poor son of a bitch on the slab back there didn't do anything wrong except have a crush on Earl Stone's daughter."

"You think Earl Stone had anything to do with his daughter's or his wife's deaths?"

"I think Earl Stone knows more than he's saying."

"And what if I told you that Earl Stone was molesting his daughter and beating his wife?"

There was a long pause. "Why would you say that?"

"I told you...Casey told me. I have her *diary*, doc. And according to this dead girl, her father belongs in prison."

I could hear him take a deep breath, followed by a long exhale. "Keep it someplace very safe, Walker. And if I were you, I wouldn't tell anyone else you have it. And you better start thinking about other countries you want to live in. Stone finds out you have something that can ruin his shot at the White House and you're not safe anywhere in this country."

"Bring it on," I snarled. And I meant it. Greller was now the second person to tell me I had to leave the country that I had defended for all of my adult life. *Are you shittin' me?* All that did was guarantee I was going to be digging deeper.

*Hooaah.*

# Chapter Twenty-Three

## Fresh Fish

I hung up with the doc after he reminded me he'd never speak to me again unless it was in court. He sounded downright scared.

I didn't know Earl Stone. Maybe if I did, I'd be scared, too. Instead, I was just pissed — pissed at myself for getting Benjamin McComb killed over something he probably never did in the first place, pissed at myself for being naïve enough to think I could just play private investigator, pissed about the fact that now I didn't want Amanda coming to this house in case some unwanted visitors showed... All in all, I was just pissed.

I went down to the basement and rummaged through my boxes of worldly possessions stored there until I found my old buddy Ice, my Mossberg. This handy little piece of equipment had accompanied me on many a night in Afghanistan and the Hindu Kush on special assignment, killing Taliban dirtbags. Up until Amanda, it had been the biggest love of my life, and there was no way it was staying behind when I returned to home soil.

For anyone who has never killed another human being, let me just say that a fair fight isn't what anyone should want. Fair fights can get people killed. The best thing is to have a weapon that will kill an enemy in one shot, even if center mass is missed. We had an old saying in the military. *'If you ever find yourself in a fair fight, your tactics suck.'* My shells were specially made by the Delta armorer and were still classified, but I can say this. They're devastating.

My Mossberg is a compact, black, tactical shotgun that has a pistol grip and holds six rounds that are pumped into the chamber manually by the handgrip and a strap that wraps around my left forward hand, up at the working end of the weapon. When I hit a human being with this weapon, it makes a large wet mess and the fight is over.

I suppose I should clarify and explain that this is not a typical weapon for an Army Ranger or Delta operator in the mountains. One would more likely find SCARs, M4s and M16s, squad automatic weapons or sniper rifles than a shotgun. But I had different kinds of assignments. I was typically a few yards away from my enemy when I killed him, not across the valley like the fancy sniper boys. Anyway, the point was now that I was reunited with my old friend Ice, I felt better.

And yes, I'd *named* my shotgun. Somehow, 'Mossberg' had turned into 'Iceberg', which got shortened to 'Ice'. Most guys named their guns after women. My gun seemed way too nasty for that. Ice and I had killed lots of people together — people who'd very much wanted to kill me. So I cleaned and oiled Ice, loaded him up with my secret shells and went back upstairs with a bottle in one hand and a shotgun in the other. Damn, I was turning country — except the wine was a beautiful Gazin Pomerol French Bordeaux, and I doubt hillbillies drank that shit.

It was now dark outside, and I was wondering how long it would take before I had visitors from Mr. Stone. *Fuck 'em.* I had Ice. Whatever progress I had made in turning into a civilian was lost. I was back in combat-mode, fully wired, blood pumping and enjoying the familiar feel of the adrenaline rush.

I called Amanda, who made me happy by picking up on the first ring.

"Hey, baby!" she said, so cheerfully that I smiled for the first time all day. "How's it going over there?"

"It's been an interesting day," I said. I proceeded to explain the events of my afternoon. She listened to every word. When I was finished, she simply said, "Sell the house." I was taken off guard on that one.

"Sell the house. Leave there tonight and come here. If they killed Ben McComb just for *talking* to you..."

That sounded very familiar. I interrupted her. "Relax. No one is coming here tonight, and if they do, it would be a very large mistake on their part."

"You almost got killed *once* already. Remember?"

"Yes, it's how I meet women."

"I'm serious. The house is very nice from the outside, but it's a house of horrors, and you need to get out of there *now*, Cory!"

"I like my house, I like my neighbors and I am *not* being forced to move because Mr. Sick Fuck thinks he can do whatever he wants."

"I want you to come here tonight. Just tonight, okay?"

"It's safe. Chill out."

"Fine, then I'm coming down there tonight."

"Okay, it's not *that* safe. You're not coming down until I get this all sorted out. Give me a couple of days and I'll figure out what to do."

"Call the police, Cory. *That's* what you do! You call the police and you stay the hell out of it before you get killed!" She was getting herself worked up, sweet thing.

"I can't call the police," I mumbled.

"And why not?"

"Because Stone and the sheriff are old buddies. For all I know, it was the guards who killed Ben, not inmates."

"The *guards*? Cory! This is insane!"

"I'm thinking about calling the Feds, maybe giving them the diary."

"Good. That's good! Do that. Call the FBI right now."

"Give me a couple of days. This is a twenty-year-old case. No one is going to want to talk to me. I need to finish reading it tonight, make some copies, then start talking to someone in law enforcement who's not connected to Stone."

We went round and round for a while, but I finally convinced her to stay put and give me some time to get organized. I put the wine in the fridge and slung Ice over my shoulder so it was across my back, the barrel facing down. I always carried him in this fashion, so if he needed to come out and say hello, all I had to do was slip the strap around and he'd come up under my right arm, ready to bark. This was probably a little over-the-top for a walk around the neighborhood, but fuck it. I have a permit and a box of medals. No cop is going to hassle me for exercising my right to bear arms, even if this weapon is technically illegal.

Oh, well. I walked out of the back door — call me paranoid — and crept through my gardens to check 'the perimeter', as we military types like to call it. There was no one around. I made a mental note. *Buy a dog — a big fucking nasty dog with huge fangs.*

When I was satisfied that there wasn't a cadre of assassins trying to kill me, I walked down the road, back to the dock where I had met the Hatfields and McCoys, aka Thomas and Caleb. The boat was tied to the dock, and 'the boys' were still there. I wondered if they ever moved forty feet from that spot. Like, *ever.*

I walked down the old wooden dock under the dim light of an overhead lamp on a wooden post. The sun had almost set and it was fairly dark now. As I walked closer, I could see they were drinking cans of beer and barbecuing some fish on an old oil drum someone had cut in half and filled with coals. *Voila!* That was what I was looking for — fresh fish.

"Evening, fellas," I called out as I approached. "I was wondering if you had caught any fish I might be able to buy."

They greeted me in their Hoi-Toider, now with a buzz on, and I didn't recognize one syllable. Caleb tried to stand up, then sat back down with a loud flop, bringing great fits of laughter from his buddies. He was *hammered.*

"Had a few cold ones, huh?" I said with a smile, trying to be one of the boys. Thomas laughed at that and spat out a bunch of gibberish, which I finally caught on to mean that the beers were only there to wash down some peach moonshine that Caleb's brother-in-law had made for them.

Caleb handed me a Mason jar of the colorless liquid. I had no interest in getting wasted with these good ole boys, but I also didn't want to offend their kind offer. I accepted the jar, offered cheers to the crew and took a slug. It was delicious. Okay, I'm totally lying.

I'm pretty sure someone had put some peaches in turpentine for a month then poured it into that jar. Drinking a bottle of that might get me another purple heart.

I smiled and told them how smooth it was, ignoring the screaming coming from my liver. I have no idea what they said in response. *Holy crud, these people need to learn some English.* Caleb rambled on and on, then I heard him use the word 'feesh' a few times. I concurred. To *what*, I have no idea, but I grunted a yes to something about fish, and the next thing I knew, Caleb was wrapping one from a cooler into some newspaper and handing it to me.

I asked him how much it was. The three of them were laughing and carrying on and were so wasted that I had no idea what to say or do. I took another sip of the lighter fluid when they offered it again, then told them I needed to get home. They smiled and waved me off, and I turned to leave, which led to Caleb exclaiming something that sounded like "God damn!"

I turned around, not sure what he was cursing about, then realized he had spotted Ice across my back.

"In case you didn't have any fish, I was going to go get me a bear," I said casually and walked back toward home. I could hear them roaring in the background about me shooting a bear. If nothing else, I had probably bonded with the locals a little bit, and they were salt-of-the-earth types who would be good to have as friends.

I walked home silently, feeling like I was on patrol, my head on a swivel. It was a familiar feeling, but not one I'd wanted in my new home. It felt as dark in my heart as it was outside.

I got home, walked the perimeter again then went in through the back door. I inspected the house, and after I was satisfied that the Boogey Man wasn't hiding anywhere, I went into the kitchen, where I set Ice down on the counter.

I opened the newspaper at the sink and pulled out the fish Caleb had given me. I looked it over. It was definitely a fish. That was about as specific as I could be. I had eaten some pretty nasty stuff in the third world, so whatever kind it was, I wasn't worried about it. At least it was fresh. I scaled and gutted it in the sink, filleted it and threw it into a pan with whatever veggies I had in the fridge. A little garlic and olive oil, and presto…dinner was under the broiler. More importantly, the wine was now cold.

I ate alone, psyching myself up to finish reading the diary I didn't want to read, and drank some wine until the feeling of dread had eased a bit. I finished eating, cleaned the kitchen and dug the journal out of my desk. Ice and I ended up sitting in the den with the bottle of wine. Ice sat on the couch next to me while I read a heartbreaking little book from a dead girl whose face now hung in front of me.

As I read, I thought to myself that I should have drank more of that peach moonshine. I'd almost been killed a hundred times in my life, and I'd seen plenty of killing, too. I'd killed people with my bare hands. I'd had friends blown to pieces right in front of me. I thought I was a pretty tough guy. Reading a teenage girl's diary made me bawl my eyes out.

# Chapter Twenty-Four

Last Entry

I read all night.

Most of her journal contained flowery girl stuff that I guess any teenager would write. Casey's crush on Ben was the main topic, with side stories about her friends on the island. I made a few notes on a legal pad, writing down the names of the friends. Maybe they'd still be around…or at least traceable. Maybe one of them knew something?

The entries about her father were limited, thank God. Either he only abused her on occasion or she didn't always want to enter it into her notebook. Her comments about her mother also became darker, although they were vague. There seemed to be resentment building there. It was hard to understand the inner workings of a teenage girl. Hell, I had a hard enough time understanding adults. Nothing stood out until I got almost to the end. The entry there made my hair stand up.

*July 29, 1991*
*He finally did it. It's not worth fighting him anymore. I just got it over with and pretended he was Ben. He didn't hit me. He wasn't even mean. When it was over, he just got up and left. God, what if I get pregnant? It didn't hurt as much as I thought it would.*

I felt physically ill again. This animal had abused his daughter for so long that by the time he'd raped her, she'd acted like it was no big deal. My head was spinning. I poured the last of the wine into my glass and drank it straight down. I looked at Ice and thought how the two of us could really wipe the smile off of Earl Stone's face. Actually, we'd wipe his *face* off his face.

I made myself continue reading. There was nothing else about that night in the diary. She seemed to just accept it, and because he hadn't verbally abused her or beaten her, she somehow seemed to think it was easier than his previous attacks. There were no entries for a few days after that one, which had been less than a week from the day she'd died. I read through to her last entry.

*August 1, 1991*
*Mom is being a total bitch. Now she's even meaner than he is. I hate this house. I'm going to leave home the minute I turn eighteen and never come back. Dad, I miss you! You would never have let any of this happen. I wish to God my mom had never met Earl Stone! I wish… Seeing Ben tonight. Maybe he'll help me get out of here. Ben is so sweet. I love him. Casey-N-Ben forever?*

*Earl Stone was her stepfather?* As horrific as that was, it made a lot of things fall into place. I considered all the mentions of Stone being her dad, even by Casey in her journal. I guessed his ego had required that she call him that and everyone had believed it.

What should have been a fun summer for a sixteen-year-old girl, soon to be seventeen, was instead the end of a long string of abuse that would end with her being strangled and dumped into the water. I wondered about what she'd written and what Ben had said in prison. The second-to-last time they had been together, she'd freaked out when they'd started to get intimate.

Then, their last night together, she had told him she loved him. She had planned on making love that night. They never had, according to Ben. He'd said he was going to die a virgin a prison. He had been right. He just hadn't known how soon.

So what had happened that night? Had she freaked out again? I'm sure she had more PTSD than I do. Maybe when she was with Ben, she flashed back to her sick stepfather's assault. Two kids in love, on the beach with their friends, enjoying a great night... What had happened?

# Chapter Twenty-Five

Trading for Leads

When I finished reading the diary, I went back down to the basement and hid it where I'd found it. If it had been a good enough hiding place for twenty years, it would work for another few weeks. Of course, I had followed this same logic with Ben McComb, now deceased.

I didn't sleep well that night.

Ice was within grabbing distance on my bed, but I tossed and turned, wondering what the hell had gone on in this house. PTSD isn't a big secret anymore. Almost all of us who'd served in combat were *some* degree of permanently fucked-up. My nightmares tended to come and go in batches — good for a few months, bad for a few months. So many times, I'd tried to grab that corporal in my sleep before he blew us both up. One more second. That was all I'd needed. Quite frankly, it just sucked.

When I woke up at dawn, I walked down the hall, inspecting the other four empty bedrooms. It was still pretty dark inside the house, and I didn't turn on any lights. They were tight rooms, typical for Victorian architecture, with lots of heavy crown molding and woodwork.

I looked around in each room, checked the small closets and wooden floors for anything resembling a clue but found nothing. I sat down in the middle of the hardwood floor in the second bedroom. I looked down the hallway toward the master.

Suddenly, it clicked! If Anne Stone had been in her bedroom, she would have heard every sound in here. There was no way she didn't know what was going on in her own house. My face got hot and my stomach flipped. Old hardwood floors tended to creak, and Earl Stone's footsteps for his unwanted visits would have been heard by anyone at home on a quiet night. Any noises, none of which I allowed myself to imagine, would echo off these wooden floors.

Was she so terrified of her husband that she let him do whatever he wanted and never spoke up? How could she not defend her daughter? She could have simply taken the child and left. Was she in total *denial*? All of a sudden, I wasn't so sure I really liked my house anymore. I knew it was ancient history. Hell — two other families had lived here since the Stones, so the ghosts were long gone. But damn, the place was creeping me out. I went downstairs, made coffee and called Amanda. I guess I should have looked at the clock first.

"Cory! What's wrong!" She sounded hysterical.

"Nothing, baby. I just wanted to say hi."

"God, you scared the crap out of me, Cory! It's five-thirty."

"Oh." Five-thirty. That kind of early for civilians.

"You okay?"

"Yeah...well, no. I finished her diary last night. I need to talk to her friends, the ones she was with the night she was murdered."

"Cory, you need to call the police or the FBI."

"I know. I will. Soon. I promise."

"Cory..."

"Sorry to wake you up so early. Go back to sleep. I love you."

I hung up the phone, knowing I had screwed up her morning. I seemed to have a habit of messing up people's days lately.

I checked my notes and found the names of the four other kids with Casey and Ben that night. Unfortunately, she had only used first names. I was hoping that Agatha Miles might remember who they were. *Darla, Mike, Lynn and Pete.* That was all I had to go on. Four first names from twenty years ago. *Super.*

I decided I would use the morning to clean up the gardens outside the house and maybe take a plant over to Agatha Miles as a conversation starter. I wasn't sure she'd remember my name from the other day, never mind four kids from twenty years ago.

I drank my coffee and headed out to the garden. By eight, the sun was already getting hot and the air was sticky. I had pulled about a hundred pounds of weeds and decided I was definitely finished for the day.

A beautiful pink and green 'whatchamacallit' plant was in one of the beds, and I decided it would be a great gift for Agatha. I dug it out and plopped the root-ball into a clay pot I had found behind the house. After I washed up inside, I took the plant next door to Agatha's. It was still pretty early, but what the hell. *Old people don't sleep late, do they?*

I walked to the door and saw that it was open behind the screen door. I sang out a cheerful "Good morning" to my lil' ole lady neighbor. A moment later, she hobbled over to the door, a large mug in her hand.

She adjusted her glasses, looked at me, then smiled broadly. "Well, good morning, Mr. *Wal-kah*!" she said so cheerfully that I actually smiled too.

"Good morning, Miz Miles," I replied. "But I really do wish you'd call me Cory. I brought you a little present from Mrs. Stone's garden." I held up the pink and green whatever-it-was so she could see it.

"Oh, my! How sweet! Seashore mallows are one of my favorites!"

Right, *mallows*—how could I forget? "Really? That was a good guess, then."

She opened the door and said, "Come right in! I was just making coffee with Timothy."

*Timothy?* I thought. Was she still hittin' it with one of the locals? That made me smile. Having changed from work boots to sandals before walking over, I followed her into her small kitchen, where a giant gray housecat was sitting on the windowsill. I mean *giant*. Siegfried and Roy's cats weren't much bigger.

"Timothy, we have company. Say hello to our new neighbor." The cat looked at me and meowed on command. It was a little freaky.

I said hello to the cat and faked a smile. I hate cats. The cat knew it. Agatha made me a coffee and tried to feed me, but I got her to settle on coffee. She spent ten minutes talking about how the plant would like the little spot in her center bed, because it got full sun.

"You just *love* the sunshine, don't you? she asked the plant.

I tried changing topics before she got into what her favorite fertilizer was. "I figured this would be like the old days for you—exchanging flowers with your neighbor in the Stone house."

"Well isn't that sweet of you, Mr. *Wal-kah*."

"Cory."

"Mr. Cory. And yes, it does bring back memories. Anne and I would trade seeds sometimes, swap flowers… She was such a dear."

"Yeah, I was thinking about what you were telling me the last time I was here, about Casey."

"Oh?"

"Yeah, about her becoming quieter as she got older. One of the locals was talking to me about her a few days ago. She seemed like a popular kid. He mentioned some friends of hers…Darla and Lynn? And a couple of guys. Pete and Mike, maybe?"

She put her hand to her mouth and seemed to be scanning her memory banks.

"Miss Darla. Darla Reynolds. Now that's a name I haven't thought of in a long time. She went away to college. Smart girl. Never came back to Harkers Island. Can't recall a Pete. Lynn Hopkins became a nurse, I think. Her parents still live here. And Mike Jackson works over at the ferry."

Jackson. It rang a bell. "Mike Jackson? Caleb's son?"

"Caleb's youngest. He used to work for Caleb on the fishing boat, but they were fighting like cats and dogs. No offense, Timothy."

Like the cat gave a shit.

"He ended up working at the ferry," she repeated.

I sipped my coffee, which was better than the pot I'd made at home, and smiled. Two solid leads.

To be polite, I let Agatha ramble on for another forty minutes and offered to plant her flowers for her, but she declined. This was evidently the most excitement she had enjoyed in years, and I wouldn't deny her the pleasure of planting something from Anne's garden. I said goodbye, promised to visit again and left, after saying goodbye to Timothy in baby-talk to score brownie points — totally demeaning.

I'm pretty sure Timothy told me to go eff myself.

# Chapter Twenty-Six

## Walkin' and Talkin'

I went home and found my machine blinking. It was Amanda. I called her back and got her voicemail. She was probably torturing some poor bastard at physical therapy. Did I mention she was a hundred-plus pounds of bad attitude who could make grown men cry? I hoped the guy wasn't staring at her ass as obviously as I used to do. I left her a message and decided to go 'feeshing'.

Kate's Diner, such as it is, was one of two or three places for breakfast on the island. We're talking a small island here. I walked to the diner, about a ten-minute walk from my house, and had a seat at the counter. The place was right out of a 1950s movie. In fact, that was probably the last time the décor had been changed.

A very nice little old lady brought me a menu. I figured she had been in Agatha's kindergarten class. I introduced myself, which turned out to be a solid move, because she then introduced me to several of the locals, most of whom spoke in the same Toider accent she did.

I wasn't ready to start grilling the locals yet and raise any suspicions. This was strictly a recon mission, getting the lie of the land, but I did meet several old-timers, which was good. The locals were slightly clannish, but now, being a resident of the famous Stone House, I was treated like one of the gang...*almost*. I'm pretty sure they all made fun me after I left.

Fully fueled on diner food, I headed over to the ferry dock at the east end of the island. It was a longer walk than most trips around the island, being at the very eastern tip of Harkers, but I didn't mind. The sun was up, and the quiet beauty was exactly why I'd purchased the house in the first place. I could see myself being very happy here with Amanda — just as soon as I solved a twenty-year-old murder case that had already been solved, as far as the justice system was concerned.

I walked along Harkers Island Road — the main highway. Homes along this street were newer, larger and more impressive than most of the others on the island. The houses along the waterside had private docks, and some of them were huge. My own house was classic-looking and I loved it — but I could have dropped three or four of mine into some of these and still had extra room. I was guessing that folks had purchased two or three small lots some years back, bulldozed everything and built one huge house on the new larger parcel. I was having a hard enough time weeding my own yard. These folks probably had full-time gardeners.

I arrived at the dock in between ferry trips. The two greasy-looking men working on a new bulkhead were the only signs of human activity. A few crabs were running around on the old wooden pier and a brown-and-white pelican seated on a wooden post looked at me with boredom. Seagulls squawked from overhead, sounding like maniacal laughter. There was a small office where travelers could purchase fares for the ferry, which would take them and their car to the southern end of the Outer Banks. The office looked deserted.

I walked over to the men. They were both hard-looking and lean from years of physical labor in the hot sun without a lot of Twinkie breaks. In another thirty years, they'd look just like the other guys I had met at the dock. "Hey," I called out as I approached. They stopped their work and looked up at me, grunting back a greeting of some type. "I'm looking for Mike Jackson. Either one of you be him?"

One of the two looked at the other, who walked toward me. "I'm Mike Jackson."

I extended my hand, which he looked at and showed me his — which was very dirty.

I reached for it anyway, and we shook hands.

"Cory Walker. I just moved here — to Harkers Island, I mean."

"Yeah, so I heard." His accent was not quite as thick as his dad's. Maybe he had read a few books in his life or traveled off the island once or twice. "My dad told me. Y'all bought the Stone House?"

"Yeah."

He cocked his head, as if to politely say, '*So what the fuck are you bothering me for*?' Instead, he merely asked, "So what can I do for ya?"

"You have a minute? Maybe take a quick walk?" I didn't want to be rude, but I also didn't know his friend, who was now standing there watching us.

He yelled over to his coworker that he'd be right back and walked toward the office. I followed him inside and he opened a small, battered fridge on top of a beaten wooden counter and pulled out two Cokes. They were in the old-fashioned thick green glass bottles, like God intended. He popped the tops and we each took a slug, then he just stared at me, waiting for me to explain why I was bugging him at work.

"I'd like to ask you about something, but I don't want to come off as being nosey."

"Um-hmm." He leaned back against an old green desk and looked at me.

"You were friends with Casey Stone. You were with her the night she died?"

"I figured that's what this was about. You been asking around about her…"

I guess the islanders had their own 'underground'. I wondered if I was a local topic of conversation. "Sort of. You, Pete, Darla and Lynn—you were all together, that night. What happened?"

"That was nearly twenty years ago, Mr.…*Walker*, is it?"

"Yeah, Call me Cory."

"Stones kin of yours?"

"No, no relation."

"How did y'all know who was there that night?"

*Damn.* I thought I was going to be asking the questions. "Like you said, I've been asking around a bit. I'm just a little curious, I guess. Did you know Benjamin McComb was killed in prison a couple of days ago?"

His face showed surprise then a flash of sorrow, then it went blank again. It seemed to me that he didn't want me to get a read on him. "Nope. Hadn't heard anything about him in twenty years."

"Did you think he killed her, Mike?"

"Why are you asking about this, Mr. Walker? You said y'all aren't family. Why'd you buy that house and start asking about something bad that happened such a long time ago?"

"Do you think Ben killed her? Raped her?"

He made a face again. "No," he said softly. "Ben was a good friend. He was poor and maybe not the smartest guy on Harkers, but he loved Casey Stone. He never would have hurt that girl. We all told the cops the same thing."

"We?"

"Me and Pete...and Darla and Lynn. We told them what happened."

"So tell me."

He drank his soda and looked outside at his co-worker. "Real quick... I need to get back to work." He stared at the ceiling as he spoke, like he was looking up into a time capsule.

"The six of us built a bonfire and were hanging out on the beach like usual. Three couples, you know? We had gone swimming, and we'd downed a few beers. Just having fun. It was summer. No school. After a while, everyone kind of found their own spots on the beach, you know. Anyway...after a while, Casey's mom found us and went nuts. I guess she had told Casey to stay away from Ben. She called Casey and Ben all kinds of names and practically dragged Casey off the beach by her hair. It was a scene, all right."

"Casey left *with* her mother?"

"Well, not exactly. Her momma dragged her away from Ben. They had been kind of making out on a blanket, you know? We all were. Her momma came out of *nowhere* and scared the shit out of all of us. Casey was real embarrassed. Started crying. Her momma left her

142

on the beach, crying. Ben tried to calm her down, but she wouldn't *talk* to him after her momma left. She was a mess, poor kid."

"Jesus. So what happened after that?"

"Well, Lynn and Darla tried to calm her down, but she told them to leave her alone. She ran off the beach, toward her house, and we all left right after. We figured Mrs. Stone would be calling our parents, getting us all in trouble, so we split up and went home. Next day, we heard Casey was dead. Thomas found her."

"*Thomas*," I said out loud, remembering the man I'd met with Mike's father, Caleb. "You know him?"

"This is Harkers Island, Mr. Walker. I know everybody…'cept you. Thomas Woods is one of my daddy's best friends. He's like family. Thomas found Casey in the water right next to his boat. It was a horrible day on Harkers Island. I never knew anyone who'd died before, let alone been murdered. Casey was a real nice girl."

"What happened?"

He eyed his coworker outside. "I gotta get back to work, sir." He looked me in the eye and added, "After Thomas found her, he called the Stones. The police and an ambulance came. Mrs. Stone killed herself when she heard the news. They arrested Ben later that day." He stood, chugged his Coke and put the bottle on the counter. "I gotta go. Y'all shouldn't keep asking about her. People don't like talking about it."

"Well, I appreciate *you* talking to me about it, Mike."

He stared at me for a long minute with a twisted expression on his face. Finally, he leaned in and spoke with great intensity, like he'd been waiting to say it out loud for a long time. "Ben didn't kill Casey."

*No shit.*

# Chapter Twenty-Seven

## Three Hush Puppies

By the time I walked back to my house, it was almost eleven and the sun was high overhead. It was another hot, sunny day on beautiful Harkers Island, summer home to a depraved psychotic who wanted to be my President. I passed Agatha's house on the way, and she waved me over. *Heavy sigh.* I had almost gotten home clean.

"Hello, Mrs. Miles!" I yelled over as I crunched up her shell-and-gravel driveway.

"Hello there, Mr. Cory. I thought you were already home. I saw you had company." My mouth went dry and I found myself looking for Ice behind my back. *Damn it.*

He was locked away at home. Maybe Agatha Miles would run next door and kick some butt for me.

"Company? You sure? I wasn't expecting anyone."

"I think so. I saw a car pull up a while ago. Come, I want to show you where I planted your beautiful flowers."

I smiled and followed her to the side yard, all the while scanning over in the direction of my house, looking for a hit team of Secret-Service-looking bad-asses. She rambled on for a bit, something about the particular leaf habit, and I tried to pay attention. Finally, I cut her off and told her I'd better see about my guests. She smiled and excused me, although she was probably puzzled when I ran through the side yard and crept up on my own house very quietly through the wall of pines and thick shrubs that separated our homes.

Then I saw the car in the driveway.

*Amanda. Holy shit.* She'd almost given me a heart attack. I ran up the front porch steps and found her inside the kitchen, making herself coffee. I was damn glad to see her, although totally surprised.

"What are you doing here?" I asked her as I picked her up off the ground and buried her in kisses.

After a warm welcome, she explained that after some asshole had awakened her at five-thirty in the morning, she couldn't sleep because she was worried sick. She'd taken the day off and driven down to make sure I was still alive. I was. I decided that what was called for after a rude awakening and a stressful drive to Harkers Island was some serious sex. Much to my delight, Amanda only half resisted, God bless her libido, and we ended up christening the dining room carpet. After a brief recovery, she leaned on her elbow and said, "You're still on my shit list."

"Shit list? I thought for sure you had an orgasm."

"*Two*, actually. But you are *still* on my shit list. You were supposed to call the FBI or the sheriff or somebody. Remember?"

"And tell them about your two orgasms?"

"I'm being serious." She hit me.

Did I mention I really loved this lady? "I told you, although you may not recall since it was a little early…"

"A *little* early! You woke me up at five-thirty!"

"Okay, a lot early. But I did tell you that I was going to talk to her friends."

"And how are you going to find her friends from twenty years ago?" she asked with a scowl on her face.

I leaned in and whispered, for dramatic effect. "Harkers Island is a pretty small place."

"And you think you know who they were already?" she asked, again the skeptic.

"Um, actually, I already interviewed one of them this morning."

She sat up. "Are you serious?"

"Yup. Mike Jackson."

"Stonewall's son?"

It took me a second to get her joke. *Everybody's a comedian.* "Might be a relative, but no, Caleb's son."

I spent the next ten minutes catching her up on the locals and tried my best to reproduce a Hoi-Toider accent. She looked at me like I had three heads. "You'll see," I said. When I had related to her just about everything I could think of, she told me she had decided she wanted to see the diary. She also told me she was starving. Did I mention some asshole had awakened her at five-thirty and she had driven all the way over? She had only stopped for coffee, then had another one at my house. Poor girl. We decided to take a shower together, although my excellent idea for making love in the shower was overruled in favor of having lunch. I now saw where her priorities were.

Having already eaten at the diner, I figured we would try Elijah's Coal Pot near the bridge. I was ready to walk it, but she preferred the air-conditioned car. It was a quick ride to the faded one-room house that was a local favorite for Harkers cuisine.

Elijah's, as it was commonly known, was a seafood place, but had just about everything on the menu that a person could think of. During duck season, hunters brought ducks. During deer season, locals would go hunting on the mainland and bring back venison. The local fishermen provided the seafood menu, and probably the calamari was leftover flounder bait. It was decorated with carved decoys to the point that it rivaled the decoy duck museum. The museum didn't have food, though, so fuck 'em.

It was early enough that we had the place to ourselves. I introduced us as the newest Harkers Islanders to the man I presumed was Elijah. Turned out he was the owner, but his name was Tad. Seriously, *Tad*? His grandfather was Elijah. Anyway, he gave us a nice welcome in the thickest Hoi-Toider accent yet. I answered him like I had a clue what he was talking about, and Amanda just stared in disbelief. He sat us at a booth next to a window that looked out at the Back Sound.

"Was that *English*?" she whispered when we sat down.

I tried not to gloat.

She smiled. "It's one of the reasons this place made my Bucket List. I've always wanted to hear the famous High Tider accent. Now that I've heard it, I have no idea what they're saying! It's awesome."

Tad returned with a basket of 'hush puppies', deep fried balls of corn bread deliciousness that should have been the main course. We each took a bite and stared at each other.

"Oh my *God*," she moaned with a mouthful of hush puppy. "These are *amazing*!"

"You didn't moan like that in the dining room," I said.

"You weren't as good."

I looked at the basket to keep from laughing. There was only one more in there. *The bastard gave us* three?

Amanda saw me looking at it. "Don't even *think* about it," she said with her war face.

We had a delicious fish lunch, conversed briefly with Tad, who quite frankly might have been speaking Old English, Latin or Gaelic for all I knew, then drove back to the house along Harkers Island Road, which follows the south coastline. 'South coastline' is a bit of an overstatement, since the entire island is only a bit over two miles long, but we enjoyed the scenery.

When we got back to the house, Amanda asked me again if I was going to call the sheriff or the FBI. I told her I would, but I still had one more person to speak with—Lynn Hopkins. Her parents still lived here, according to Agatha Miles, my detective agency personal assistant who just didn't know her job title yet. I found the listing for Mr. and Mrs. Robert Hopkins and saw that they lived a few streets over from my house. Well, that made sense. The girls had been friends and hung out all the time.

I decided to pay them a visit. Amanda insisted on coming along. I tried to get her to stay home, to protect her from what they might say, but she was having no part of it. She was not going to miss my ongoing investigation. I decided that she probably thought it was sexy, watching me work as a super detective.

We walked over to the Hopkins' house and up the oyster-shell driveway. The house was a medium-sized bungalow, with a faded cedar shake front that might have been painted green twenty years ago. It was a typical Harkers-looking house. I knocked on the front screen door, and a man who looked to be in his late sixties opened the door. He left it closed and said hello through the screen.

"Hi," I said in my cheeriest voice. "I'm Cory Walker. This is my friend Amanda. We're trying to locate your daughter, Lynn. I heard she moved away and is a nurse now. Could I trouble you for her address?"

"You the ones bought the Stone House?" he asked in his thick accent.

"Yes, sir."

"Well, you should learn to let sleeping dogs lie. I heard what happened to Ben up in Maury. Lynn's got nothin' to say to you." He shut the door in my face.

I looked at Amanda. "Well, *that* went well."

We started to walk away and I heard some voices behind the front door. It opened back up and Mrs. Hopkins was standing there behind the screen.

"He didn't mean to be rude, Mr. *Wal-kah*," she said, trying to sound polite, her accent even thicker than his. "But please, leave our *daughtah* outta this. Now y'all go on and have a nice day, hear?" She gently closed the door.

I looked at Amanda. "Well, that was a *much* more polite version of 'go fuck yourself,'" I whispered.

She wasn't amused. "These people are *scared*, Cory. That should tell you something. Now let's get your shit together and go home."

"I *am* home, remember? And I'd like you to make this home, too."

She shook her head, walked past me and headed for my house. Man, that girl had a bit of Irish in her or something.

In the kitchen, we both saw it at the same time — the answering machine blinking. I didn't get many calls other than Amanda and potential witnesses to a capital case, so I was intrigued as I hit play.

"Hello, Cory. This is Grant Williams over at the County Prosecutor's Office. Sorry to ruin your day, but it looks like your case may be going to a grand jury. I didn't think it would happen this way, but it looks like you should be expecting some mail. The Eastern District of North Carolina will be seating a Federal Grand Jury in about four weeks. We'll be in touch."

Amanda looked as shocked as I felt. "This is ridiculous!" she burst out. "A bunch of thugs try to rape me and kill you and they want to prosecute *you*? This is outrageous!"

I nodded, wondering if Congressman Earl Stone had made a few phone calls.

# Chapter Twenty-Eight

## A Tough Read

It took me a while to get Amanda to calm down. It was good that she'd freaked out. It prevented *me* from doing that. I had all but been promised that I could forget the whole thing had ever happened. That was before I had flown onto Congressman Earl Stone's radar.

We sat down in the library after I dug Casey's diary out of the basement crawlspace for Amanda to read. As I handed it to her, I warned her it was going to be pretty intense. I was happy to have a second opinion on what was in it, but I also knew that Amanda would be very upset after reading it.

I sat down and put the TV on while she read. Almost like it was planned just to piss me off more, as soon as the power came on, the newscaster was talking about Earl Stone's bid for the White House. I listened and watched the clips of this lying-sack-of-you-know-what from the comfort of the old couch that had come with the house. I could feel my face getting hot as I watched him. When the news showed a still shot of him with his new wife and son, I turned it off. Amanda was totally engrossed in the journal, and I excused myself to the backyard. Maybe pulling weeds would relieve some stress.

The sun had gotten lower and the pines provided a bit of shade in my yard, so it was pretty nice outside. I spotted Agatha in her yard clipping her roses, and waved. She walked over, and I cursed myself for being so friendly.

"Hello, Mr. Cory. Did that reporter talk to you?" she asked, brushing white hair out of her face with a gloved hand.

"What? What reporter?"

"That nice young man who was here earlier. He was from the *Carteret Inquirer*. He's writing a story about Congressman Stone. He wanted some comments from his old neighbors out here on Harkers Island. I saw him on your veranda, but I think you were out with your lady friend."

I smiled to myself. *My lady friend.* "He didn't leave a business card. Did you talk to him?"

"Just for a moment, really. He asked me if I knew who lived in the Stone house now. I told him I did and you were a lovely young man."

That didn't sit quite right. If he were doing a piece on old neighbors, why would he want to talk to me? I asked Agatha, "What did you tell him about the old days with the Stones?"

Agatha put her hand to her mouth. The blue veins so visible in her bony hand reminded me just how old she must be. "You know, come to think of it, he really didn't ask me very much at all. I think he must have been more interested in the house."

I felt the hair stand up on the back of my neck. "Did he walk around my yard for a while?"

"I don't believe so." She scanned the sky, trying to recall. "Timothy was making a big fuss over a bird in the yard, and I got distracted. Your house *is* pretty famous now, though. If the congressman becomes the next President, you'll be living in quite a famous residence."

I thanked Agatha and told her I needed to make a call, then hustled back inside and started checking all the windows to see if they had been tampered with. Quite honestly, how the hell would I know? My special forces training did not include the fine art of breaking and entering, unless I was blowing a door off and tossing in a grenade.

Amanda was engrossed in the diary and didn't notice my strange behavior until I walked past her with Ice across my back.

"Cory!" she screamed, as I passed by her toward the kitchen.

I stopped. "Yes, dear?"

She just stared at me. She knew I knew damned well what she was thinking. I played dumb. "Hmm? You say something?"

She put the diary down in her lap and folded her arms. I used my thumb to point to the Mossberg on my back, my eyebrows raised. "That's just my home security system."

"What's going on, Cory?"

"Not sure. I guess you didn't get to the good parts yet. Keep reading."

I walked out to the kitchen and hunted through some old phone numbers. It took a while searching my very sophisticated filing system to locate the business card I was looking for. It was one of about fifty cards all jammed together in the front of a very old phonebook. Organized people are just too lazy to look for stuff.

Kim Predham of the *Carteret Inquirer*. She had been one of the reporters who had covered my story when I'd had my ass kicked on date number one with Amanda. Her story had been *huge* in my being treated as a hero instead of a trained killer picking on some poor defenseless locals.

I picked up the phone as Amanda walked in behind me. She had tears in her eyes. I *knew* she was going to be a mess. She walked over and gave me a hug, then just buried her face in my chest and hung on for a while.

"I warned you," I whispered.

"That poor girl," she said softly.

"He wants to be President of the United States, Amanda."

"No way that's going to happen, is it, Cory?"

"Not if I can help it."

"Can we call the FBI or the sheriff now?"

"I have one better — the power of the press."

I called the number for Kim at the *Inquirer* and got her voicemail, which gave me her cell number. I called that, and she picked up, announcing her name. I put her on speaker phone.

"Hi, Kim. I'm not sure if you'd remember me, but you covered my story a few months back. My name in Cory Walker…"

"Oh my God, of *course*, I remember you, Cory! How are you feeling?"

She sounded a little too happy to hear from me, according to Amanda's face. Amanda raised an eyebrow at me, and I stuck my tongue out at her, mature person that I am. "I'm fine, actually. I was wondering, though, if I could ask you a few questions, if you have a minute?"

"Sure, how can I help you?" she asked.

"Well, first of all, I moved to Harkers Island..."

"Down south? Below the Outer Banks?"

"Yeah. You've been here?"

"Only once, in college, while I was taking a class on linguistics."

I laughed out loud. "Did you save your notes? Maybe you could translate for me."

Even Amanda laughed.

"Yeah, *really*! That Hoi Toider accent is bit different, huh?"

"No kidding."

"Wow. So you *really* wanted to get away, huh? Harkers is tiny."

"Yes, and very peaceful. In fact, I bought Earl Stone's old house." I had just cast my fishing line.

"Earl Stone? As in *Congressman* Stone?"

"The very same."

"That's so cool! Is the house *great*?"

"It is...for a lot of reasons. We fell in love with it right away. I was wondering... Do you know if someone from your newspaper is down here doing a story on Earl Stone? Someone was nosing around my house today when my girlfriend and I were at lunch. He told my neighbor he was from the *Inquirer*."

"Did your neighbor get his name?"

"No...and he didn't leave his card."

"Hmm...I'll ask. By the way, how is the woman who was attacked with you that night at the bar?"

Amanda made a face, and I paused long enough to get a punch in the arm. "She's fine. She's here with me right now. We'd love to have you come down and see the house."

I heard her say a quiet, "Wow."

"Wow?" I asked.

"I'm Googling your house. I was about five years old when the daughter was killed. God. And his wife hanged herself? That's terrible."

"Yeah, there's a lot of talk out here about all that. Forget the human-interest story. You might want to get an investigative reporter down here for *that* one." I was now reeling in my fish.

"Why? What do you mean?"

"Well, I think there's a *big* story down here, but no one talks about it to outsiders—close-knit community and all. The deaths of his daughter and wife. Maybe you could come down here and do little digging."

"I'm not an investigative reporter. I do local interest. What kind of story?"

"It might be dangerous." I *was* baiting her, true enough—but I wasn't kidding about the dangerous part.

There was a pause. "Do you *know* something, Cory?"

I had to trust somebody, and the same cops who had let Stone off twenty years ago might not be the best place to start. "When I was in the hospital, some folks were looking to arrest me for murder. Your story was a big help and I owe you one, so I *will* tell you this. After I started asking questions down here about Stone, my case was coincidentally re-opened for a grand jury."

I could almost hear her nod. "I'll talk to my editor."

"You can tell him you have something that will be front page news all over the world."

"All over the *world*? Are you serious?"

"Dead serious."

"And you can't talk on the phone, right?" I could hear the skepticism in her voice. "Okay, don't talk to anyone else about this, okay? Let me get back to you."

She hung up and I smiled at Amanda. "Are you happy now? I called in the cavalry."

"She covers local fluff. She said it herself. You need more than that, Cory. And what was that about a reporter already being here?"

"Not sure." I pointed to Ice, still on my back. "But I intend to find out."

"You missed him? You didn't see him? Did you ask Agatha how long he was here?"

"No. Why?"

"He could have come into the house."

That stopped me cold. There were no locks on the doors. He could have walked in and looked around. But why? Nobody knew there was a diary...or did they?

# Chapter Twenty-Nine

## Tuckers

Amanda finished reading the diary, and looked completely wiped out afterward, pretty much the same reaction I'd had. I made her walk upstairs with me and go into what must have been Casey's room. I pointed at the master bedroom. She understood without me saying a word.

"Right down the hall from her mother?" Amanda said. "No wonder she hanged herself."

"Funny thing about that, Amanda. The medical examiner doesn't think she did."

"*What*?" she exclaimed.

"The gist of what he told me is that when a person is strangled, it's a different injury from hanging. He says she was choked to death *then* hanged."

"*What*? Why didn't anyone do anything about that?"

"That's the deal. Even twenty years ago, Earl Stone had some juice. The guy I spoke to *did* ask about the deaths and ended up being transferred to the moon. Same thing with a cop who asked questions. Some old doc ready for retirement did the exam and the paperwork. I think he wrote whatever he was told to write. Stone got away with murder."

Amanda leaned back against the wall, looking grim. "We should leave here right now, Cory. Who knows who that guy was, asking questions? If you have to walk around with a huge gun in your own house, there's a serious problem."

"Some chicks think it's sexy. And besides, this isn't a gun. This is Ice. He and I have traveled the world together. He's a trusted friend."

"I'm scared."

"Even with me here?" I asked, trying to be very Clint Eastwood about the whole thing.

"*Especially* with you here."

The phone rang, interrupting what may have been a great segue to me taking off Amanda's clothes again. It was Kim.

"I'm coming down there!" She sounded *very* excited.

"Yeah? The editor gave you a shot at the big-time?"

"I told him you bought Congressman Stone's old summer place on Harkers. I'm driving down there tomorrow."

Kim asked for the names of the cop, the coroners, the neighbors and a million other details. She was off and running, a hundred miles an hour, her reporter blood on full boil. She wanted all the details of what I had discovered so far, which I wasn't about to share with anyone except Amanda.

I gave Kim most of the information she wanted but left out the part about finding the diary. That was worthy of a face-to-face conversation.

"If I go through a woodchipper tonight," I told Amanda, "at least Kim will have some suspects."

Amanda didn't think the woodchipper comment was funny, but I was only half kidding.

I showed Amanda where I'd found Casey's journal, then hid it again in the same spot.

"Let's go talk to Thomas Woods. He's the guy who found Casey's body."

I hid Ice in the hallway closet and we walked down to the pier where I had met Caleb and Thomas that first time. They weren't around, but we kept meandering around the dock area until we came across Mike Jackson. *Small island...* We exchanged pleasant hellos, and I asked him where his dad's buddy Thomas might be.

"Where he *always* is if he isn't out fishing. Tuckers."

Now there was a name I hadn't heard yet. "Where's Tuckers?" I asked.

Mike laughed. "You really are a dingbatter. Just keep following this road until you hear music and see drunk old men."

*Ah. The local watering hole.* I thanked him, and Amanda and I walked arm-in-arm along the sandy road until, sure enough, we could see an old shack that was full of local fishermen drinking beer on the outside patios. Large garage-type doors were left open in the front of the bar so anyone could see right inside. There was a fire going in the backyard, with fish grilling and an old set of speakers cranking out some music that sounded like Johnny Cash on acid. We walked in and caught a lot of stares. I just squeezed Amanda's hand and smiled, having a flashback of our first date that hadn't ended so well. I rolled my bad shoulder out of habit.

The tavern, such as it was, was a one-room shack with an ancient wooden-plank floor that had probably had more beer spilled on it in the last hundred years than most bars would ever pour. There were a few wooden picnic tables inside and a long wooden bar along two sides of the room. Mismatched chairs of wood and plastic were mixed in among the barstools, and white Christmas-like lights were strung on the porch outside to add to the 'just throw anything anywhere' decor.

I felt better when I spotted Thomas and Caleb at one end of the bar. They noticed me then spotted Amanda and forgot I was on the planet. I introduced them to Amanda and they immediately started chatting with her, although I'm pretty sure she only caught every third or fourth word. They were tough enough to understand *sober*. I finally realized they were arguing over whose wooden decoy duck looked more realistic.

They decided Amanda would be the judge. For ten minutes, that end of the bar paid very close attention as Thomas and Caleb each explained why *their* duck was better. Amanda, sharp girl that she is, remembered that it was Thomas we wanted to talk to. By coincidence, his duck won the contest. Caleb was only playfully a sore loser and had to buy the next round for that end of the bar, which was met with a loud cheer, roaring laughter and back-slapping. As the bartender served mugs of cold beer on the wooden bar, I felt very much at home here on Harkers.

I made small-talk with Caleb, and Amanda started easing into local history with Thomas. By the time she'd mentioned Casey being found by his boat, he was fairly hammered, but Casey's name seemed to sober him right up. I tried to listen to her politely grill him.

"It must have been awful, finding that poor girl."

"Nothing you ever want to see, miss," he said, and chugged his beer, I guessed to wash away the memory. "Why you two always asking about that girl?"

*Oops.*

I talked fishing with Caleb to keep him busy while Amanda worked her magic but kept one ear on the conversation.

"I guess living in that house made us start wondering about what happened," she said, being very cool. "And I don't think everyone believes that Ben McComb killed her. He was just killed in prison."

Thomas sat back and changed his expression. I didn't like how it looked. "Yep. Might have started talking about things that should just be left alone. Might be a lesson in that for everyone." His face looked hard, and quite frankly, a bit scary.

Amanda bounced back beautifully. "Oh, I'm sorry, I meant no offense, Thomas. It was just bothering to me, that's all. I had a friend who was killed when we were about her age, and I guess it hit a nerve."

Man, she was good. She'd just pulled that right out of her ass.

Thomas faked a polite smile, but I could see he was upset. He was done speaking with Amanda. I interrupted their conversation and handed them each a beer. "How's the fishing been?" I asked Thomas, with my stupid innocent grin on. I sometimes worry that my stupid face comes to me way too naturally.

He looked like he was a million miles away. "Der's feesh out there," he said, almost to himself. His mood had changed and his face looked dark, and I turned back to Caleb, who was still going on about his decoy duck to the old-timer next to him.

I told Amanda it was getting late and we should be heading back. She took the hint, said diplomatic goodbyes to everyone, and we left the bar. It was dark outside, and the island was eerily quiet. What should have been a nice romantic walk home was instead troubling. I found myself 'on patrol', and I hated that feeling. Amanda had polished off a few beers and was content to just rest her head against my shoulder as we walked, oblivious to me being back in combat mode.

The entire walk home, I looked for tripwires, checked for fields of fire and kept my head on a swivel. It was hard enough to shed a lifetime of combat training under the best of circumstances. My quiet island home now felt like the Hindu Kush.

# Chapter Thirty

A Visit from Timothy

Amanda and I got home and undressed, slipped into bed and, much to my dismay, she passed out almost instantly. I got up, took Ice out of the closet and checked the perimeter. I hated feeling like that in my own house, but those were the breaks, I guessed. When I was satisfied that we weren't under attack, I double-checked the door locks and went to bed.

It felt nice to curl up with Amanda. She was soft and warm and looked very happy sleeping. I, on the other hand, ended up awake most of the night, listening to every noise outside, wishing some other guy in my squad would take a turn on watch. When the sun came up, I pushed myself out of bed and made a large pot of coffee. I filled two mugs and brought them upstairs. Amanda was still out like a light, so I sipped mine in silence and enjoyed the view of my sleeping beauty. She was great-looking, even sound asleep with her hair all over her face. I was a very lucky man.

I ended up drinking her cup, too, threw on a pair of shorts and went out into the backyard. It was cool out, with dew on the grass that made my bare feet cold and wet—a nice change from the hot, humid days. I looked over at the statue of the two angels, so white against the dark green pine-tree border, and saw condensation on the white marble. It looked like tears were running down their faces. *How appropriate.* I heard something move in the bushes, and without even thinking, I dropped and rolled across the wet grass, grabbing for a weapon that didn't exist. I spotted the source of the noise—a very large, very fat gray cat. *Timothy.*

As soon as my heart rate slowed down, I sat up and shook my head at my own nerves. It was lucky that I hadn't puked coffee on myself. I walked over and called his name, and the fat bastard walked over to me and sat up on his back paws. I bent over and picked him up. *Jesus.* It was like holding a dog, he was so big. I carried him back into his yard, where I found Agatha on her back porch, dead-heading some flowers in large clay pots.

"Look who I found," I announced, as I walked over into her yard.

"Oh my!" she exclaimed. "I didn't know he'd gotten out! You naughty boy!"

I was hoping she was talking to the cat. I put him down on her back porch and he ran to the door, which Agatha opened to let him back inside. She thanked me ten times and told me that he rarely strayed from the house and almost never from the yard.

"He must really *like* you," she surmised.

*Great.* He'd probably taken a dump in my yard.

"You're up early," she said.

"Yeah, an old habit of mine. I usually wake up with the sun. Nice part of the day, though."

"I think so, too. Some folks are sunrise people, some are sunset people. I like the promise of a new day — especially at my age."

We both chuckled. She was a pretty cool old lady.

"My angels were crying this morning," I said, for no particular reason.

"My dear young man, whatever do you mean?"

"The condensation. The water running down their faces. It looks so sad."

"She was a sad girl," said Agatha quietly.

"Casey looked sad all the time?"

"Not Casey. Anne. She was always so blue. She spent so much time in the garden. I think she tried to cheer herself up with the flowers. But she always looked so heartbroken to me." She folded her arms like she was embarrassed. "I don't mean to speak ill of the dead," she said, almost apologetically.

"Not at all. You were just making an observation. You said you two were good friends. Did she ever talk to you about what was bothering her?"

"No. I considered her a friend and a nice summertime neighbor. I think I may have been her *only* friend, though. She was *very* quiet. If we hadn't both spent so much time in our gardens over the years, I'm not sure we ever would have met. She rarely left the house, poor thing. I never saw her out at the restaurants. Maybe she just went to fancier places in Carteret County, but it was a bit strange, how she kept to herself. Might not have been a coincidence that she planted so many Bleeding Hearts in her yard."

She looked depressed to me as she spoke about her old friend. "What about Mr. Stone?"

"Mr. Stone... I don't think I said more than a few sentences to him in all the years he was here. He was away a lot. And not really an Islander, no offense. He never tried to get to know anyone here. Sort of 'above it all', if you know what I mean."

"Folks here didn't like him?"

"I wouldn't say that. Folks here respected him, maybe even were a little afraid of him. But he did a lot for the island. I know without him we never would have gotten that bridge when we did. He pulled lots of strings in Washington to get the money for that. He had the jetties fixed, the beaches replenished after the hurricane, got insurance money for the fishermen when they lost their boats... He was a powerful man, even back in those days. Everyone was very upset when the tragedy happened. When he sold the house and moved away, most folks here figured we'd be forgotten about. Now that he's a congressman, though, Harkers Island has done pretty well. He always gets money for projects here."

"So I guess he gets your vote for President," I said.

"I wouldn't vote for that son of a bitch if he was the last man in the country," she snapped, suddenly red-faced. Then she caught herself and apologized.

I was shocked but started laughing out loud. "*What*? I thought everyone on Harkers Island *loved* him? Didn't you just tell me all the wonderful things he did for the island?"

"I apologize, Mr. *Wal-kah*. I shouldn't have said that."

"Come on, Agatha. This is Cory you're talking to. Don't apologize. Why don't you like him?"

"Woman's intuition," she said.

I folded my arms. "I just rescued your cat. Fess up."

She stared at me hard with blue eyes that were still clear and sharp in her wrinkled face. "Anne was miserable. She had the prettiest house and garden on Harkers Island, and she was sad all the time. I don't think he was *ever* nice to her. And," she whispered to me, like anyone else was listening for a hundred miles, "I think he hit her." She blushed and instantly looked very uncomfortable. "I've never said that out loud before to anyone."

I patted her hand. "Your secret is safe with me, Agatha." We had just bonded, and I really liked her more now. Too bad she hadn't put a round through Earl's forehead about twenty years ago. "Did you ever see him hit her?" I asked.

"Oh no, of course not."

"But...?"

"I saw her face enough times to know, makeup or not."

I was finally getting somewhere. "What about Casey? Think he hit *her*?"

She made a face, then said a quiet "No."

"But...?" I asked again.

Agatha let out a tired sigh. "I don't think he hit her, but I think she was scared of him. She avoided him. *That* much I do know. Anytime he was home, she found an excuse to be somewhere else. She only visited me when he was around." Then she added, "Not that I minded. She was a sweet girl, and always welcome here, bless her heart."

"Did she ever talk about Stone? Ever say anything about him hitting her mom?"

"Oh, heavens, no. She would never say anything like that. She was quiet, too. But I've always had cats here, and she used to love to sit with my kitties. Anne had her garden, and Casey had my cats. I think they were both just finding ways to avoid *him*. Anyway, enough of that talk. Oh, look, here comes your little friend."

I turned around and spotted Amanda in the backyard wearing my T-shirt and not much else. Damn, she even rolled out of bed looking hot. She called my name. I told Agatha I'd better go and make Amanda some breakfast before she got cranky, and she laughed. I promised her I'd bring Amanda over when she was dressed, and I walked back to my own yard.

I gave Amanda a hug and said good morning, and she informed me that I had once again scared the crap out of her by leaving her alone so early in the morning. And I thought *I* was jumpy. We went inside and I caught her up on my conversation with Agatha.

# Chapter Thirty-One

## Phone Call

Over scrambled eggs and toast, I told Amanda how Earl Stone had funneled a lot of money to Harkers Island. And although he wasn't exactly loved for his charm, he was respected. I also told her that Agatha hated his guts.

"Smart woman," she said.

We finished breakfast to a darkening sky. The phone rang, and I hit speaker phone to hear Kim's voice on her cell phone.

"Morning. How's it going down there?" she asked.

"It's another beautiful day on Harkers Island," I responded.

"Really? It's raining so hard here I can barely see my hood. I might be a little late, but I'm on my way."

"No worries. Drive safe."

"Cory, are you going to give me any clues about what you found? I was up all night googling old news articles and going through every file we have on the Stones and Harkers Island. What did you find?"

"Oh, come on now, Kim. If I told you now, it wouldn't be any fun. When you get to the bridge, give me a call and I'll tell you how to get to the house." I didn't mention to her that I was no longer comfortable speaking about this on the phone anymore, even in my own house.

"You're already in my GPS. See you in a bit."

Amanda made a dramatic gesture of throwing her hair back and said, '*You're already in my GPS...*'

"Oohhh...somebody's *jealous*," I teased.

"And somebody better be a good boy if he wants any more booty before I go home."

"You *are* home," I said.

She made a face. I knew the place was creeping her out more and more. The diary gave me the same feeling, like I needed to take a shower or something after I read it.

We turned on the weather channel and watched a front moving in from the mainland. It didn't look nearly as nasty as the hurricane that was forming down in the Caribbean. The Outer Banks had been hammered, and Harkers Island had been devastated by hurricanes. At least my house was rock solid. The weather could huff and puff all it wanted.

I suggested a walk around the island before the weather got lousy, and Amanda obliged me. Cape Lookout National Park was a decent walk from the house, not far from the dock where the ferry tied up. The east end of the island, being federal parkland, was undeveloped and pristine. We walked through the sand dunes and dune grass, watching the squawking sea gulls zip back and forth between their nests and the ocean to catch their lunch.

When we arrived at the shoreline, the waves had picked up a bit, perhaps a foreshadowing of the hurricane that was heading our way. It really was a beautiful spot, with a picturesque lighthouse standing atop the dunes. I'd have to blame the natural beauty of the park for my next outburst.

"Do you think you're going to marry me?" It just sort of popped out.

She looked at me and laughed. "I don't know. I guess that would depend on if you ask me."

"If you told me ahead of time, I wouldn't be so nervous when it was time to actually pop the question."

"And I get to take my time and think about it? And possibly say no?"

*Damn. Tough crowd.* "Okay, well, I was just taking a survey anyway. We'll discuss this again in a few years."

"Uh-huh."

We walked and walked, eventually with our sandals in our hands as we let the saltwater roll in up to our knees. Boats were coming in from fishing. I looked at my watch. It was still early—not quite eleven—but maybe the weather had swayed them. I saw flags flying by the lighthouse and recognized them as small craft advisories.

Actually, that was total horseshit. Amanda, walking encyclopedia of miscellaneous facts, told me that, which led to a conversation about an old boyfriend who'd had a boat.

It started to drizzle, and we headed back toward the house. By the time we got home, the rain was getting heavier. We toweled off and changed into jeans and T-shirts. I suggested an afternoon delight, but she informed me that I was a nymphomaniac who was only interested in her for the great sex. I admitted it *was* in the top five reasons I was interested, but managed to save myself by having the other four reasons at the ready for recitation.

"So now what? Are you going to give the diary to Kim?"

"Not now. I need to hang on to it. I *will* let her see it, though. If she reads it, she'll know exactly what kind of animal Earl Stone is."

"You know he can just deny it, call it a forgery for political reasons and make you look like the bad guy. He'd get a lot of sympathy as the poor father of a murdered girl. We have to be really careful."

"We don't have a ton of options. I'm still thinking about trying to find a hook to get the FBI involved. No way I'd trust the cops in Carteret. Maybe Kim has some ideas."

"Kim isn't an investigative reporter, Cory. You should have called someone with more experience."

The doorbell rang. I glanced at my watch. Too early for Kim. I looked through the side window and saw a mailman on my porch. I opened the closet, took out Ice and had Amanda open the door. She looked fairly terrified when she saw me level Ice toward the door and take off the safety. He asked her to sign for a certified letter, and he left.

As soon as the door closed she turned and looked at me, red-faced. "Jesus Christ, Cory! What were you going to do? Blow the mailman's head off?"

She threw the letter at me.

"Sorry. I wasn't expecting a *real* mailman."

She stormed off into the kitchen, and I put the safety back on then picked up and opened the letter, which was from the Eastern Carolina Justice System, informing me that the Prosecutor's Office was seeking a Grand Jury indictment into the deaths of three scumbags, and the aggravated assault of another couple of assholes. I am paraphrasing.

"Motherfucker!" I screamed at the letter.

Amanda walked back in. "What's the matter?"

I held up the letter. "Guess who's going to jail?"

She walked over and looked at the letter. "You aren't going to jail. It just means they want to see if there will be a trial. I'm sure they'll throw it out."

"Yeah? You can bet Earl Stone will pick the names of the jurors himself. *Fucker*. I'm gonna pull the switch on him myself."

Amanda gave me a hug. "Are you ready to go home now?"

"I told you, I *am* home. And I'm not being chased out of it by *that* sick fuck. Game *on*."

"You aren't in Afghanistan, Cory. Earl Stone is a very powerful man. This is nuts."

"Bring it on." I meant it. The phone rang. I figured it was Kim, and hit speaker. Instead of Kim's ever-cheerful voice, I got a gruff man's snarl with a Southern accent.

"You should have minded your own business, Cory Walker." The line went dead.

*Great. Just fucking great.*

Amanda looked at me and started crying.

# Chapter Thirty-Two

## In from the Rain

I have to admit, Mr. Nasty on the phone had shaken me up. It was just so, I dunno, 'unexpected'. *So much for finesse*. When Kim knocked on the door, we both jumped. I had Ice nearby, much to Amanda's consternation, but put him back in the closet when I saw Kim through the side window. The rain was now coming down sideways. It was dark and blowing pretty good out there.

I opened the door. Kim stepped in, her game face on.

I greeted my visitor from the press and invited her into my house of horrors. She said hello to Amanda as she peeled off her wet windbreaker and sat down with us in the library, which was right off the entryway. After a brief exchange of pleasantries and weather observations, we got down to business.

"Kim, I'm giving you first crack at a story that is so big it will have major ramifications on a *national* level. It will also probably put Earl Stone in jail — or get all three of us killed." *That* got her attention. "I bought this house out here to find some peace and quiet and learn how to relax again. I was *really* trying to leave the battlefield behind me. It hasn't quite ended up that way. I was working downstairs and I found an old diary. *Casey Stone's* diary."

Kim stared at me wide-eyed for a second, unable to hide her shock. "She kept a *diary*?" She shifted gears from thunderstruck back to investigative reporter and began asking questions at a hundred miles an hour.

"Oh my God, Cory! She kept a diary and you *have* it? Do you know what this *means*?"

"Yeah. I know *exactly* what it means. Twenty years buried in that basement, and if Earl Stone finds out I have it, the three of us may end up at the bottom of the sound. I want you to read it. And when you get *done* reading it, *you* tell *me* who raped and murdered that girl."

I walked over to the roll-top desk, where I had shoved the diary prior to Kim's arrival. I took it out and handed it to her. She looked at it with amazement, made sure her hands were completely dry and took it from me like I was presenting her with the Dead Sea scrolls.

"You go ahead and read. I'll make us all a pot of coffee. This is going to take you a while."

For the next two hours, Kim drank coffee and read page after page of Casey's diary. At one point, she started sobbing uncontrollably. Amanda brought her some tissues and put her arm around her. When she got control of herself, she told Amanda and me that she had been raped in college and had never told anyone. This was the first time she'd ever said it out loud since it had happened. Reading Casey's diary had brought it all back.

Amanda hugged her, and the two of them just rocked back and forth for a moment until Kim regained her composure. Kim blew her nose and wiped her face, apologizing softly.

"Don't apologize. We're way past apologizing. We all have to get this stuff out in the open." Amanda patted her thigh. "I'll get us some more coffee. Finish reading."

Finally Kim closed the book gently and just held it on her lap, staring at it. "I don't know what to say," she said, still staring at the faded cover. Then she looked up at me. "I don't know where to start. You're right. This is huge. I need to call my editor." She stared at the diary in her hands again, lost in thought.

"Do whatever you need to do," I said.

"And see if your editor has any contacts in the FBI," Amanda suggested.

"Somebody he trusts," I added. "I don't trust the local cops."

"I think Stone owns the whole state," Kim said. "There's no way to know how far the police corruption goes."

"What if you run the story as is?"

"No way my editor would run a story like this about Earl Stone without all kinds of proof. Those names you gave me? I found one guy — the medical examiner."

"Greller? I talked to him. He was shut out of the daughter's autopsy. And later, when he questioned the findings, they dumped him. Same thing happened to a cop I told you about on the phone, Arthur McDade. They forced him out. He's so scared of Stone he won't say where he is. I'm telling you…this whole thing stinks."

"Tell her about the phone call," said Amanda.

"Yeah, right. Before you got here, someone called and told me to mind my own business then hung up."

"This is extremely serious, Cory. Who would know that you were looking into this?" Kim asked.

"I went to see Benjamin McComb at Maury…"

"Oh my God. You spoke to *McComb*? When? Do you know he was *just* murdered in prison?"

"Yeah, I know. Right after I went to see him, a few guys worked him over real good and killed him. Just for talking to me, they killed him."

That last sentence hung in the room like the dark clouds outside. My stomach felt the way it did after I had to write an after-action report explaining why one of my people had died.

"Then some guy said he was a reporter and was snooping around the house," added Amanda.

"I asked about that at the paper. No one at our paper is doing a story down here. It doesn't mean anything, though. Reporters from all over the country are covering Earl Stone. Can I take the diary and show my editor?"

"It stays with me for now, but you can make a copy to show your editor."

Kim grabbed her purse and pulled out her phone and a camera. "This will be good enough for what we need." She opened up to various parts of the diary and started taking pictures with both, using the cell phone camera to shoot off quick messages to her boss. I sat back and waited for her to finish. *Life in the twenty-first century.* Then she called the paper. I listened to her try to explain what she had just read to her boss. She was so excited. I could hear her editor yelling at her to slow down.

Amanda and I gave her some space. The rain had tapered off and we walked out back, admiring Anne Stone's work in the colorful flower beds. In the eerie gold light of the stormy sky, the flowers seemed extra bright and colorful, and the angels glowed white and pure.

Amanda put her arms around me from behind. She whispered that she was scared.

I turned around and gave her a hug. "Kim is going to do a story, the Feds are going to arrest Stone and you and I are going to live happily ever after."

Kim walked out after us and excused her interruption. "You said you wanted me to tell you who killed Casey. I assume you think it was Earl Stone."

I nodded. "I think he killed his wife, too."

"*What?*"

"The M.E. told me that Anne Stone didn't die from being hanged. She was choked to death, just like her daughter."

"My God! He killed his wife then made it look like a suicide?"

"Exactly."

"And the medical examiner tried to report that?"

"He asked a few questions and got shit-canned."

"It's unbelievable. It's like everyone knew and nobody did anything about it."

A huge crack of lightning, followed by booming thunder, made us all jump. The rain started coming down again. We headed back into the house.

"Hurricane Eduardo is off Florida now, you know," said Kim. "It looks like it might be turning north. If it does, you'll probably get slammed in a couple of days. While I'm down here, I want to talk to some of the locals."

"They won't say much," Amanda told her. "I tried the other night with the guy who found Casey's body. He got kind of angry. They don't like us bringing it up. You definitely can't say you're a reporter. They'll never talk to you at all."

"The islanders are a pretty tight bunch," Kim acknowledged. "You could be here another hundred years and still be an off-islander. What about your neighbor? The one who told you about the reporter or whatever he was."

"Agatha? She hates Earl Stone's guts. She was friendly with his wife, and I think Casey used to hide from Earl over at her house."

"She *knew* about the abuse?"

"Only suspected, I think."

Kim bit her lip.

"Let's go talk to her." We stood on the back porch, watching the torrent, and decided to forego the visit.

When we walked into the kitchen, Amanda was saying, "Wait. He just walked in."

# Chapter Thirty-Three

## Early Signs of Trouble

Amanda handed me the phone.

"This is Michael Greller."

To say I was surprised to hear his voice would be a major understatement. I put him on speaker phone. "I thought you said you'd never talk to me again unless I got Stone in court."

"Did you talk to anyone about our conversation the other day?" He sounded agitated.

"Why?"

"Yes or no? You tell anyone I gave you information on that case?"

The only person I had spoken to about him was Amanda then Kim, just a couple of minutes earlier. There was no way anyone else could know what we'd discussed. I told him so.

"Are you sure?" he asked, sounding very upset.

"What's wrong, doc?"

"I got a phone call. You been asking a lot of questions down there?"

"I've been asking around a little. I didn't mention *you*."

"Listen to me real good. Do *not* fuck with these people. You hear me?"

"What's going on? What did the caller say?"

"Mind my own business or I was a dead man. And I'm giving you the same advice. He told me to go look at Benjamin McComb if I needed any reminders. These people are connected, Walker. They know everyone. They hear everything. Whatever you're doing, drop it."

"But—"

He hung up on me.

Kim smiled.

"You think that's funny?" I asked her.

"No. This is scary as hell, but this will be the biggest scoop of all time, and it's *mine*!"

I shook my head. *Youthful exuberance.* "Watch for the tripwires, kid."

"Look… Since I'm not talking to the locals right now anyway, I want to get back and start working on this. Obviously, Dr. Greller won't talk to me. But what about that cop? Can you give me his number?"

I mulled that over. I guess she'd find it without my help anyway, the same way I had. I gave her the number. She gave Amanda a hug and left, excited to start working on her Pulitzer, and told us she'd call. I hid the diary back down in the crawlspace.

She ended up calling a lot sooner than we'd expected.

\* \* \* \*

Amanda and I were contemplating a grocery store run to stock up before the hurricane hit—if it did—

when my cell phone rang. We just looked at each other. *Another psycho ready to threaten me?* Instead, I saw Kim's number on the caller ID. When I said hello, she started shouting so loud that Amanda could hear her without the speaker on. She sounded furious.

"Kim?" I could hardly make out what she was saying. "What's wrong?"

"He fucking *stole* it! Right out of my briefcase!"

"What are you talking about?"

"That cop! He pulled me over as soon as I crossed the bridge and told me to get out of the car in the pouring rain. I went to get my license and he pulled out his fucking gun and told me to freeze, like I'm a drug dealer or something. He said he was going to check my briefcase for a weapon! A weapon? Are you kidding me? So he made me get back in the car, took my briefcase back to his car and rifled through *all* my stuff. He stole my camera and took all my notes from today. Can you believe this shit? The balls of this guy! I'm a reporter! He can't do that!"

"Did you get his name? A badge number?"

"I demanded his badge number. He *has* to give it to me, but he refused! He just threw my stuff at me, walked back to his car and took off at a hundred miles an hour. With the rain, I couldn't even get the license plate number."

"Tell her to come back here," Amanda said.

"You want to come back here?"

"No, I'm going home. That son of a bitch! He can't do that! He's gonna be pretty shocked when this hits the papers! Thank God I emailed those pictures to my editor! Listen... Put the original in a safe deposit box. The banks are closed now. Do it first thing in the morning."

"Okay. Just get home and call us when you get there."

Amanda looked scared shitless.

"It's gonna be fine," I assured her. "As long as we all don't get killed."

Amanda stared at me. "That cop who stopped her...?"

"What about him?"

"What if he wasn't a cop?"

*Great. Just great.*

# Chapter Thirty-Four

## Visitors

Amanda and I decided against the grocery trip. Leaving the island with dirty cops on patrol—or Stone's guys dressed like cops—didn't seem like a great idea, even with all the doors and windows locked. We opted for a quick drive around the block to Tuckers for pub grub and a beer. Amanda didn't even argue when I wrapped Ice in a beach towel and shoved him under my seat.

Tuckers was fairly crowded. It was raining again, and the wind was blowing pretty hard. The temperature had dropped a bit, and honestly, the cooler salt air smelled clean and refreshing.

I said hello to Mike and his dad. He and Caleb were sitting on stools at the bar, drinking beer, when we walked in. Amanda and I slid into a booth and ordered the catch of the day, which I was figuring was probably the catch of *yesterday*, since no boats would be out in *this* mess.

"Your boyfriend's not here," I said to Amanda as I scanned the bar for Thomas. She looked around, same as me, and shrugged.

The door to the bar opened and a sheriff's deputy in a rain poncho walked in. He took a slow walk through the place, like he was looking for somebody, but ignored us. I saw him stop and talk to Caleb for a minute, then he left. Caleb left not more than five minutes after he did. Mike appeared troubled as he sat by himself at the bar.

I couldn't stand the suspense. I told Amanda that I was going to try to get him to join us so I could ask him who the cop was. I walked over to Mike. "All by yourself? Want to join us for dinner?"

He didn't look happy to see me. "I'm fine here, thanks."

"Aw, come on. There's no sense sitting by yourself. Come have a beer with Amanda and me." He hesitantly slid off his bar stool and walked to our booth. Amanda moved over and he sat next to her. She gave him a warm smile and he said a quiet hello.

"Who was that cop?" Amanda asked. "Is everything okay with your dad?"

He gave me a hard look across the table. "You been asking a lot of questions. Folks around here don't like it. The cop was searching for Thomas. I think he wanted to know if Thomas talked to *you*."

"Where *is* Thomas?" I asked.

"I don't know. My dad went to go find him before that cop does."

"Does that cop mean trouble?"

Mike shrugged. "Never saw him before."

"Isn't that unusual? You know most of the cops around here?"

"We don't see many. They come over from Carteret County. Lots of new faces lately."

"Mike, why does everyone treat those murders like a big secret?"

"*Those* murders? You mean a murder and a suicide," he corrected me.

"Maybe. Maybe not."

"Why won't anyone talk about it?" Amanda asked.

He glanced around the bar and leaned closer. "My job on the ferry? Stone. The new pier and the new ferry itself? Stone. The bridge reconstruction? Stone. The beach restoration? Stone. The marina money? Stone. He *owns* this place. Everybody felt real bad about what happened. He let everyone know afterward that he never wanted it discussed. That's just the way it's always been. Nobody ever wanted to cross that man."

"You scared of him?"

"Why would I be scared of him?"

"You tell me."

Mike glanced at Amanda and slid out of the booth. "I best be heading home." Amanda and I ate dinner but didn't speak much. I paid the check and we went back out into the rain. When we pulled into the driveway, my front door was wide open. And I was pretty damn sure I hadn't left it that way.

"D-d-don't go inside," she stammered.

"Bullshit. You stay here. Lock the car doors. Slide behind the wheel, and if there's trouble, get back to Tuckers."

I grabbed Ice and hopped out before she could debate me on this. Ice was chambered, safety off and up in front in the make-a-mess position. I slipped into my house. *Son of a bitch!* I had just started to get the place cleaned up and somebody had come in and tossed it. I moved silently through my wrecked house, very much hoping to blow the head off some motherfucker who had rearranged my furniture without my permission.

I was dying to check the basement and the diary but needed to check the bedrooms first. It was slow going, room to room, waiting for someone to take a shot at me. Bad memories from Iraq and Afghanistan... I was really missing my Delta boys at that moment — and grenades.

The house was clear. I ran downstairs to the basement. It had been thrown around like the rest of the house, with my boxes of clothes dumped out everywhere. I reached over the small opening in the wall and felt for the diary. It was still there, thank God! I left it. I ran back up and got Amanda, who looked terrified. When she saw the house, she turned white and started crying.

"Call the police!"

"Call the police? Shit, Amanda! They're probably the ones who did this!"

That didn't go a long way in allaying her fears. She started on me about leaving — right then! I relocked the doors — the locks weren't broken — and checked all the windows. The lightning and thunder were getting worse, and I could hear the rain drumming harder on the windows.

I called Kim's cell and she picked up right away.

"Hey, Cory, glad you got my message."

"What message?" I walked to the kitchen. There were zero messages on my machine. I was pretty sure there had been a couple of old ones on there when we left for dinner. "What did you say on the message?"

"Just that I got home safe. Oh, and I tried to call Greller. No answer. I left a message."

Shit! "Kim, my house was just ransacked."

"They broke into your *house*?"

"Yeah, we were at dinner. They made a mess, but we're fine."

"The diary?"

"It's safe. I had it hidden. Listen, Kim, whoever was here listened to your message and erased it. Do me a favor. Leave your house. Go stay with a friend or something. And don't say where now on the phone. Just go. And ask your editor about what we talked about before. Don't say *anything* on the phone now. Just talk to him as soon as you can, okay? Get somewhere safe and check in with me tomorrow."

‘

# Chapter Thirty-Five

Arthur McDade

After I hung up with Kim, I called Dr. Greller, to warn him about Kim's message being listened to by folks who weren't invited into my house. I got his voicemail and told him to call me immediately. I tried his work number, even though I knew it was late. Again, I got voicemail and a message with the office hours. Starting to feel desperate, I called Arthur McDade to see if anyone had threatened *him* yet. Another voicemail. I was striking out all over the place and getting worried.

Amanda walked in with a garbage bag full of what *used* to be a lamp. I'd hated that lamp anyway. She didn't say anything, but I could see she was scared and probably not very happy with me. She dropped the garbage bag unceremoniously at my feet and went upstairs without a word.

I turned on the television to check on the weather. We were due for shitty weather that would turn even shittier. Very excited meteorologists were discussing projected paths of Hurricane Eduardo. They lived for this crap. Something about storm bands moving in over the next few days, yadda, yadda, with all watercraft being told to find safe harbors. *Great.* That meant the ferry would be closed and there'd only be one way in and out of Harkers Island — over a bridge that could be easily watched by the same guy who had stopped Kim and taken her stuff. Just how far would these guys go? I looked around at my fucked-up house and said out loud, "Pretty far."

My phone rang. I got that feeling in the pit of my stomach again. A phone ringing never used to do that. I picked it up, waiting to hear today's latest threat, but instead was surprised to hear Arthur McDade's voice.

"You must be rattling some cages down there on Harkers, Mr. Walker."

"I guess so."

"How are you doing? Everything okay out there?"

"I'm okay. Somebody broke into my house and wrecked the joint, but other than that, I'm just fine. And you?"

"Oh, I'm just fine. Hunting up in the mountains at the moment. But I think I had some visitors, too. A neighbor called me on my cell to give me a heads up. I called in for my messages and wasn't surprised to find one from you. You stirred up a hornet's nest down there, Mr. Walker."

"Yeah, well, there's no turning back now, is there?"

"I 'spect not. I been smiling all day, though. Keep picturing Earl Stone shitting his pants while he runs around the country shaking hands and kissing babies."

"You're not worried about his people going after you?" I asked.

He laughed out loud, like I'd said something hilarious. "Mr. Walker, I got more guns and ammunition than the sheriff's department. I have a few real good friends up here that I've been hunting with for years. I don't 'spect that Stone's boys could find me where I am, but if they ever try, they'll sure be sorry. I'll hunt them down and mount their heads right next to the elk and bear. But you? You better start being careful. If they are looking for me, it means they're serious. You might think about getting off Harkers Island. I warned you about digging around."

"Yeah, you did. But I'm not going anywhere." Damn, I was sick of saying that. I was *not* being thrown out of Harkers Island.

"Well, I was just calling you back to warn you, Mr. Walker. I hope they put Earl Stone in prison for a hundred years, but I wouldn't count on it. And you better go real slow, son. His boys are pros. And they *will* kill you without thinking twice if you got something that will put Stone away for murder. You take care now, hear?"

He hung up. I pictured the former cop holed up in the mountains in a fortified cabin with a bunch of hillbillies and shook my head. Was this my future, too?

Amanda walked into the kitchen with a duffle bag stuffed under her arm. "I'm leaving. Are you coming?"

"Amanda! You are *not* leaving! First of all, there is a hurricane on the way and second of all, the same dirtbags that wrecked the house and stole Kim's notes and camera are *still* out there! There's only one way outta here right now, Amanda, and they'll be sitting on it, waiting. Just chill until tomorrow."

"And what's going to change by morning? Goodbye, Cory. When you're finished playing detective, call me."

She stormed out through the kitchen, kicking stuff out of her way as she went. I chased after her, shouting, "Amanda!"

Catching up, I grabbed her arm.

She spun around, removing my arm and leaning forward practically spitting her words. With her finger pushed against my chest, she began ripping me a new one. "Don't you *touch* me! There's an army of crazy people coming here to kill you, and you just want to stay here and play superhero? This isn't Afghanistan, Cory! This isn't how it works for normal people! I'm leaving. I'll go to my mother's or a friend's or anyplace but here. And if you gave a shit about our relationship, or your life, you'd come with me!"

"Amanda! I love you! But this is *our* house! We're not getting chased out by anyone, and that piece of shit doesn't get to be the next President if I…"

"You have fun playing soldier!"

She threw the front door open so hard that I thought it would come off the hinges. I wanted to grab her, but what could I do? I followed her out to her car and stood in the rain as she started the engine. When I banged on her window, she rolled it down only about an inch and gave me a hard look. "Are you coming or not?"

"No, *I'm* not going anywhere. Just *please* drive safely. And call me the second you get to your mom's or wherever it is you're going. The weather is only going to get worse. Please, Amanda, keep your phone plugged in, okay? I love you. Just stay hidden for a day or two until I can get this all figured out."

She rolled up her window and peeled out of the driveway into the street. She sped off through the rain and never looked back. *Shit.* Well, maybe it was better that way. Stone and his thugs were after me and the diary, not Amanda. At least she would be safe off Harkers Island.

# Chapter Thirty-Six

Mark?

I went inside and wiped the rainwater off Ice. The safety was back on, but there was a round pumped into the chamber, which I was leaving there. "Make my day." The phone rang. I prayed it was Amanda calling to say she was coming back. No such luck.

"Hello?"

"Cory Walker? We haven't had a chance to speak yet, but Kim probably told you I'd be calling. It's Mark Rosman, from the *Inquirer*."

"Oh, hi, Mark. Yeah, Kim said you'd want to talk to me."

"Quite a fantastic story you have there, Mr. Walker. We don't print something like this without incontrovertible proof."

"Of course not. I understand. Kim sent you the photos of the diary. You saw them, right?"

"I saw the pictures, yes. But that's not enough for a story like this. I'll need to see the original. You have it there with you now?"

My hair stood up. Literally. Like a few times when I was on a goat trail in Afghanistan or in house to house fights in Iraq—sometimes I just *knew* when someone was in a room waiting for me. I don't know how, but I knew something was wrong.

"No, Mark. I don't have it here."

A brief awkward silence. "Oh? Kim said you had it there in the house…"

"Yeah, well, I did, but then some *asshole* tore my place up looking for it, and I thought I'd better find a safer place." I had said asshole real loud, in case they were listening to my call.

"Good thinking. But you can get to it quickly, right? I mean, I'd like to get started on this story, and I need to see it personally and have it tested for fraud before I put this on the front page. You realize how big a story this is, I'm sure. We can't make any mistakes with something like this."

"I can have it within twenty-four hours. When do you want to meet?"

"I can come out there tomorrow morning," he said eagerly.

"Tell you what… Why don't you call me in the morning, and we'll figure out exactly when. I have to get it back. I'm sure you know the weather out here is a mess."

"Okay, that's fine. Raining pretty good here, too. I'll be in touch tomorrow morning."

He hung up.

I pulled my cell phone out and called Kim. I was begging her to pick up when she answered. "Hey!" she said happily, "I was just going to call you. I'm sitting here with my editor. He wants to talk to you. I'll put you on speaker phone."

"He's there, right next to you, right now?" As I spoke, I picked up Ice and took the safety off. Son of a bitch. I was waiting for the door to burst open and twenty guys to run inside my house.

"Excuse me?" asked Kim, puzzled.

"A guy just called my house two seconds ago and said he was Mark Rosman. He asked me if I had the original diary on me right now."

"You're on speaker phone, Cory, but it's my cell, so you have to speak up and talk slowly. The storm is messing up the reception. You want me to call you on your land line?"

"No. I don't trust the phone."

"Cory Walker? This is Mark Rosman." He sounded a lot different from the Mark Rosman I had just spoken to a few seconds ago. "This is the first time we've spoken. You need to understand that."

"Yeah," I mumbled, moving around my own house carefully with Ice at the ready, safety off. "I believe you."

"I suggest you get to a different location, Mr. Walker. You know that Kim was stopped by someone claiming to be a cop, correct?"

"Yeah, she told me what happened."

"I filed a formal complaint with the county. No one there knows anything about it. I have a contact for you with the FBI. I suggest you get someone there to listen to you directly. I wouldn't trust the sheriff's office. You realize the sheriff and Earl Stone are old friends, right?"

"So I gather. You saw the diary?"

"I saw parts of it, and I read what Kim has put together so far. Quite frankly, I'm speechless, and trust me, I'm *never* speechless."

"When are you going to run the story?"

"I can't do it tomorrow. I need to see the original diary. We need to speak to some of the people Kim mentioned to me. This is huge, Cory, but we really need to get our ducks in a row on this. We mess this up, even a little, and I'll be delivering newspapers from my bicycle on the moon."

"Maybe tomorrow I can drive up and bring the original, but honestly, I'm worried about being stopped by a cop and having it taken from me."

"I understand. Is there any place you can go that's safe?"

"Not really. The only way off the island is by bridge at the moment. They probably know my car. If I have the diary on me, they get it. If I leave it, maybe they come back and find it."

"Call the Feds, Cory. Any neighbors out there you can stay with tonight?"

The only neighbor I knew was Agatha Miles, and there was no way I was getting that little old lady involved in this mess. She'd have a heart attack.

"I'm cool here. I'll call your guy and see what we can come up with."

"Cory—it's a hell of a story. I want to thank you for giving Kim the exclusive."

He gave me the name and number of his contact at the FBI. I tried calling Amanda first but got her voicemail, which worried the hell out of me. One of the downsides of being in love with someone? You worried about them all the time. Now I genuinely understood Mom's tears when I'd left for boot camp. *Sorry, Mom.* I left a message asking Amanda to please call me, then dialed the number Mark Rosman had given me.

# Chapter Thirty-Seven

FBI

I called the cell number of Special Agent George Bauman, over in the Carteret field office. It was already after nine but he picked it up, sounding very official.

"Special Agent Bauman," he snapped.

"Agent Bauman, my name is Cory Walker. Mark Rosman gave me your number. I have evidence of a double murder that was committed on Harkers Island twenty years ago, and I need your help."

I have to admit, Bauman was a pretty cool customer. "I know Rosman. What type of evidence, Mr. Walker?"

"A diary. It's more than just a double murder. It was a series of sexual assaults from a father on his stepdaughter, a rape, a few hundred good beatings of his wife *then* a double murder. And the guy who did it is a sitting United States congressman."

"On Harkers?" I could hear his wheels turning.

"That's right. You getting an idea of where this is going?"

Everyone knew Earl Stone's life story on Harkers Island. "What kind of evidence?"

"This *congressman*," I began — then I thought, *oh fuck it.* "Earl Stone." There, I'd said it. "His stepdaughter Casey's diary. It tells the story of a teenage girl who was sexually abused by her stepfather." In my head, I added *that Sick Fuck, who was also beating his wife.*

"And you believe the congressman killed his wife and stepdaughter, Mr. Walker?"

"Now you're tracking."

"And does the diary mention any threats of murder?"

"No. But it gives you way more details than you want to know about what was going on in this house. Oh, I should tell you… I live in the Stones' old house. I just bought it. That's how I found this diary…by accident."

"You are the current owner of Earl Stone's former summer house on Harkers Island?"

*Holy crap, am I speaking Chinese?* "That's what I just said."

"I want to be correct, Mr. Walker. What other evidence do you have that Congressman Stone may have been involved in the deaths of his daughter and wife?"

"I spoke to the doctor who did the autopsy and got shit-canned for opening his mouth about it, and I spoke to a cop who questioned the investigation and was shipped off to nowhere."

"You have been doing your own investigation, Mr. Walker?"

"Not on purpose. I just bought a house, that's all. All this shit just sort of happened." I explained, as best I could, what the medical examiner had told me about hyoid bones and a hanging that had happened after Mrs. Stone was already dead. I told him how Dr.

Greller had been threatened. Then I explained the deal with Arthur McDade.

"Oh, and another thing—and you can check this all out yourself. I went to go talk to Benjamin McComb, the kid who was arrested and put away for the murder of Casey Stone and was also accused of raping her. He said he loved her and she loved him, which is in her diary, and that he would never hurt that girl. I spoke to him in person at Maury Correctional Facility. And right after we spoke, he ended up being beaten to death."

He was silent for a second. "Please hold."

I listened to elevator music in my ear as I crept around my house with Ice in my right hand, his strap over my right shoulder, and the phone in my left. It seemed like I was holding on for a long time.

"Mr. Walker, this is a closed case from twenty years ago—a closed case considered solved. One does not just re-open a case because someone calls the FBI and says he has found an old diary."

That pissed me off. "Well, how about I tell you that since I started looking, Ben was murdered, my house was ransacked, I've gotten threatening phone calls, I'm pretty sure my phone is *bugged* and that someone is watching my house. The reporter I spoke to got pulled over and had her notes and camera *stolen* from her by a guy who was supposedly a cop. And I just got a phone call with a guy who said he was Mark Rosman from the *Inquirer* and wanted the diary, except he *wasn't*, because Mark called me five minutes later, and I'm standing in my own fucking house with a shotgun. How about *that*?"

"Mr. Walker, I can't promise you anything, but tomorrow I myself will drive down to Harkers Island to meet with you."

"Fine. Come on down. But it's BYOS. Bring your own shotgun, I'm not sharing."

"Mr. Walker, you'll need to secure your firearms before I come down. Do you have a license to carry?"

"Of course I do. And I am in my *own* house. There are guys out there who want to kill me because their boss is a fucking animal. Ice stays with me! Oh, and Ice is my shotgun...from Afghanistan."

"Were you in the service, Mr. Walker?"

"First Special Forces Operational Detachment, Delta."

There was a pause. "I named my rifle 'Jenny', but that's just me."

I smiled for the first time all day.

"Yeah, well, Ice is a Mossberg 500 tactical. Somehow, a girl's name just wasn't working."

"Sit tight, Mr. Walker. I'll be there tomorrow morning by ten."

# Chapter Thirty-Eight

Storm's a' Comin'

I hung up with Special Agent George Bauman and decided to try to find Thomas. Why was that cop looking for him? Caleb was trying to warn him before the cop found him? Why was that? Something was up, and I hated being the only guy on the island who didn't have a clue.

I checked outside. It was pitch black but the rain had let up a bit. Must be between those 'bands' that the guy on the weather channel had been talking about so happily. I slid Ice around behind my back and threw a rain poncho on to conceal him.

I put a bar in the sliding glass door, double-checked all the window locks, then re-locked the front door behind me. I shoved a tiny piece of twig between the door and the frame, and if anyone picked my lock again while I was out, I'd know it.

I decided to take the car, in case it started getting nasty out again, and cruise around to see if I could locate Thomas. The island was so tiny. Where could he possibly hide?

I drove very slowly with the windows down, trying to hear anything that sounded like human activity over the roar of the surf and the occasional howling of the wind. The air was wet with ocean mist blowing off the Back Sound, and there wasn't one star visible.

I drove past the ferry office, which was closed and dark, and noticed the ferry wasn't docked. They must have docked at the mainland to ride out the storm.

I wondered if Mike Jackson was still on the island or if he had gone out with the boat. Lots of houses I passed were dark and a few were boarded up, the owners having headed off the island. I felt sort of trapped. One way out, and the enemy held the bridge. Where was the Air Force when I needed them? I could call in an air-strike, clear the far side of the bridge and send the light armor over it. *Oh well.* A different lifetime…

I passed Tuckers, which was still open and looked busy. If all else failed, one could always find a drink on Harkers Island. The blackboard sign on the porch read 'Hurricane Specials'. At least they kept their sense of humor. I guessed it wasn't their first hurricane party.

Driving slowly, I passed a few small bungalows and decided I was probably wasting my time. That was when I spotted that old fishing boat that Caleb, Thomas and that other guy had been working on the day I'd met them. It was anchored just offshore, which seemed completely ridiculous, seeing as how there was a hurricane rolling this way and the boat belonged in the dock. Who would want to sit out there rocking back and forth all night? Or maybe it was safer out there? The waves were crashing against the boat like the TV show *The Deadliest Catch*.

I pulled over and walked to the pier. It was maybe a thirty-yard swim, but the water was black and the current was insane. There was no way I was leaving Ice and trying to swim to the boat. Hell, I didn't even know if Thomas or Caleb were out there, although I could see lights on in the wheelhouse and below deck.

I spotted a small rowboat bobbing up and down, tied to the pier. I wasn't actually *stealing* it, just borrowing it. I climbed down, untied the lines and grabbed the oars. The current was much stronger than I anticipated. I'd figured it would take me two minutes to row over to the fishing boat. *Holy crap*. The tiny rowboat was full of water and rocked back and forth so badly that I thought I'd drown for sure.

After what seemed like fifteen minutes of killing myself against the current, I finally worked my way over to the fishing boat. Combat could be terrifying, and this was every bit as bad. Mother Nature was not to be trifled with, and she was *pissed*. It took every ounce of energy, backed up by terror-driven adrenaline, to get the dinghy alongside the boat.

There was no one on deck, so I just grabbed the side of their boat and tied my line to it as best I could. One quick grunt and I was on the deck. I slipped Ice around in front of me but kept him under my raincoat. The wheelhouse was empty, but there was definitely noise from below deck. I strained my ears against the whistling wind. It was that God-awful country music again. I worked my way over to the door that led below decks and stood out there in the blowing mist trying to explain my presence on their boat in my head. I really had no idea what I would say, so I just said fuck it, and opened the door.

I stepped inside into the warm, dry cabin to find Thomas plastered at the galley table all by himself. He had a mason jar of moonshine in front of him and there were several empty beer bottles on the table. He was so hammered that he just looked at me with a blank expression. His blue coveralls were stained with black grease, and the T-shirt under it might have been white at some time in the past.

"Hi, Thomas," I said, like I just happened to be passing through the neighborhood. "Pretty nasty night out there."

He handed me the moonshine, which I accepted and faked taking a sip. "Whatcha' doin' out here all by yourself?"

"*Wal-kah?*" he slurred, trying to remember who the hell I was. He ran his calloused fingers through his long salt and pepper hair.

"Yeah, Thomas, Cory Walker. You had beers with Amanda and me the other night at Tuckers. Remember?"

He smiled, I guessed remembering Amanda, and said her name out loud. "How's that girl of yours?"

"Really pissed off at me at the moment."

For some reason, that was quite hilarious to him, and he took another slug of the shine. He offered it to me, but I asked if he had any beer left. He pointed to the old fridge on board, and I dug out two Buds.

"There's a hurricane coming, Thomas. What are you doing out here by yourself?" He made a noise that sounded something like, "*Phhhfffft...*" and threw his hands out, to show me he didn't think much of the hurricane. After a slug of beer, he mumbled, "I been through plenty of storms out here. This ain't nothin'."

"Why was that cop looking for you, Thomas?" I asked.

"Caleb tell you?" he asked.

God, he was hammered. "Yeah," I lied. "He said you'd tell me the whole story."

And he did.

# Chapter Thirty-Nine

## True Story

Thomas leaned against the hull and let his head fall back against the worn wooden bench seat. He closed his eyes. At first, I thought he was going to fall asleep, but he wasn't sleeping. He was thinking back twenty years to a night he had tried to forget by drinking hard every night since then. He didn't move for a while, and I didn't say a word. The boat creaked and groaned in the storm. The sky lit up outside the portholes for a second, followed by a crack of thunder that made me jump.

Then he told me a story.

"It was a nice night. Warm. The stars were out. Lucy and me were still married, before she passed...God bless her. I had been out on Caleb's boat working that day. We had a good catch. I'd gone home and seen the missus, then headed back to the boat to finish offloading. I'm telling you, the hold was so full of fish." He was smiling, his eyes scanning back through a sea of time, probably picturing the boat so full of fish that it was low in the water.

Outside *our* boat, the wind howled and rocked us.

"I worked late that night. Then I cleaned up the boat and went topside to have a smoke and a beer. I fell asleep. When I got up, it was late. I secured the boat and walked home along the beach. It was such a pretty night. First thing that happened was I passed a group of kids. They looked upset, and I remember them talking about how they were going to be in big trouble. They had beers on the beach and a fire going, but they were Islanders, good kids. Mike was there — Caleb's boy. He's like my nephew. I don't know why they thought anyone would bother them. I just let them be and kept walking. That's when I saw Casey and her mother."

He looked at me, his gray eyes so tired and sad.

"She didn't mean to do it."

"Who? Casey? She didn't mean to do *what*?"

Something crashed up on deck, blown by the wind.

"Mrs. Stone. She and Casey had a terrible fight. Terrible. Casey was on her knees. At first, I was so far away that I didn't get it right in my head. I couldn't make sense out of what I was seeing. Then I heard Casey and her mother screaming awful things at each other."

"What were they saying Thomas? *Think!* It's important."

"Casey, she kept screaming, *'How could you let him do that to me? You knew!'* and her mom kept screaming, *'Shut up!'* Casey was still screaming about her mom knowing and not helping her. She screamed, *'You let him!'* over and over and finally Mrs. Stone lost it. It was terrible. She had Casey by the throat and was screaming *'Shut up!'* I think she was just trying to get Casey to stop talking and she squeezed too hard and too long. That poor girl fell into the sand and her mom ran off. I ran over and found Casey…dead."

"Thomas, what are you saying?"

Thomas looked at me again, this time with tears running down his cheeks. "I saw Mrs. Stone choking that girl. Casey's eyes were wide. Her mouth was open like she was trying to scream." He stared right through me. "She looked so dead." He wiped his face and took a long drink of the moonshine.

"I shook her. I tried to give her mouth to mouth. I tried everything I *knew* to save that little girl. She was so young…" He was crying now, twenty years of guilt pouring out of his soul.

My head was spinning. "I don't understand. *Anne* Stone killed Casey? You *saw* it? How did Ben get blamed for that? And how did Casey end up in the water? She wasn't found on the beach. Thomas, what the fuck happened?"

Thomas composed himself. "I sat on the beach for a long time with that girl. I'd watched her grow up, summers on this island, every summer for sixteen years. She was such a beautiful kid. I just held her in my lap, rocking her. I couldn't help her. After a long time, I left her and went to find Judge Stone. He had always been real generous with us, always made sure the bank loaned us money when things were bad. I trusted him. I ran to his house and banged on his front door so hard. When he opened it, he was a worse mess than me. I started screaming about what I saw. I told him to call an ambulance, call the police, somebody. He said he knew what had happened. Ben had raped Casey, and Casey and her mom had had a terrible fight. He knew she'd killed her daughter. It was an accident, he said. Then Mrs. Stone hanged herself. It was too much for her."

"Wait. Earl Stone said that Ben had raped Casey that night?"

"Yeah. Said Casey told her mom before they had their fight. Mrs. Stone blamed Casey for it somehow, and they got out of control. She would never have killed her own child. It was a terrible accident. Judge Stone said that there was no reason to ruin his wife's reputation. The poor woman was dead. She'd killed herself in her grief, you see."

He took a huge slug of moonshine. The boat rocked back and forth hard as a big roller must have broadsided us. "Why tell anyone what happened, when it was an *accident*?"

"Because Ben didn't *kill* her, Thomas! Why would you let him take the blame for killing her?" I didn't mean to scream at him.

"He *raped* her. Earl Stone *told* me. He deserved to go to jail, and Mrs. Stone didn't *mean* to kill Casey. He said that after a few years, he'd see that Ben was released, after he paid for what he'd done." Thomas was crying silently.

"He didn't do *anything*, Thomas!" God, I wanted to start screaming and never stop. "Did you *see* Anne Stone that night after she killed Casey on the beach?"

"No. Judge Stone said he found her. She hanged herself."

"But you didn't see her body, did you? And what about Casey? The paper said you found her in the water? You told me you left her on the beach?"

"It wasn't my idea."

"*What* wasn't?"

"Judge Stone... He said he'd take care of Casey himself. I brought him down to where I'd left her on the beach, and he sat down there and started crying. He told me to leave and not say a word to anyone about anything. I didn't know what to do. I went back to the boat that night, got blind drunk and passed out. When I got up the next morning, Judge Stone was still sitting on the dock right near my boat. He'd been up all night."

"And where was Casey's body?"

"In the water. Judge Stone had carried her down to the water and laid her in the ocean. I think he sat with her down by the water's edge most of the night. Then he walked up the dock and waited for me to wake up. When I saw him, he was a wreck. His wife and daughter were both dead the same night. I mean, can you imagine?"

I shook my head, trying to get my mind around all the lies.

"He asked me to go along with his version of what had happened. I don't know why he wanted it that way, but I felt so terrible for him. I just said yes. He made me say it over and over again, like a hundred times. Casey was missing. Me and him and Mrs. Stone went looking for her. Mrs. Stone said, *'Don't worry. Don't make a scene. Don't call the police. She's with one of her friends, and she'll come back in the morning.'* That's the story I told the police next day."

"That you found her body by your boat?"

"In the morning, I found her by my boat and called him, Judge Stone, then I called the police. That part is true. I'm the one who called the police. Judge Stone later told the police that while we were all waiting for them to come, Mrs. Stone went back to the house. Judge Stone found her dead later on."

I was shaking my head in disbelief. Thomas didn't seem like a bad guy, but could he be that naïve? Rain drummed against the windows, louder. The wind howled like an angry animal.

"He said he didn't want his wife called a murderer. That's all. I felt so bad for him. What's the difference? They were both dead. Why drag her name through the mud? It was an accident, and she paid for it with her life…"

"*No*, Thomas! Ben McComb paid for it with *his* life!"

"He raped that girl…"

"No he *didn't*! Earl Stone did!"

Thomas stared at me blankly.

"That's right, Thomas. Earl Stone was molesting his own stepdaughter and beating his wife. *He* killed Anne. She didn't hang herself!"

"*What*?" Thomas was drunk, but beyond that, he was totally shocked. His face was twisted as he tried to get his head around what I'd just said. "But…he couldn't… He wouldn't…not his own stepdaughter. His wife?" Thomas' face showed more than confusion. It showed horror.

"Thomas, why was that cop looking for you? Does Caleb know what happened that night? Did you tell him?"

"Caleb? No. No one knows…except you now. Caleb knew *something* happened that night but I told him never to ask me about it, never to speak of it. Earl Stone got us this boat after all that happened. Told us it was a government program for Harkers Island fishermen, but I knew it was just payback for keeping my mouth shut. No one *else* on the island got a new boat."

He stared at the floor, like he'd been hit by a bus. He started crying again. "I didn't know, I swear."

"I know, Thomas. But the time has come to make amends."

# Chapter Forty

## Hitting the Fan

Thomas and I sat on that boat for a long time, rocking hard in the storm. He sat with his back against the hull, staring off into nothing. I felt bad for him. It was a lot to keep inside for twenty years, and the truth was, he was just a simple guy who hadn't asked to be put in the middle of this mess. Come to think of it, neither had I. Outside, the wind howled and waves crashed over the deck.

"Caleb tell you to come out here to the boat?" I finally asked him.

"Yeah. He said a cop was asking about me. He figured it was something about the Stone murder. You been asking a lot of questions. A lot of new faces out here the last couple of days asking about *you*, too."

"Is that right?"

"You should have let it be, Mr. Walker."

"And let Earl Stone be the next President of the United States? Not on my watch."

"He couldn't have done what you said. He's not like that."

"I read Casey's diary, Thomas. He's *exactly* like that. And he killed Anne."

"Why? Why would he kill her? It was an accident..."

"We'll let the FBI ask him that one. Where's Caleb?"

"I don't know. He took the dinghy back to the dock. Told me to stay put out here until he came back."

A crack of lightning lit up the sky outside, and the rain started harder again, this time so intense it made the bilge pumps kick on. The rolling roar of thunder that followed sounded like a B-52 strike.

"Thomas, the storm is getting worse. We should move this boat back to the dock and get off it."

"Caleb said to stay put."

"Thomas, you have to help me move the boat. I don't know shit about boats. You hear me?"

There was another crack of lightning followed by what sounded like artillery. I stood and pulled him to his feet, but the boat was rocking so bad that I had to use the walls to hold us up. We staggered together through the galley, and half crawled up the stairs to the rear deck. When I opened the door, it was like stepping out into Hell. The waves were breaking over the rail, and the rain was coming down in sheets. When the lightning lit up the sky and we could see the storm waves, it was so terrifying that I preferred the dark. We've all heard that expression, 'the roar of the ocean'. Now I truly knew the meaning, and I was petrified.

"Come on, Thomas! We gotta move!" I was screaming as loud as I could, and I could barely hear my own voice over the wind.

We stumbled over the deck to the wheelhouse, barely keeping our feet, and closed the door behind us. We were both soaked to the skin.

"Turn the engine on, Thomas! How do I pull up the anchor?"

Thomas bobbled across the room to the controls and pressed the button for the engine. He was so calm that it helped me maintain my composure. He was either the world's bravest sailor or just that drunk. I could hear the powerful diesel kick in and said a quiet 'thank you' to God Almighty.

Thomas flicked another switch and told me the anchor was being winched up. I tried to look out, but all I could see were waves crashing over the bow in the lightning flashes. I remembered why I hadn't joined the navy.

Drunk as he was, Thomas did okay in the captain's chair. When the anchor was up, the boat immediately started moving in the current, but Thomas cut the wheel, gunned the engines and headed back to the dock. He stood, holding the wheel with his game-face on, all business. He hit a few other buttons and powerful spotlights kicked on overhead, aiming ahead of us as we chugged through the waves. The boat might not have been fancy, but it was just what anyone would want in this kind of weather.

We were back at the dock within minutes, and I ran topside to cast a line at the piling once we pulled alongside. Thomas came out and threw the rubber bumpers over the side, then helped me tie us off. For a drunk old-timer, he was impressive. Guess he could do this in his sleep. When he was satisfied that we were finished, he turned off the lights and cut the engine.

"Now what?" he asked.

Excellent question. I thought for less than a second, standing in the roaring wind and rain. "My house. Come with me."

Back on the dock, and I again thanked God. If I'd had more time, I would have gotten down and kissed the wooden planks of that dock. I grabbed Thomas by the shoulder and we ran through the rain to my car. It felt like the wind might just pick us up and carry us away, which might be the safer option.

It was my turn to operate heavy machinery while almost totally blind. The storm was relentless. When we slid into my driveway, I pulled off my rain slicker and checked Ice, taking him off safety. Thomas' face showed his surprise at the shotgun.

"Just stay behind me, Thomas. Seriously. *Behind* me, okay?"

"Your girlfriend here?"

"No, I told you. She's pissed at me."

He nodded, and we jogged up the walk to my front door, Ice leading the way. It was still locked, and the twig was still place in the door jamb. I breathed a sigh of relief at the twig, opened the door and we stepped inside.

"Jesus Christ!" said Thomas as he looked at my wrecked house. "She really *was* pissed!"

I realized he meant Amanda and smiled. "Wasn't *her*."

He could drive a boat wasted, but his stream of logic was questionable at best.

"Stone's guys were here, looking for something."

We walked carefully through the house, and once I was satisfied that we were alone, I pushed the safety on and slid Ice around to my back again. I went into the kitchen and saw the machine blinking. It was almost midnight. Amanda would have been home long before now.

I smiled and reached for the machine and hit play.

"*Cory!*" she was crying, hard to understand. "*Cory!*"

A man's voice cut her off. "Mr. Walker, you have something we want. We have your girlfriend. A little trade is in order. You bring us that book and we give you Amanda. Call her cell phone and make the arrangements for the trade. You call anyone else and we'll know. And I'll mail you your girlfriend in ten different packages. Call the cell phone *now!*"

My breath had left my body and I thought my heart was going to come through my chest. A wave of nausea rolled through me. Thomas was standing in the kitchen next to me, stunned.

"They got your girl?" he said, almost to himself.

I could feel the room spinning. I thought I had seen it all, but that threw me off balance. My mind was racing with questions, trying to be rational and fight off the feeling of panic. I never played defense, only offense. There was no way I'd let these guys call all the shots, but shit! They had Amanda.

The phone rang. It showed Amanda's cell phone. They must have been watching the house. I picked it up.

"Mr. Walker, you didn't call. Don't you want this pretty girl back in one piece, or did you want me to start cutting her up and Fed-Exing her to you in little boxes?"

"You fucking touch her and I'll kill you."

"No time for macho bullshit, Walker. You have Casey Stone's diary. No one else is ever going to see it. You understand me? No one. *Ever.* You are going to drive to Cape Lookout now and bring that diary to the lighthouse in a waterproof plastic bag. We'll see you. We'll come get it. And if you're smart, you won't fuck around. You deliver the book, and we'll tell you where to find Amanda."

They must have done something to her at that moment because she started screaming in the background.

"No! You bring Amanda to the beach. We swap right there, otherwise I'll have every news network on the planet asking Earl Stone questions he don't wanna answer! You hear *me*?"

There was a hesitation on their end, probably a few guys working it out.

"We'll bring the girl. You be on the beach at midnight or you'll never see this pretty girl in one piece again."

The line went dead.

I raced down to the basement, Ice in front of me, safety off again. The diary was where I'd left it. Thomas saw it and looked at me.

"That's where it says things about Mr. Stone?"

I ran past him. "Thomas. Go home."

"You're gonna need help out there, Mr. Walker. You don't think they're just gonna trade and let you go, do ya?"

I hadn't really gotten that far yet. "Thomas, go home before you get killed."

I grabbed a box of custom-load shells for Ice and my old K-Bar combat knife from one of the strewn boxes on the basement floor.

"Do you even know where the beach is he was talking about?"

"Yeah, I do. By the lighthouse. I can be there in two minutes."

"Uh-huh. *Then* what?"

I really didn't know. I was being stupid to think they'd just let us go. I needed to calm down and get my head out of my ass. Damn it. I hated not being able to control my situation — *think!*

I pulled out my cell phone and scrolled through to Special Agent George Bauman's number and hit send. To my relief and surprise, he picked it up.

"They've got Amanda! They've kidnapped my girlfriend! They want to swap her for the diary. I have to meet them in ten minutes!"

"We can't be there that fast. We're at least forty-five minutes to an hour away. We're already on our way to you."

I was confused. "You said you were coming down tomorrow?" I blurted out.

"That was before we started checking on your story and found out that Arthur McDade was killed tonight. His hunting buddies found him beaten and murdered."

"Jesus, they got to *him*, too? I just talked to him tonight."

"We can't get a chopper up in this weather, Mr. Walker. We'll be there before one a.m. but not much before. You're going to have to stall them as long as you can. I have to advise you… If you meet these people with that diary, they're not going to just give you Amanda and just let you leave. You both know too much."

"Yeah, no shit."

"I'm afraid the local police may not be your best bet, either. Stall them. That's all I can tell you. What do you look like? I have night vision with me."

"Look for the pissed-off looking motherfucker with the Mossberg lighting up Harkers Island. Cape Lookout. I gotta' go."

I saw my old boonie-hat lying in a pile of clothes on the floor and slapped it on my head. When I turned around, I realized Thomas was gone. It was just as well. *No sense in both of us getting killed.*

I grabbed my old sidearm out of my duffle bag and way too much ammunition. I retrieved the diary and ran upstairs, the shells jammed into my pockets making them look so fat that I looked ridiculous. *Fuck it.* I wasn't going down without a serious fight.

I grabbed a plastic bag from the kitchen, wrapped up the book and shoved it into my waistband in the small of my back. Ice was strapped on, ready to rock and roll. I ran out to my car, threw it in drive and tore up my lawn as I roared away down the dark, deserted street.

It was miserable out. Full-on hurricane. *Good.* Maybe they didn't have night vision either, and we'd be up close and personal in the dark. That was nothing new to me and Ice. In fact, it was just how we liked it.

# Chapter Forty-One

Combat

I slowed down and killed my lights as I approached the east end of the island. The east end of Harkers is mostly federal land and completely undeveloped, except for the lighthouse, the little duck museum and a few old buildings.

I pulled over by some trees, got out and started jogging through the dune grass toward the lighthouse. In the ominous night, the beam of the lighthouse was the only thing visible. A hundred years ago, that beam had represented safety and hope for sailors in a dark storm. I was praying it would mean the same thing for us.

Slowly, I started moving—controlling my breathing and using every nerve ending in my body to feel danger. I moved and stopped, moved and stopped, picking my way through the dune grass toward the lighthouse. When I got closer to the actual beach, I spotted a narrow beam from a flashlight.

Going prone, I crawled silently across the cold, wet sand in the direction of the light. What I would have given for binoculars or a sniper rifle. A crack of lightning conveniently showed my two enemies on the beach, holding the flashlight and weapons. I scanned as far as I could, trying to find their buddies. How many were out there? I scanned the lighthouse. If I were them, I'd have a sniper up there. If he was up there, he was hunkered down pretty tight, and I couldn't see shit.

Knowing where the two guys were on the beach, I circled around them and worked my way to the rear approach of the lighthouse. It was slow going, and I was barely moving when I heard a man's voice whisper, "Any sign of him?"

A radio crackled, "Not yet."

I crawled so slowly that I was part of the sand. I eased the K-Bar out of my waistband and slithered toward the guy hiding in the scrub. The dune grass gave me excellent cover, and unlike him, I wasn't sitting up high trying to watch the beach. I came up behind him and slapped my left hand over his mouth while my right hand shoved the K-bar into his kidney so deep that it almost came out his front. I hung on hard to his mouth, yanking his head back, pulled the knife out and shoved it back in two more times into his neck, twisting and tearing as hard as I could. I couldn't remember feeling so much hate killing another human being.

I dropped him slowly and gently into the grass and slipped his radio from his belt, listening while I went through his gear. He was carrying an MP5 submachine gun with a banana clip and scope. These guys weren't fucking around. The scope made me very happy. I slipped the weapon on over my shoulder so it hung behind me, and kept Ice up in front of me. The radio chirped.

"Anything?"

"Shut up. Stay off the radio until you see something," said a second voice.

*Hmm-m.* I chewed on that for a second. They had state-of-the-art weapons, but obviously hadn't worked together before and lacked discipline and training. They weren't the state police or local cops, which I figured was a good thing. I started working around toward the lighthouse again. The two guys on the beach started walking toward the area where I had left my car, maybe figuring I was coming in from the road, which I had.

The rain stopped, just like someone had thrown a switch. Between the bands again, I guessed. I went prone and froze, scanning in every direction. My cell phone vibrated in my pocket, and I saw it was Amanda's cell calling me. *Damn it.* I didn't want to answer. I also didn't want to get her killed. I pressed send but didn't speak.

"You're late, Walker. Where are you?"

"I'm close. It was a long walk in the rain. I should be there soon. Where are you? How will I find you?"

"Just walk up the beach, down by the water and we'll find you. You have two minutes. I suggest you start running before I kill your girlfriend."

He made her scream again, except this time I heard it live as well as through my phone. I was *close*. The fucker was near the small building by the lighthouse. I picked up the MP5 and scanned up at the lighthouse through his night vision. I knew there had to be a guy up there. I lay there in the sand, not moving, trying to find any sign of motion. Nothing. The guy was good — or he wasn't there.

I moved toward the lighthouse and my stolen radio came on again.

"Everyone move toward the waterline. He should be coming down the beach any second. Nobody shoots until we get the book."

Two men hopped up not twenty yards from where I was and started jogging down the beach. Jesus—in another ten seconds I would have crawled right into them. *Must be getting rusty.* I watched them through the scope as they approached a group of three other men. Damn—how many of these guys were there? Five on the beach, maybe one in the lighthouse, at least one with Amanda by the building. This was *so* not cool.

In a typical combat situation, I'd take out the group on the beach first and cut their numbers down before they knew what happened, but I couldn't do that with Amanda being held by the house. I checked my watch. No help would be here for another forty minutes at least. I was fucked.

I crawled toward the building where I'd heard Amanda scream. My radio popped on again. "Rogers? Where the hell are you?"

I smiled. They called him again. "Maybe his radio's out," said a voice.

"I haven't seen anything from up here."

Ah, my little friend up in the lighthouse. I knew it. Okay, that would make it a bit tougher. I scrambled through the tall dune grass until it ended, about forty feet shy of the building. The sniper was in the lighthouse fairly high overhead, and I was so close now that he'd have to practically hang over the edge to see me beneath him.

I made a dash for it, sprinting across the sand as fast as my legs would move, and dove for the base of the lighthouse. I was now directly under the sniper and looking at the building less than twenty yards away where they had Amanda. The lights were off inside. My guess was they were shielding themselves behind the building, not inside it. I looked around. The sniper would be looking at the beach for my approach, not straight down the tower. My radio came on again, and I quickly decreased the volume until I could barely hear.

"You guys see that? What the fuck is he doing? Is he fishing at night in this weather? What the fuck?"

I looked out at the water. It was dark and hard to see in the waves, but sure as shit, that old fishing boat was chugging toward us. *Thomas, God bless ya, you crazy old bugger!* It had its floodlights on, bobbing like a cork on the choppy waves. The sea was so rough that the ship rocked to and fro. White foam blew over the bow, but the old diesel engine chugged on.

One of the guys on the beach jogged toward the fishing boat, probably in utter disbelief. The weather was better than it had been an hour ago, but it was still no night to be out in a boat. The water in the sound was wild, swirling and crashing from every direction. While they were distracted, I made a run for the building and hit the sand by the back wall of the structure.

Belly crawling to the corner, I peered around so only my eyeballs were past the edge of the wall. Sure enough, Amanda was seated with her back against the building, her hands tied behind her and a gag in her mouth. There was one guy with her. He was looking around the front corner of the building with his back to me. As much as I wanted to use Ice to blow him into a million pieces, I knew the MP5 was much quieter with its suppressor attached. If I got lucky, nobody would even hear it.

The guy at the front of the building still had his back to me, and he started talking to Amanda. "Where's that little boyfriend of yours, missy? Maybe he got scared and left your ass here. Maybe we'll all take a turn on you before I shove you in a crab trap and drop your ass in the ocean."

"I don't fuckin' think so," I said, and fired a suppressed three-round burst into the back of this asshole's head, neck and back. He dropped with a quiet plop into the sand, and Amanda's scream was muffled by her gag, thank God. I moved quickly to her and shushed her, then pulled my K-Bar and cut the ropes behind her back. She pulled the gag out of her mouth, threw her arms around me and squeezed so hard that I fell over.

"Be quiet!" I whispered in her ear. "There's a ton of these fuckers still out there."

"I know," she sobbed.

I pulled the dead guy back away from the corner and found his nine-millimeter semiautomatic. Taking the safety off, I chambered a round and handed it to Amanda. "Point the gun and pull the trigger. Use two hands. It'll kick up after you fire. The safety is off, so try not to shoot me. There's a sniper up in the lighthouse, and at least five guys on the beach. The sniper can't get a shot at us down here without exposing himself. I'm going to try to pick off the guys on the beach. You watch the back of the house, okay? Stay low and quiet. Anyone comes up behind me, point and shoot."

I crawled back to the front corner and spotted the guys still standing on the beach looking at the fishing boat, which kept moving closer to shore. It was high tide with a storm surge, and the boat could practically anchor ten feet offshore.

Looking through the scope, I watched the five guys, then opened my cell phone and called Agent Bauman. I told him I had Amanda, two bad guys down, and six to go. "Sniper in the lighthouse."

Taking aim at the group on the beach, happy to have a scope, I started squeezing off double-taps. Two went flying, and the other three hit the deck in total shock. They were screaming into the radio, "*Russo*! What the hell are you doing! That's *us* out here! Cease *fire*!"

I sent another burst at them, which I guess woke them up to the fact that I wasn't Russo. They started firing back. They were low in the sand and using the two dead bodies as cover, and all I could do was keep their heads down and wait for the cavalry. I was figuring the FBI when I thought of the cavalry, but that wasn't how it went down.

The fishing boat opened up both diesel engines and roared up high out of the water. It was like a killer whale surfing in for a seal and made a bee-line for the guys on the beach. With the floodlights on them, they were temporarily blinded, and I scrambled forward to the front of the house and started firing again. One more down.

Thomas didn't slow the boat down, and the two guys left on the beach turned their guns on him. I moved forward as fast as I could, using the building to shield me from the sniper as I worked closer to the guys on the beach. The boat continued its course straight into the enemy gunfire, which would have been great if the boat were armed with a bow gun, but it wasn't. I fired and moved and fired again.

A loud *boom* resounded off the water. It was so loud that I stopped and looked. There was Caleb on the bow of the boat, firing a shotgun at the guys on the beach. The crazy son of a bitch was going to get his head blown off.

The guys on the beach tried to make a run for it as the boat hit the sand like a landing craft at Normandy, beaching itself and sending Caleb flying across the deck. Tons of sand and water shot up out of the stern of the ship as the screws made contact with the shore.

I used that split second to charge, dropping the MP5 and pulling up Ice. I don't remember doing it, but according to Amanda, she could hear me screaming bloody murder as I charged their position. The switch in my head had flipped, and I ran into the crowd firing round after round at everyone I saw. Ice was a wicked friend and blew holes in those dirtbags that were big enough to read a newspaper through.

A round impacted near my foot and I realized I was giving the sniper too large a target. I hit the ground and pressed into the sand as hard as I could. I could hear Caleb and Thomas on the boat, screaming.

I yelled, "There's a sniper up in the lighthouse," but there's no way they could hear me over the wind.

Caleb fired a few rounds with his shotgun, but the tower was well out of range. I yelled at him to get inside and stay down.

Thomas ran out on to the deck and grabbed a floodlight, repositioning it to hit the lighthouse. The sniper started firing at the boat, and I sprinted for the house. He only managed one shot at me. I was moving way too fast. I got back to the house and yelled to Amanda not to shoot me when I came around the corner. I found her crouching with the gun, looking terrified. When she saw me, she shouted my name and started to cry. *No time for that now, babe!*

Running past her to the rear corner of the building, I looked up at the lighthouse. I still couldn't see him or his rifle. I pumped three rounds back into Ice and told Amanda to sit tight. I didn't stick around to wait for an argument.

Thomas and Caleb were trying to aim their lights at the lighthouse, but the sniper kept shooting their lights out and making the poor guys scramble for cover. They had balls, those two old guys. Sporadically, I'd hear their shotguns go off, useless and out of range, but providing emotional support.

I opened the door at the base of the lighthouse and entered slowly. There was a tight spiral staircase leading to the top, made of waffle-print metal that had been painted black a hundred years ago. I looked up but couldn't see anyone. I heard him fire and breathed a sigh of relief. As long as he was firing at the boat, I had a chance to reach him.

I held Ice out in front, in two hands, starting my long run up the staircase, trying to be as quiet as possible. The sniper fired another round. I heard him shout, "Got you, you fucker!" Damn. I was praying he hadn't just killed one of my Toider friends, but there was no way to know.

Moving quickly and quietly up the last twenty stairs, I stopped at the top, near an open doorway. The huge lens inside the top of the lighthouse was shielded in the back, I suppose to protect the lighthouse-keeper's eyes. The front part of the room was as bright as you'd imagine with a gigantic lighthouse beam blasting a few thousand watts. Under the light, on his belly, there was the sniper with a bi-pod rifle and scope.

Crouching, I moved up behind him. "Freeze, asshole!" I wanted one of them alive.

He didn't freeze. He rolled over on his back and tried to bring his rifle around on me. Ice roared as I fired two rounds on autopilot and left his splattered mess all over the lighthouse.

I ran down the spiral stairs as fast as my legs would take me.

# Chapter Forty-Two

## Hoo Aah

I blew through the door at the bottom of the lighthouse. Amanda raised her pistol at me with both hands! I screamed at her not to shoot. She threw the gun in the sand and covered her face with her hands.

I ran over to her, picked her up and squeezed so hard that I think I adjusted her spine.

She cried, and I'm not sure, but I think I might have, too. It was all a bit overwhelming.

Combat was one thing. Having someone I loved in the middle of it was another.

"We need to check on Thomas and Caleb." I grabbed her hand and we ran along the side of the house, Ice still out in front of me in case we had missed anyone. I stopped and tried a fake-out move on the radio.

"Help — is anyone out here? Help…"

I waited for a full minute. No one responded.

I started jogging down the beach, dragging Amanda along behind me. The boat was beached, sitting at a funny angle in the sand. Half of the floodlights had been shot out, and the remaining ones shot beams of light in different directions. With the wind making strange sounds in the background, the boat appeared like an otherworldly being.

I yelled at the boat, waving my arms as I ran with Amanda. I had slid Ice back behind me so they wouldn't mistake me for a bad guy and take a shot at us. Caleb's face appeared over the rail.

"Over here! Help!"

*Shit. Thomas.*

I started running as fast as I could, dropping Amanda's hand as I hit the surf in full sprint and pounded through the breaking waves to the side of the boat. I climbed up and saw Thomas on his back with Caleb holding an old rag over his shoulder. I moved over to them and checked for a pulse. He was alive!

He opened his eyes. "You get 'em?"

"Yeah, how you doing?"

"All of 'em?"

"Yeah, Thomas, all of them. How do you feel?"

"Best I have in twenty years," he said, and closed his eyes. He had a silly grin on his face, and I swear some of the ancient stress lines seemed to disappear.

I pulled my phone out of my pocket, pressed 'send', handed it to Caleb and told him to tell Special Agent Bauman that we needed an ambulance immediately.

While he talked to the Fed, I ripped open Thomas' shirt and looked at his wound. It was from a high-powered rifle and had made a large hole. I rolled him over on his side and saw the bigger hole in back. It had gone through. I was relieved. Thomas had lost a lot of blood, but Caleb had only been putting pressure on the entry wound. I wadded up a piece of Thomas' shirt, cut off a piece of a plastic rain slick and went to work. Plastic first to try to seal it off, the wad second, with a homemade pressure bandage last. I gently eased him back onto the deck and pushed my hand over the entry wound.

"Hang in there, buddy. Help's coming."

He tried to talk.

"Just rest, Thomas. Help's coming." I felt his carotid artery. The pulse was slow and weak, but it was steady. "You're gonna make it, Thomas. Just hang in there. And thanks, man. You saved our lives tonight."

He smiled.

While I was working on Thomas, Caleb was helping pull Amanda aboard the fishing boat. As soon as she was on, Caleb ran to the wheelhouse and started gunning the reverse engines. Behind the boat, tons of sand began shooting over the water as the props dug a hole in the sand under us. Caleb didn't care about the boat. He kept full power up until enough sand had been moved that the boat slid backward. He was a pro. His right hand moved around the wheel and controls while his left one held the radio.

"Coast Guard, Coast Guard, Coast Guard! Mayday, mayday, mayday. This is Harkers Island fishing vessel *Lucky Lucy*, *Lucky Lucy*, *Lucky Lucy*… We are en route to Morehead City. Advise Carteret General that we have a gunshot victim on board. He's lost a lot of blood. Have an ambulance at the Thirty-Fifth-Street pier."

As used to medics and self-reliant Special Forces operators in the field as I was, I was taken aback by Caleb's professional demeanor on the radio. Shocked, actually. He was cool as a cucumber.

Thomas looked like shit, but I'd seen plenty of guys who looked worse come through just fine. Of course, they'd been forty or fifty years younger and in battle-ready shape. I pulled off my belt and wrapped it around Thomas, tightening it as best I could to try to stop the bleeding. He was unconscious now, but his pulse was still steady and his breathing seemed okay. Amanda knelt down next to him on the other side, holding his head steady against a makeshift pillow as we bounced along the surf.

I felt my cell phone buzzing in my pocket. *Agent Bauman.*

"What's your situation over there?" he shouted into the phone.

"We're on a fishing boat, headed over to Carteret General. One of my buddies got shot helping me out, and he's lost a lot of blood."

"What about the hostage?"

"I have her. She's safe." I looked up at Amanda, who was holding on to Thomas—and *maybe* her sanity.

"And the kidnappers?"

"All dead. We got 'em all. And I still have the diary. Can you meet us at Carteret General?"

"Listen… By boat, you can make it in thirty minutes. By car, we're screwed. We'd have to take Route 70 all the way back the way we came and hook around. We're already at the Straits. Damn it! Let me call you right back."

Caleb kept chugging along through the Back Sound, way faster than was prudent in the dark and the weather. The sound had plenty of shallow spots which could wreck us, but I prayed the storm surge and high tide might help us out.

A few second later, the radio on the boat squawked.

"*Lucky Lucy*, be advised that we have military choppers inbound from Camp Lejeune and Cherry Point. ETA ten minutes. Put on as many lights as you can and be prepared for aerial boarding. Special Agent Bauman has arranged for emergency transportation to Carteret General. Over."

We were closer in miles to Carteret General than the choppers were to us, but they'd cover twenty miles a lot faster at a hundred and fifty knots than we would at twenty-five.

I breathed a sigh of relief. He'd sent in the Marines. My cell phone buzzed again.

"Walker, you there?"

"Yeah — the Marines are sending choppers."

"Ten-four! They'll have a combat team on board to personally escort you to the hospital and stay with you until I can get there. No one is getting within five miles of you without an invitation."

Not even fifteen minutes later, two Marine helicopters banked in over top of us, bathing us in their searchlights. Caleb cut the engines and dropped anchor right where he was in the middle of the Sound, and within a few minutes, the chopper was dropping ropes and lowering a gurney. It was a sight for sore eyes. A Marine staff sergeant was the first on the deck, having fast-roped down in the wind and rain like it was no big deal. He ran forward to where we were working on Thomas.

"Staff Sergeant Cruz!" he shouted over the rotors. "We'll have your man in the hospital in fifteen minutes. Leave this vessel where it is, anchored. You're all to board the chopper and come with us!"

I looked at the wheelhouse. Caleb was *not* going to want to leave his boat in the middle of the sound in a hurricane. "You better tell the skipper yourself!" I screamed back at him.

Two medics ran forward with their kits and knelt beside Thomas.

"He's lost a lot of blood," I yelled over the rotors. One of them nodded at me and broke open his kit. Within seconds, they had real pressure bandages on

Thomas and had popped a bag of plasma into his arm. They were writing Thomas' blood pressure and heart rate on his forehead with a felt-tip marker, along with the time — *1:30 a.m.* I remembered seeing that happen in Afghanistan.

Caleb came out of the wheelhouse behind Staff Sergeant Cruz and yelled over at me. "How is he?"

"I think he's going to make it, but we need to go!"

"They want me to leave Lucy right here in the middle of the Sound?"

"That's right! We're out of here! Let's move!"

The medics slid Thomas onto a board, strapped him down tight and ran aft with him. Within seconds, he was clipped to a caged gurney and hoisted up to the chopper. The gale-force wind was howling, and yet the helicopters were perfectly still. Damn, they were some pilots. The chopper dropped more lines and hoisted us up, two at a time. Within seven minutes of when they had arrived, we were all aboard the chopper, leaving *Lucky Lucy* anchored by herself in the middle of the Back Sound.

We sat in silence as the medics worked on Thomas, and as I glanced around the chopper at the young faces from Lejeune, I felt very old.

SSgt. Cruz moved over to where I was sitting with my arm around Amanda and leaned close to me. "I have no idea who you people are or what this is all about, but when the base commander personally tells me to guard you all with my life in the middle of a hurricane, that's what I do. My men are to escort you to the hospital and not leave your side until we are relieved by FBI Special Agent Bauman. Anyone else tries to get near you, we're ordered to fire." He stared into my face. "What the fuck is going on, sir?"

"You don't want even want to know. Hopefully, you'll read about it in the news very soon."

He nodded and moved back with his men. Amanda buried her head in my shoulder and closed her eyes, obviously totally exhausted. I was pretty damned beat myself.

# Chapter Forty-Three

Recovery

With the wind whipping, I was seriously worried, but our ride was pretty smooth, all things considered. The choppers landed on the front lawn of the hospital. Two attack helicopters from Cherry Point had escorted us halfway through the trip and now circled the hospital. These guys were the best of the best.

I have no idea what Agent Bauman had said or what kind of juice he had, but I was pretty damned impressed. The Marine bases in North Carolina — and there were several — didn't get involved in civilian police activities. Whoever Bauman had spoken to, or whatever connections he had, had come through big-time.

The Marines literally escorted us into the hospital and wouldn't leave our side. I'm not sure the President would have had so much security. I was very happy to have them with us. Thomas was sent on to surgery, with two Marines posted outside the doors of the OR. The three of us were taken to a doctors' lounge, where we collapsed in exhausted heaps.

Amanda and I curled up next to each other and were sleeping within minutes, the adrenaline having been replaced with complete physical exhaustion. The doc had given Amanda something to help her calm down, and she was snoring, which made me smile. I'm sure Caleb wasn't far behind.

It seemed that immediately I was awakened by the same Staff Sergeant. "Sir, the Federal Agents are here to see you."

I looked around and tried to remember where the hell I was. I checked my watch. It was four-thirty. "Is Thomas okay?"

"He is still in surgery. Special Agent Bauman is on his way up."

I sat up and moved gingerly around Amanda, who was out cold. I walked out into the hallway to meet my hero. Special Agent Bauman greeted me in his FBI windbreaker, a 9mm and badge on his belt. He had two other agents with him. "Cory Walker?" he said as he stuck out his hand.

"That would be me," I said. It hurt to talk. I was so tired.

"You've had quite an evening. How are you doing? The hostage is unharmed?"

"Yeah. She's shaken up pretty good, but she'll be fine."

"I had another couple of field agents head to Harkers Island. We changed course and came directly here. Apparently, you left quite a pile of bodies over there." He attempted a smile. "We're going to need to go through the events of the past few days in detail, but we can debrief after you get a few hours of sleep."

I reached behind me and pulled the diary from my waistband in my lower back, where I had kept it for so many hours. I slid it out of the plastic bag and handed it to Agent Bauman. "You're one of the few guys on the planet I'd give this to—maybe the only one."

He nodded. "Roger that." He looked at one of his men. "Find a copier and copy every page of this book. Give Mr. Walker the copies. The original will be logged into evidence." He looked back at me. "You okay with copies?"

*Like I have a choice?* "Sure."

"Get some sleep. This place is safer than Iron Mountain. When you all wake up in a few hours, we have a lot to discuss."

\* \* \* \*

Amanda stirred and that woke me up. I had my arm over her waist, curled up behind her on a couch. I sat up, feeling like I had been run over by a truck. I looked around the room and spotted Caleb sipping black coffee in a chair by the window. I patted Amanda's fanny until she woke up. We both did our share of groaning and stretching, then stood.

"Coffee's free from the machine," Caleb said.

"Coffee," I mumbled. I sleep-walked over, grabbed two Styrofoam cups from the pile and filled them. It was a very happy moment. I handed one to Amanda, who returned to the table to add cream and sugar. I was too tired to do anything but drink it black and wait to feel like a human again.

"Good morning," said a voice from another corner of the room. It was one of Bauman's agents, who I had seen last night. He didn't look nearly as crappy as we did, but then again, he probably hadn't been fighting for his life all night.

"Morning," I managed to croak. He hopped up and walked outside, returning a few minutes later with George Bauman, who also had coffee in hand.

"You're Amanda Jensen?" he asked, turning to my lady, who still managed to look pretty damned good. "How are you feeling?"

"Better now, thank God. Thank you so much for last night. How is Thomas?"

"He's in recovery. Critical but stable. We need to get statements from each of you. It might be a long day. How about we grab breakfast and take a ride?"

"What about Thomas?" I asked.

"He will have a security detail. Too many folks involved in this case have been threatened or killed. We picked up Dr. Greller last night after I found out about Arthur McDade. He's in protective custody with his wife until we get to the bottom of this."

"What about the guys on the beach?" I asked. "Have you figured out who they are?"

"Sorry... I can't tell you much, as it's an ongoing investigation, but I can tell you those guys were all very dead." He paused and looked at me, likely thinking about what the crime scene guys had told him. "You have special loads for your shotgun?"

"Yes, sir. The exact nature of which is classified and most likely illegal in the civilian world." I refrained from telling him how happy I had been to kill them. I looked over at Amanda. Even exhausted, she was beautiful. "Amanda has attracted the wrong guys since the day I met her," I said.

"Well, *that's* pretty obvious," she responded.

Yeah, I had set myself up for that one.

Caleb, Amanda and I started to head out after Agent Bauman. I stopped and shook Caleb's hand. "I didn't get a chance to thank you. You guys saved our lives."

"That was Thomas' doing," he responded. "Never seen that man so excited. He practically threw a shotgun at me and dragged me down to the dock. I've known him all my life. He'd never say no to me if I told him I needed him. So what could I do?"

# Chapter Forty-Four

## Plans

The next twenty hours were a blur. We were transported to Camp Lejeune for safe keeping under the watchful eyes of thirty thousand United States Marines. We spent hours doing individual interviews with the Feds in offices they'd borrowed from the jarheads.

It felt good to be able to explain the whole unbelievable mess to people who seemed to understand what had happened. They didn't treat us like criminals. They were professional and courteous, and they made me proud, as an American, to have an agency like the FBI.

At the end of the second day, I was introduced to Special Agent in Charge Jeffrey Hess from the Criminal Investigative Division out of Charlotte. The FBI isn't very revealing about their ranks like we were in the army. Hell, I wore my stripes proudly on my sleeve. *These* guys made it a mystery. But I *could* tell by Special Agent Bauman's behavior around Hess that Hess was certainly the boss.

Everyone seemed to tiptoe around the guy. I'm not great with ages, but I'd guess he was in his late fifties. He could probably still run a marathon. He had lost most of his hair and decided to go *au naturale*. That is to say, he was totally clean-shaven from the neck up and looked like some of the hardcore guys I'd worked with back in the day. He walked into the cramped office, shook my hand and introduced himself, then sat on the opposite side of the desk.

"Quite an interesting story," he said. Then he sat back, crossed his legs and just looked at me. I stared back him, not sure what he was up to. After a moment, he leaned forward and spoke softly. "Here's the thing, Cory. I've got a diary which forensics may or may not be able to prove was actually Casey Stone's. I've got a witness to a murder that occurred twenty years ago that wasn't a murder then, who remained silent while another man went to jail. His credibility may not hold up in court. I've got bodies all over the place on Harkers Island, courtesy of you, and a dead ex-cop who worked the case twenty years ago."

He started ticking off points on his fingers. "I've read the reports. I've spoken to Dr. Greller. I've examined the diary. I've personally spoken to the agents who were on the scene at Harkers Island as well as to Special Agent Bauman. And this morning, I spoke with Thomas Woods myself about the events of August third, 1991. Let's assume for a minute that everything happened exactly the way that you and Thomas say it did." He folded his arms. "Now what?"

I was somewhat stunned. "*Now what*? Now you arrest that sick fuck!"

"And charge him with a murder that was considered solved twenty years ago, by the conviction of a man, coincidently, who isn't around to give his side of the story? For that matter, neither is the newly accused Anne Stone."

"Are you shittin' me?" I yelled. I stood without even realizing it.

"Sit down, Mr. Walker. I'm just asking you what you think expect to happen next."

"I'm just a civilian, Mr. Hess. I don't know how it works. Hey — wait a second. I haven't seen a paper in days. Did the *Inquirer* run the story?"

"They're holding off, awaiting a chance to speak with you."

"What about the shootout on Harkers Island? *That* must have been in the papers? No?"

"The incident occurred on federal land. Federal jurisdiction. We sealed off the east end of the island, did our work and sanitized the scene. No one knows what happened there."

*Whose side is this guy on? Holy crap* — they had the diary. What if Stone had gotten to them? I could feel myself starting to lose it. I guess he saw my wheels turning, and he raised his hands and cut me off.

"Mr. Walker, I want to see Earl Stone stand trial for the murder of his wife and the sexual assaults on his daughter. But here's the thing... We don't have enough. He's a powerful man with deep pockets. His lawyers will use every trick in the book. He'll make the O.J. trial look normal."

"He gets to run for President when we all know he's a raping murderer? Are you fucking kidding me?" I was standing up again, my hands squeezing the edge of the desk, feeling sick to my stomach. My version of low-key. "So he's just gonna walk?"

"Not if I can help it. But we need your help. Have a seat, Mr. Walker."

I sat back down.

"As of right now, Earl Stone has no idea what has happened to you. He doesn't know the FBI is involved. All he knows is that he had another witness silenced and one is in the wind. As far as he knows, you still have the diary, and he wants it back."

As he spoke, I was trying to think ahead to where this was all going. "He'll never admit anything."

"He might...if you have the diary." He let that sink in.

"You want me to wear a wire? Try to set him up?"

"That *is* one possibility."

We just sat and looked at each other for a second.

"You think he'd meet with me *alone*?"

"He has to know soon that his effort has failed. He isn't President *yet*. And he's not even an official candidate at this point, so he doesn't have a Secret Service detail assigned to him—just a few goons he likes having around him to look impressive. A few less than he had yesterday, but he can call them off and do whatever he wants."

"And how would I possibly get to him? I mean, to ask him to meet. He ain't exactly in the book."

"Actually, he *is*. He's a congressman. They're *all* in the book. And I just happen to have his office manager's number. It's public information. You'll tell her who you are—Cory Walker, the guy who's living in his old house on Harkers. You think you have something of his, and you'd like to speak to him personally. He already knows what you've got. Trust me... He'll call you."

"And...?"

"You set up a meeting, and we'll have you wired up and covered from a dozen places. All we need is for him to talk about the murder of his first wife."

We spent the next two hours planning my conversation. An FBI psychologist named Jan came in and gave me a bunch of pointers. She told me to use his first name and get personal with him. Use Casey's first name, too. Then I realized she had introduced herself as Jan — not doctor so-and-so. *Very funny. She's using her psych-ops on me, too?*

"Be specific about things in the book," she said. "Use a calm voice."

That one made me laugh. She didn't know me very well.

She shook her head when I laughed. "Look... If you can get him riled up, just keep pushing those buttons, but you have to try to remain calm. *You* have to control the conversation."

That made sense. I always wanted to control the battle-space. Now the battle-space was the conversation. It would literally be a war of words — *interesting concept.*

"Paint the picture for him, Cory," she said. I was so aware of her using my first name that I wasn't sure if she was screwing with me or not. "He's probably suppressed these memories for decades and might have managed to seal them away in some brain compartment somewhere. Your job is to make it real again and piss him off. Get him talking."

"One thing I'm good at is pissing people off."

When we were finished, I asked to call Kim at the paper and catch her up a little, off the record. The paper wouldn't sit on the story forever, unless I promised them something even better. Hess agreed, and we called from the same office. While Mark Rosman wasn't delighted about waiting another day or two, this was worth biting his fingernails over.

There was only one last person to discuss this with. Amanda. I had go talk to her myself. I preferred to face armed men on the beach.

Long story short, it didn't go over that well. Miss Worrywart was quite sure I would get my head blown off. No matter how many times I explained that the Feds would have my back, she didn't want to hear it. She *'was a prisoner on a Marine Base'* and just wanted to go home. And by home, she was referring to Twin Oaks, far away from the house of horrors. When I told her she couldn't until Earl Stone was arrested, it just upset her more. Even my usual charm and wit was useless. The woman had had it with the house and with me. It sucked.

The Feds told Amanda that she had to remain in protective custody until the operation was over. They apologized for the inconvenience and got to stand there and have *their* asses chewed off, too. My girl was *spunky*. I'll give her that much. I tried to give her a hug as I left the base for Harkers Island, and she pushed me away. That hurt.

Thankfully, by the time I got to the door, she yelled, "Be careful."

That was *something*, I guess.

I said, "I love you," and left. I'm pretty sure she was bawling her eyes out again.

*Women.*

# Chapter Forty-Five

Phone Call

Thomas was recovering. Caleb and I paid him a visit. He still had a Marine guard posted outside his door. The young Marine stood at attention, facing straight ahead, her weapon across her chest at the ready. She was hard and squared away. The future looked bright for the Corps.

Thomas was a tough bugger and never complained about pain or the numerous tubes and hoses running all over his body. His chest was wrapped up like a mummy under his stylish green hospital gown, reminding me of my own beat-down on my first date with Amanda.

I thanked him for his heroics. Thomas said he owed it to Casey and Ben, and I forced a smile and patted his shoulder gently. He'd be released in a few days and taken home, when he was up for it. The Feds gave Caleb and me a ride back to Harkers Island on a boat borrowed from the Marine Corps base. They'd already had Sea-Tow bring the *Lucky Lucy* back to the dock, and that news delighted Caleb.

There were nine FBI agents on the boat with us, all in jeans and T-shirts, looking like tourists...or FBI agents trying to look like tourists. In any event, I didn't mind having them around. Maybe I could get them to clean up my house.

The storm had moved out to sea, headed for Rhode Island, and the water in the Back Sound was calming down. We docked next to the *Lucky Lucy* and piled out onto the dock. Caleb's wife and son Mike were there waiting for us. There were a few other tourists around the dock, the kind with mirrored sunglasses and ear buds. They didn't say much, but it was obvious they were pros who had worked together before.

George Bauman, who had come with us on the boat, said he'd give us a lift home. He informed me that he was now 'my old army buddy' and would be staying with me for a few days, along with a couple of my other 'old friends'.

*No problem — just pull up a broken lamp and make yourself at home.*

The Feds had sent men ahead in several cars and they split up and gave Caleb and me rides back to our houses. I told Caleb I'd be in touch. He didn't love having the Feds hanging around his house but didn't complain.

When we arrived at my house, I saw Agatha working in her front yard. She was sawing away at a huge limb that had fallen during the storm. *Damn, she's a tough old bird.* I made George pull over, and we all piled out. She gave me a hug and told me she had been worried about me, asked me where I had been during the storm, the whole nine yards.

I made up a bunch of bullshit, introduced my buddies, and the four of us tough-guys sawed her tree limb into little pieces and stacked it in the rear yard for firewood. If Agatha had had her way, we all would have stayed for dinner and dessert and coffee and stories about the old days, but we had serious business ahead of us.

The Feds went into my house first, and searched every room for intruders, explosives, booby-traps, you name it. Then they checked all the phones and swept the rooms for bugs. The land line *had* been bugged, and the bug was removed.

When they were satisfied, I sat at the kitchen table, by the phone. I watched as they hauled duffle bags from their cars and hooked up all kinds of devices to my phone. They'd be recording all calls and trying to locate the positions of any callers who dialed in. It was impressive to watch them work. Reminded me of *me* in the old days, back when my shit was still wired tight and I had two shoulders that worked equally well. *Oh, well…*

When they were finished, George put on some headphones and handed me the phone. It was almost three in the afternoon. "You ready?"

"Ready as I'm gonna be." I dialed the number for the congressional office of Earl Stone.

"Representative Stone's office," she said in a professional voice. "This is Susan speaking. How may I assist you?"

"Hello, Susan. My name is Cory Walker. I live in Congressman Stone's old house on Harkers Island. It is extremely urgent that you give the congressman a message."

"Yes, sir? And what is the message?"

"Please tell the congressman that I have something of Casey's that was left in the house when he moved. I know he'll want it back. I will only give it to him in person, though, because it is a *very* personal item. This is *very* important."

"Yes, sir. Would you like me to read back the message to you?"

"No, Susan, I'm sure you have it right. I'll give you my home number. I'll be here for a while yet..."

"I have the number you're calling from. Is this the best way to reach you?"

"Yes, ma'am." I gave her my address, although Stone obviously knew it. It was *his* old house, which seemed to go over Susan's head as she wrote it down. She promised to get the message to Stone as soon as possible.

"Susan, if you have the congressman's cell phone number, no matter what he is doing or where he is, I suggest you give him this message now. As soon as you hang up with me. It's *that* important." I hung up.

"Perfect, Mr. Walker," said George.

"Please, would you call me Cory?"

He tried to smile and said, "Sure."

One of the Feds, a guy named Ronnie, walked into the kitchen, stepping over a broken drawer on the floor. "I love what you've done with the place! It has sort of an Early-American post-apocalyptic feel to it."

"Thanks a lot, man. Feel free to pick up whatever shit you step on. Stone's boys rearranged the place without my permission."

"*Allegedly* rearranged your place," Ronnie said. He was a big Italian guy with thick dark hair and an easy smile. He looked more like a mobster than a Fed. I guessed he had come to that crossroads sometime earlier in life and had decided on the 'law and order' road.

I started picking up the place, and the guys were kind enough to give me a hand. We were anxious about the return phone call, and it helped keep us occupied. When the phone finally did ring ten minutes later, I almost shit myself.

George looked at me stone-faced. "Just be cool. Stick to the script."

I picked it up and said "Hello," to the blocked caller ID.

"You have something of Mr. Stone's?" said a man's voice.

George shook his head.

"That's right. And as I told his office manager, I will only speak to him about it." I hung up.

The phone rang again in seconds.

"Mr. Walker, don't be an idiot. Mr. Stone is never going to meet you face to—"

I cut him off. "In person. Or my next call is to the newspaper. He has five minutes." I hung up. Everyone around me smiled. I guessed I'd done well, at least so far.

The agents fanned out around the house in predetermined locations, and they started checking in with other folks I couldn't see stationed all over the island. *These guys don't fuck around.* I liked that.

Two and a half minutes later, my phone rang again.

"Earl Stone here," he said an affable voice. "I believe you have something of mine that you want to return to me?"

"Not *yours*, actually. Casey's."

Silence. I was wondering how many guys he had sitting around *his* office.

"Do you want me to start discussing the contents now over the phone?"

"I don't think that's called for, Mr. Walker. Have some respect for my stepdaughter."

"I have a lot more respect for her than *you* ever did. Now I'm gonna say this one time, so pay attention, Mr. Congressman. I want my life back. I bought a house because it was a great house. I didn't ask for all this bullshit. I found Casey's diary, and I know what happened that night. All I want is to be left alone. I'll give you the book, and you give me your word you'll leave me alone."

"Who have you told about the diary, Mr. Walker?"

"I'm the only one who knows what's in it. A reporter has some information in case anything happens to me. I give it back to you, and you give me your word to leave me alone. Or you keep fucking with me, and I call the newspapers and the cops. I already met a couple of your friends, and in case you're wondering why you haven't heard back from them, it's because I killed those motherfuckers and dumped their asses in the ocean so far from land that they'll never be found. I'm retired Special Forces, Stone, and if you come after me again, I'll make you very sorry. Now do you want to meet me and end this, or would you rather read about it in the paper?"

"I know your military record, Walker. And I've read the police reports regarding the triple homicide. It would be a shame to see you indicted and do time for trying to defend your girlfriend."

"That's right, Stone. I was *defending* her. And now you see how nasty I can be when someone comes after me."

"Touché. Perhaps you're right. We should end this. How much money do you want?"

"*Money*? No money. Just you to call your goons off. I only meet with *you*, Stone. No one else. And we meet *here*, on Harkers Island where I'll know if you bring any friends with you. Just me and you. That's it. I give you the book, and you forget you ever heard of me."

"Just like that?"

"Just like that."

"I'm in Washington. Might be a few days before I can get there."

"You have until ten o'clock *tonight*. You don't show tonight at exactly ten o'clock, the newspaper gets a phone call. I have a friend over there dying to hear about what's in the diary. Don't fuck with me, and don't be late. I'll be waiting for you in the backyard by the angels. You remember *them*, don't you?"

I could almost hear his veins popping out of his head. "I'll be there at ten, Walker. Have the diary."

*Stone is coming*!

George gave me a thumbs-up and called Special Agent in Charge Hess over at the CID.

# Chapter Forty-Six

## Pizza and Prep

Ronnie left the house for a while, and when he returned, he had five large pizza boxes. I didn't even know Harkers Island had a pizza place. *Leave it to the Feds to find it.*

"I thought you guys ate doughnuts," I said when he walked in.

"That's before ten in the morning. What are we, *animals*? Jesus, Cory, be civilized." The guys ate in shifts, and I had three slices myself. It was either better than I expected or I was just starving. I mentioned beer, but they said not until Stone was in custody. At eight, George told me it was time to 'get wired'. I was expecting all kinds of wires to be taped on my chest or something, but that must have been old school. Instead, he popped a tiny plastic thing into my shirt collar and said, "All done."

"That's it?"

"That's it. Microphone, GPS, infrared sensor. We got you covered nine ways from Sunday. You'll be in a dim environment by design. My guys will be all over with night vision. Your job is to get him to incriminate himself on tape. We can't swoop in and arrest him unless he physically threatens you, but that's a weak charge unless he tries to shoot you, and frankly, the congressman isn't that stupid."

"Glad to know that," I deadpanned.

"Push his buttons. Make him talk. Try to rile him. In other words," he smiled, "just be yourself."

"I'm cool. After the other night, this is child's play."

"Yeah, well, remember," George cautioned, "that this isn't about killing the enemy. If you harm him physically without a definite threat against your life, we'll end up having to arrest *you*. The guy's a *congressman*, Cory. Please don't forget that."

"Well, that would be ironic, huh? We do a sting operation against a child-raping murderer, and you end up arresting me? Sounds like a military operation."

"It's going to be fine. You have that copy of the diary?"

"Yeah, it looks exactly like the original."

"The lab boys are good. Plus he hasn't seen it in twenty years…if he ever saw it. He'll never know. Try to relax. We're watching the bridge, the ferry dock and the waterways from the mainland. No matter how he gets here, we'll know before he wants us to. You carrying?"

"No. I lost my Mossberg at the lighthouse."

"No you didn't. We have it. We'll give it back to you after this is all over. No other weapons on you now?"

"You want to pat me down?"

"Nope. But *he* may want to. If he does, let him. We want him to know you are unarmed and alone."

"I'm *never* defenseless. I'd prefer to kill him with my bare hands anyway."

"Yeah, I get that," he said seriously. "You aren't here to kill him, understand? We have you protected in case he brings friends or tries something stupid, but you are *not* to physically assault the congressman. Remember… Get him talking."

"I get it. I get it. I'll be a good boy and just try to give him a stroke or heart attack instead."

"Natural causes would be fine," said George. He looked me deep in my eyes and repeated himself slowly and deliberately. "Do *not* assault the congressman. You may need the most restraint of your entire life."

I exhaled and nodded. "Wilco."

Ronnie walked back in. "We got him…in a limo coming across the bridge. Spotter says maybe three guys plus the driver. Everyone's in position. Showtime, Cory. We are *go*. Good luck."

# Chapter Forty-Seven

Stone

At nine-forty-five, I walked out to the backyard with the forged diary and sat on the ornate bench next to the garden. In the dim light, the pink flowers looked grayish white, and the white marble angels gleamed eerily. I looked up at them and my heart ached.

Three FBI agents in black jumpsuits and Kevlar vests jogged past me with their weapons out and night vision goggles on top of their heads. Their faces were covered with black masks, and Ronnie whispered, "Just be cool, bro," as he passed me and moved into the pines and shrubs that surrounded the property.

I sat on the bench, the book in my lap, and waited. Fifteen minutes felt like fifteen lifetimes. If he walked in with guns blazing, I guessed I'd just read my obit in the *Inquirer* from Hell the next day.

I heard a car pull into my driveway. Three car doors opening and closing.

The sounds of footsteps on the slate walkway around the side of the house made the hair on my arms stand up. I should have been sitting in a foxhole with my SCAR or Ice, not sitting on a bench with a book for protection. All I was missing was a large bullseye on my chest.

My house was locked up and dark inside. The outside lights were on, and the Congressman knew his way around. He emerged around the corner of the house and stood. I didn't move. For a moment, we were just frozen in time.

He finally started walking warily to me and stopped a few feet away. He looked up at the angels, and I saw his expression change. That psychologist from the Bureau had *said* they'd help get him talking. I hoped she was right.

I stared at this man who wanted to be the next President. He was tall and fit, with salt-and-pepper hair. He didn't look like a child-raping murderer. He looked more like a congressman, complete with suit and tie. I found that disturbing.

"You have something of mine?" he said quietly.

"Like I said before…not yours. Casey's."

"All right. Casey's. I'm her father. I'll take it now."

*Her father?* The asshole's ego just wouldn't stop.

"Why'd you do it, Earl?" I asked, using his first name, the way the psychologist had told me to.

"Kids… Who knows what they write in their diaries? You got kids?" He was staring at the two beautiful angels.

"You didn't kill Casey. I know that. I mean, why'd you kill Anne?"

His head snapped in my direction, away from the angels. "I didn't kill Anne. She was heartbroken over Casey. That McComb kid raped and killed our daughter. It was too much for any mother to endure."

"Holy shit, Earl. You've been telling that story for so long you actually *believe* it now, don't you? I would, too, except I read Casey's diary. And I spoke to Detective Arthur McDade, who was mysteriously murdered this week. And I spoke to Dr. Greller, the medical examiner, who seems to have disappeared. And I spoke to Thomas Woods..."

The mention of Thomas hit a nerve. I could see it in his eyes. I'd hold that in my pocket for now. "I've learned a lot since I moved here and bought your house, like what a hyoid bone is. You know what a hyoid bone is, Earl?"

"I'm not interested in speeches, Walker. I'm here for the diary."

"The one where she writes about how you used to take her panties off and spank her while you jerked off, you sick *fuck*?" I'd been waiting a long time to call him that personally. "How you *raped* your stepdaughter? *That* diary?"

"Give it to me, Walker. Don't be a fool."

"Going to send more of your goons after me? Were you *there* when they killed Detective McDade? No — you wouldn't have the balls. You have people to that do that *for* ya, don't you?"

"I have people that do lots of things for me, Walker. This conversation is over." He held out his hand. "The book."

"Yeah, it's still here on my lap. Want me to read you the last part? The part where you raped her? She was so dead inside that she didn't even protest. She pretended you were Ben. Did you know that?"

I could see his face turning purple, even in the dim light. The congressman had looked like a handsome candidate when I'd first seen him. Now he was just a dark, evil entity, emitting an ugliness that was palpable.

"That's *enough*," he snarled.

"Hardly. Thomas told me about that night. How Anne caught Casey on the beach with Ben. Thomas said it was an accident, that Anne didn't mean to kill Casey."

He took a step toward me. He started talking through teeth clenched so tight that I could hardly hear him. "That's right, you piece of shit. It was an accident. She snapped when she saw Casey with that white trash—"

"*Oh*! So it was all right for Casey to fuck her *stepdaddy* but not her *boyfriend*?"

"You're a dead man," he growled.

If he could have, I know he would have killed me himself right then.

"Why'd you kill her, Earl?"

"She killed my daughter!" he bellowed. "That jealous bitch killed my *daughter*!"

"You're a sick fuck, Stone. Casey was your *step*daughter, so luckily she didn't have any of your fucked-up DNA. I'm gonna love watching you get the needle."

"You're not going to see anything. *Anton*!" he bellowed.

A large man appeared from around the side of the house, carrying a pistol. He was followed by another man, who was also carrying a gun.

That was when I heard Agatha's voice. "Mister Cory? Is that *Earl* I hear out there with you? *Earl*? Is that you?"

Agatha Miles walked into my yard in her pajamas, holding her oversized cat. "Oh my, it *is* you! Earl! It's been so long!" She approached him, her eyes open wide. He looked like he had just seen a ghost. He whispered to the big man in front to get the diary.

"Agatha! Stop! Turn around and go home!" I said, as controlled as I could.

"Cory? Is everything all right?"

"Go *home*!"

The cat leaped from Agatha's arms and disappeared into the bushes. She stood still, looking confused as the mountain named Anton stepped forward and raised his pistol at me. When I heard the gunshots, my heart was pounding through my chest like a freight train. I waited to feel the same pain I had felt in Afghanistan.

Anton dropped to the ground, with multiple holes in his chest and face. The man behind him also dropped, dead before he hit the ground.

The Feds started charging through the brush, guns drawn. I could see Earl's face. He stood by himself below the angels. He knew it was over.

"FBI! Don't move, Earl Stone! FBI! Freeze!"

Agents were appearing out of nowhere, the red dots from laser sights dancing on Earl's face and body. I held up the book for him to see and smiled.

He reached down for Anton's gun.

"Don't do it! Freeze! Stop or we'll shoot!"

Earl Stone looked into my eyes and continued reaching for the gun. It seemed strangely quiet in the yard at that instant. I was aware of everything around me, like the old days in combat. I could see Agatha standing in my yard, in total shock and horror. I could see Ronnie and George and other agents charging out of the bushes in black combat gear, guns drawn. I could smell cordite from the shots that had been fired. It was all happening in slow motion, and total silence, and I was totally at peace.

The last thing I remember was George's voice commanding Stone to stop. Stone picked up the gun and aimed right at my chest. Then the loudest noise, like submachine guns, started popping off.

One of the rounds went through Stone's neck, and the arterial spray shot up so high it sprayed the angels' faces. He dropped into the flowers at the base of the statue, his own blood dripping down those cheeks, like the angels were crying blood. I think maybe they were.

They seemed so tall and majestic over Stone's bloody corpse.

# Chapter Forty-Eight

### And Just Like That...

I'd never been in shock after a firefight, never been frozen in combat. I've seen some shit. I had always been totally cool. But as I sat on the bench watching the blood run down the faces of those angels, my legs wouldn't move when I told them to stand.

Earl Stone, United States Congressman and Presidential hopeful, was lying dead in my flower garden, under the statue of his girls. I watched as the Feds scrambled around, checking vitals and calling for ambulances. I heard Ronnie yell that they had the driver in custody. But I just sat there, hearing it all somewhere far away in the distance, feeling like I was on a different planet. It was Agatha's voice that snapped me back.

"*Cory? Cory?*"

I looked over and saw her standing there, helpless and terrified, and I remembered how to walk again.

I stumbled off the bench, the diary falling at the feet of Earl Stone, and ran to Agatha. I wrapped my arms around her and gave her a hug. "It's okay, Agatha. We're gonna be fine."

"Is that really *Earl*? *Earl S-S-S*...?" She was stammering.

"It's okay. It's all over now."

A female agent wrapped a blanket around Agatha to walk her home.

"But my Timothy..."

"Her cat," I said.

"Don't worry. We'll find your cat," the agent promised her as she led her into her own backyard.

* * * *

My yard was crawling with state police. Light towers with generators flooded my property like it was daytime. The locals were complaining because they weren't being allowed into the rear yard, but the state police and the FBI were already having a pissing match about jurisdiction, and the Sheriff's Department wasn't going to trump either of them.

George pulled me inside my house and took my bug off. He got a cold beer out of the fridge and handed it to me. "You earned this one." He handed me his cell phone. "Just press send. It's ready to dial. Take it into your room, if you want. It's Amanda over at Lejeune."

He was a solid guy, that George Bauman.

Amanda was frightened, upset, mad and exhausted, but when I told her Stone was dead and it was all over, she broke down, cried and somewhere in her hysterical-sounding rambling, she did tell me that she loved me.

"Me too."

I told her to go to sleep, and I'd make sure she got a ride over to Harkers Island as soon as she was ready in the morning.

"Like I can sleep," she said.

We hung up, and I wondered if we'd be okay. We'd only been dating for such a short time, and had already been through more than couples who were married for a lifetime. I hoped so. I loved that woman.

When I walked back downstairs, I could hear a state police officer giving George a hard time. He was demanding to interview me personally. George told him to call Special Agent in Charge Hess. No one was talking to me other than the FBI.

That was fine with me. There was a lot of testosterone downstairs. I just sat on the stairs and listened to them argue until the state police officer left, then I walked downstairs, feeling whatever it was that comes after complete exhaustion.

"Thanks," I said to George.

Ronnie walked up behind him. "Good job tonight. I'd share a foxhole with you." Where I come from, that's the ultimate compliment. "Thanks, man. I guess it worked out how it was supposed to. You got enough on tape to prove he killed Anne. He's dead. You saved some taxpayer money and prevented him from fucking up my country."

"Well," George said, "I'm not sure how much the tapes will prove, but it was a justified shooting with plenty of eyewitnesses. Now comes the paperwork. Go upstairs and get some sleep. We'll be at this all night. There's no sense in everyone feeling like shit tomorrow."

I thought about Stone dead in my yard. "Actually, this is the best I've felt since I found that damn book."

George and Ronnie walked off with their computers to begin their massive pile of paperwork, and I remained in my kitchen, looking out of the window to my rear yard and gardens. I could still see the dark red blood, dried now on the angels' faces like permanent tears.

Casey had been avenged...and so had Ben. And Anne? Well, I'd leave her judgment for a higher authority. I'd never know how much she knew about Casey's abuse at the hands of her twisted husband. I suppose she'd been dealing with her own hell on earth. But still, she should have protected her child. Where I came from, a person always sacrificed their personal safety for their battle buddies. Always. I didn't know how to process it. Those were moccasins I'd never walked in.

I went upstairs and flopped face-down on my bed. I may have been asleep before my head hit the pillow.

# Chapter Forty-Nine

It's Over

I woke up at sunrise to the sounds of people walking around downstairs. I smelled coffee brewing in my kitchen, thank God, and got out of bed with a groan. While stretching my shoulder a bit, it dawned on me that I felt like I'd been hit by a bus. I threw on some fresh jeans and a shirt from the piles that were still strewn all over my room. One of these days, I'd have to pick all that stuff up.

I washed up in the upstairs bathroom and walked downstairs. Ronnie was the first person I saw, and he had a Styrofoam cup of beautiful coffee in one hand and a doughnut in the other. He presented them to me with fanfare and a slight bow.

"Good morning, Sleeping Beauty," he said with a smile. "I *told* you, doughnuts before ten. *Then* we switch to pizza."

I took the coffee and considered kissing Ronnie. "You guys been to sleep yet?"

"Sleep is overrated. Who needs sleep after a hundred coffees? You'll be happy to know that we picked up around the backyard. You have a young lady waiting for you out there. She's been here since two a.m."

"Amanda's here?" I could feel my heart speed up. God, I wanted to see her!

"A reporter. Kim's her name. Agent Bauman said she's 'part of the deal', whatever that means. She's been on her cell phone back there since before sunup. There were bodies everywhere when she arrived, and she was smiling from ear to ear. You hang out with some strange people, Cory Walker."

I laughed. *Her big break.*

I thanked Ronnie for the coffee and headed out back. I guess I was expecting to see bodies, blood and Feds everywhere. Instead, the yard was completely empty, except for Kim, and the sun, shining in a blue sky. They had sanitized everything like nothing had ever happened back there. Someone had even been considerate enough to hose down the angels.

But there was no missing the yellow crime scene tape that screamed *Do Not Cross* that had been stretched around the perimeter of my property, and as word spread from the tiny community of Harkers Island out to the mainland — and by that, I mean China — dozens of reporters began finding their way to our sleepy little island. The Feds and local deputies kept them off my property, and they were complaining about why Kim was allowed back there. *She saved our asses, and you didn't, so go eff yourselves.*

I found Kim sitting on the same bench I'd sat on when all hell had broken loose, smiling and typing like mad on her laptop with ear buds in. When she saw me, her face turned serious, and I heard her say, "He's here. I'll call you back."

She put her laptop down and ran over to me. "Cory!" She threw her arms around me and gave me a hug. She pulled back and looked at me. "Are you okay?" she asked, sounding ever-so-serious.

"I'm fine. They sure cleaned up the yard," I said, almost to myself as I looked around.

*Hell, maybe they weeded for me, too.*

"Yeah, but not until I got here and took about a thousand pictures last night under their lights. I had the scoop in this morning's paper—front page, above the fold. It'll be all over the world by now, but I had it first. I owe you—and that George Bauman—*big* time."

"So you've got your Pulitzer in the works?"

"You never know. The sheriff's department wasn't even let in, and they were going crazy. The FBI had sealed off the entire area, and other than some state police guys who were allowed, I was the *only* one! And I'm the only one who will have an interview with Cory Walker. A Kim Predham *exclusive*! I was just waiting to talk to you. I need some quotes."

"Quotes? 'The sick fuck is dead and his daughter can rest in peace.' How's that for a quote?"

"I may have to paraphrase that."

"Ask your questions, and let's get this over with. I really just want all this to be over and done with. You know what I mean?"

"Totally. On the record, how did you find the diary?"

I answered every question for the next thirty-five minutes without complaint. Kim had helped me more than I'd helped her, and I always pay my debts. As soon as she was finished, she thanked me and hopped back on her laptop and her phone.

George walked out to the yard and told me they were wrapping up.

Kim had thanked me a hundred times and raced off to get back to the office, although her story was already filed via email and the paper was already on the newsstands. She had Rosman thank me personally, although the gratitude was quite mutual.

"This story is on every news source in the country. Harkers Island is going to be a very busy place," George said. "You may want to take a trip somewhere quieter, Cory."

"Yeah, I was thinking about trying to re-enlist," I said.

"Special Agent Hess already started making some noise in Washington. You can rest assured the grand jury will never hear your old case, and the prosecutor who pushed for a grand jury will be looking for a new job tomorrow. I'm doubtful we'll ever find the shooter in the McDade murder. If he was connected to the guys on the beach, we have a shot. The lab is working up IDs on them. In any event, you can put this all behind you. For whatever it's worth, you did a great job."

"Wanna buy a house?" I asked him.

He laughed. "Not on my salary. Besides, with the next news cycle, all this will be forgotten and you'll have a beautiful place to live happily ever after in. I got a call. They're bringing Amanda over."

Lejeune was only sixty miles away, which meant she'd be back soon. I couldn't wait for her to get here.

George gave me a light smack on my good shoulder. "We'll get out of your hair. I'm leaving an agent out front for the next couple of days, in case the press or anyone else goes overboard. Oh, and I left your illegal Mossberg that I never saw up in your room. Even had it cleaned and oiled. That's a nasty little weapon you have there, Cory."

"An old friend. Thanks for everything, George. You ever want to come out 'feeshing', just call. Bring Ronnie and we'll hang out some weekend."

"Yeah? I might just take you up on that."

# Chapter Fifty

## Six Hush Puppies

By the time Amanda arrived from Lejeune, I was the only one left at the house. The Feds had left, pretty much without a trace. One lone 'tourist' with mirrored sunglasses and a bulge on his hip was parked out front, occasionally getting out to walk around the block.

I was standing in the kitchen, making a halfhearted stab at putting things away, when Amanda walked in. Suffice it to say, there was a lot of hugging, kissing and saying 'I love you'. We spent the entire day cleaning the house. It was cathartic, and when we were finished cleaning, I think we both felt 'cleaner' ourselves. We finished the day with a long hot shower and some personal time. It was after five and we were both famished.

"I know a place that makes great hush Puppies," I said.

"You buying?" she asked.

"You know it. And, if we get a *double* order, then each person can have equal amounts so there won't be any long-held hard feelings."

We were going to walk, but the agent out front insisted on playing chauffeur. We sat in the back, holding hands.

"This feels like another first date," I said. Then I leaned closer to her ear and whispered, "Are you gonna marry me or what?"

"Maybe," she said. "Let's see how dinner goes. I've had some pretty bad first dates."

Together, Amanda and I read the front page of Carteret *Inqurier*.

*Congressman Killed in Shootout*

*Harkers Island*
*Kim Predham*

*Earl Stone, sixty-two, U. S. House of Representatives, D-SC and Presidential hopeful, has been fatally shot by FBI agents on Harkers Island. Stone has been implicated in the death of his late wife, Anne Stone, who allegedly committed suicide in 1991 after learning of the brutal rape and murder of their daughter, Casey, sixteen. Cory Walker, a veteran of the Iraq and Afghanistan wars and a decorated Special Forces soldier, purchased a house in late August of this year on Harkers Island that was once owned by the Stone family. While doing renovations, he discovered a diary believed to be written by Casey. The diary has been turned over to the FBI.*

*According to a confidential source close to the investigation, the diary reveals a pattern of sexual, physical and mental abuse perpetrated by Earl Stone. The sources claim that Anne Stone did not commit suicide as had been originally reported. Earl Stone is alleged to have strangled her and hanged her body in the family residence. Stone allegedly used his influence to cover up the murder, as well as evidence of sexual assault. Benjamin McComb, then seventeen, was found guilty for the rape and murder of Casey Stone. After being interviewed by Walker in Maury Prison, McComb was brutally murdered. Several prison guards have been suspended with pay, pending further investigation. Stone allegedly sent a team of professional hit men to kill Walker, in an attempt to end the investigation. Walker, with the assistance of two local Harkers Island fishermen, Caleb Jackson and Thomas Woods, killed what has been described by the FBI as 'a number of professional hitmen', who were seeking to obtain the diary.*

*The FBI has announced that Walker, Woods and Jackson will not be charged. The three men will be awarded the FBI's Civilian Meritorious Service Medal. The FBI continues its investigation into undue influence peddling by the late Earl Stone, including charges aimed at the Eastern Carolina Prosecutor's Office. Carteret County Sheriff Wade McFadden has announced his retirement, pending formal inquiries into his involvement in this case nearly twenty years ago.*

*Regarding this case so unbelievable that it has sent shockwaves through the entire country, FBI Special Agent George Bauman said, "Heinous crimes occurred almost twenty years ago which were considered solved. As a result of corruption and manipulation by Congressman Earl Stone, an innocent man, Benjamin McComb, was sent to prison, where he was recently murdered. If not for the courage and conviction of Cory Walker, this case might never have been properly solved. The country owes the North Carolina native a debt of gratitude for his service, once again, to his country."*

*In an* Inquirer *exclusive, Walker said that while he wished the entire event had never occurred, "I am satisfied that the truth has finally come to light and that Earl Stone has finally been given his proper sentence." Walker expressed his deepest sympathies for Casey Stone. Tomorrow — an exclusive in-depth interview with Cory Walker.*

\* \* \* \*

*The real estate section, two weeks later*

*For Sale —*
*276 Turtle Cove Road, Harkers Island*
*Magnificent estate home, a short walk from the beach.*
*Turn-of-the-century Victorian, four bedrooms, three-and-a-half baths, two*
*fireplaces, open kitchen, wine cellar. Hardwood floors throughout.*
*Magnificent gardens. A must-see. $450,000.*

\* \* \* \*

I woke up to the smell of coffee. When I opened my eyes, the first thing I saw was my amazing Amanda, wearing my T-shirt from the night before and a beautiful smile. She was holding my coffee in her left hand, her engagement ring sparkling in the sunrise through the window.

"Wow. If I had known you were going to make me coffee in the morning if I gave you a diamond, I would have done that a long time ago," I said.

"I might not have said yes a long time ago," she said, handing me my hot cup of joe. No macchiato vente soy bullshit—just a regular ol' cup of joe. Unlike mine, her coffee always came out perfectly. She sat on the bed next to me and asked, "So now what are we going to do?"

We had sold the house on Harkers Island in three weeks to a lawyer from New Jersey named Lou Scalzo, who was looking for a quiet summer home away from the typical tourist places. An avid fisherman, Scalzo quit his practice, moved to Harkers Island full-time and opened a charter business with his first mate, none other than Mike Jackson. Their first week, they broke the North Carolina record with a ten-foot long, one-hundred-eighty-pound sailfish.

We were in her apartment in Twin Oaks on a month-to-month lease, since she had gotten out of the lease to come move down to Harkers Island with me, and *that* hadn't gone so well.

"What are we going to do now?" I echoed her early morning question. "We are going to travel around the United States of America and have the best time ever. And when we find a perfect spot, we are going to settle down, get married and live happily ever after."

She leaned over and gave me a kiss, even with my morning breath. She was leaning close, her eyes smiling, when she asked me, "Can I do a background check on the house *before* we buy it this time?"

# Heat: A Love to Kill For
## Conor Corderoy

### *Excerpt*

I parked my TVR Daemon outside Noddy's Diner on the Portobello Road, put my 'Doctor on Call' sign on the windshield, loped through the gray rain and pushed through the door. Chandler once described a woman as the kind who'd make a bishop kick holes in a stained glass window. This one would have had him burning down the Vatican with the Pope strapped to the roof of the Sistine Chapel. It wasn't just that she was a drop-dead looker. She was. She had all her curves in the right places, bobbed black hair, crimson, Cupid's-bow mouth and slow sea-green eyes. But more than that, she managed to look vulnerable and lethal at the same time in a way that stirred your primal urges till you had smoke billowing out of your sphygmomanometer. Yeah, look it up.

In my book, all women are bad news. They make you feel this thing called 'love', so you'll let them chew you up, suck you dry then spit you out before they move on to their next victim. But even by those standards, I could see this lady was the kind of bad news they interrupt regular broadcasts for. Fortunately, I'm immune to bad news.

She and Noddy both saw me as I pushed in, but I noticed his eyes pleading in a way I had never seen before. I ignored him and eased onto a stool next to the vamp, pulled out a Camel and asked Noddy for a Martini, dry. He stared at me like he was astonished I wanted that drink instead of another and said, real urgent, "This is Caffrin, Liam. Caffrin 'oward. I told you abaht her."

I nodded that I knew and he went to get the Martini. While he put it together, I flipped my Zippo and lit up. She watched me do it the way a cat watches a fly — cute and patient, and ready to eat it alive the minute it gets close enough. Finally, I blew smoke and said, "Noddy thinks I can help you. Want to tell me how?"

She made a slow, green blink. When she spoke, she had that absence of accent the English call cut glass, but husky with it.

"I'm being blackmailed, Mr. Murdoch. I've arranged to make a payment and collect the incriminating material, but I'm afraid that when I do, I may be murdered."

I'm not easily fazed and this didn't faze me, but I wasn't expecting it. I took a moment to study the olive in my Martini. It floated, so I bobbed it up and down a few times. I took a sip and, as I put the glass down, I said, "So you want me to get murdered for you."

She didn't even have the decency to blush. Whether she said yes or no, it was going to be the wrong answer. So she said, "Not exactly, Mr. Murdoch. I'd like you to make the drop and collect the material. I shall pay you very well for that. Clearly, I don't want you to get murdered." Something like a smile played across her face. "That wouldn't help anybody, would it?"

I nodded. "Especially me. You want to give me some background?"

She hesitated and pointed at my glass. "Can I have one of those?" While Noddy fell over himself in four different directions assembling a second Martini, she gestured at my cigarettes. I nodded and pushed them along the bar with the lighter. It's hard for a woman to make a Zippo look graceful. In her hands it was triple-X-rated exquisite. She let the smoke drift out through red lips and read my face for a while. I put a blank page there. After a moment she said, "I used to work as a high-class prostitute. I had highly placed clients. I was expensive..."

I said, "Class usually is."

She blinked sea-green at me and carried on. "I didn't waste the money. I put myself through university. I read biology and did a master's in business. Just over a year ago I bought myself into a biotechnology research and development company as a partner." She sucked on the Camel, frowning at the ashtray. "There are films and photographs. They're held by a man. We used to call him the Don. He used to be my..." Her look turned resentful, like it was the ashtray's fault she'd once had a pimp. She tapped a little ash into its mouth and said, "Manager. I bought myself out a couple of months ago, but now he wants money for the films and the photographs. If I don't pay, he'll send copies to the board."

I took a long drag on my cigarette and squinted at her through the smoke. "I've known a few pimps in my time, Miss Howard, and a few blackmailers too. Most of them weren't smart enough to know a biology degree from an amoeba's ass, but most of them weren't dumb enough to kill a goose that laid golden eggs, either."

She tilted her chin and smiled. Her voice was so husky it could have pulled a sled across Alaska. It was getting to me. She said, "You don't believe me."

"Me and Descartes, sugar. I believe I exist because I can hear myself think. Outside of that, I don't believe shit. I'm not a hit man, Miss Howard. I'm not going to kill your blackmailer for you."

Outside, the rain had turned torrential. A rumble of thunder shook the ceiling and the lights in the diner winked off, so we were sitting in shadow. She shook her head. "That isn't what I'm looking for."

"If everything you say is true, he can keep the squeeze on you for years. Why should he want you dead?"

She stubbed out her cigarette, smoke trailing from her nose. She sipped and licked her lips with a very pink tongue.

"It's a little more complex than that."

"So tell me the complex bit. I can recognize an amoeba's ass."

"How colorful…" She watched me a while in the half light. Then the lights came on and somewhere a fridge began to hum. "During the time the Don managed me, I accumulated a lot of information about him, his operations and his clients. I told you some of them were important men — and women. People in the public eye. If I should ever decide to write my memoirs, Mr. Murdoch, it would cause a lot of people a great deal of embarrassment. More than that, it could bring down important political careers and, with them, the Don's power. I don't think I need to paint you a picture. It's in the Don's best interest — and his clients' — to make me very dead."

I nodded. "Have you anything more concrete than a general theory of his motives?"

"Yes, the way he's set up the drop. He's done it before to other people. I'll be extremely vulnerable." Her cheeks flushed incongruously and she smiled. "I'm between a rock and a hard place, Mr. Murdoch. I daren't risk not going—not making the drop. But I know if I do, he'll kill me. He has to."

What she said made sense. A man like she described could not afford a loose cannon, especially one as smart as Catherine Howard. But even so, I knew she was lying. For one thing, if she were for real, she'd work for Russian Pete, not some anonymous Don. And Russian Pete would have introduced her to me by now. My gut told me that every word out of her mouth was a lie that concealed layers of deeper lies. But I also knew, as I sat looking into her level, green eyes, that I didn't give a damn. I crushed out my cigarette and said, "So what do you want me to do?" And just so she didn't think I was as soft as Noddy, "And how much does this caper pay?"

She took a swig of her Martini and said, "I just want you to go in my place."

"What makes you think he won't kill me?"

"Does that worry you?"

"Yeah. I don't like getting killed. It gives me a headache."

She didn't smile. She shrugged. "Why should he? He has no interest in your death. In any case, he is expecting a weak woman, not"—she paused and gestured at me with a look that was both insulting and flattering—"someone like you. And even if he should try, you are forewarned and I'm sure you can take care of yourself. I'd advise you to be armed." Now she smiled. "Have you got a weapon, Mr. Murdoch?"

The innuendo was obvious and vulgar and made me unreasonably mad. I grunted. "Yeah, I have a weapon. What if he won't give me the material?"

"Again, you're a big boy. I'm sure you can persuade him. In any case, I think he will. The money he's asking for is considerable."

"Okay. What makes you think I won't take the money for myself and leave you in the lurch?"

She turned to Noddy. She went a little pale and her eyes were beseeching. She should have been in Hollywood. She deserved an Oscar. He looked deep into her oceanic green eyes, read a thousand impossible promises there, swallowed hard and turned to me, stabbing a big, ugly finger in my face. "'Cos if you do, Liam, I'll kick you dahn the fahkin stairs, tear yer fahkin 'ed off and stuff it up yer fahkin backside, so you'll be watchin telly fru yer fahkin arse for the rest of yer miserable fahkin life! Don't mistreat the lady, awright?"

Noddy was from the East End of London, where they speak a language all their own. She smiled at me, telling me silently that she could make him do it. I gave Noddy a look that told him what I thought of him and his 'fahkin telly' then sighed. "Okay, how much does it pay?"

Something strange happened to her face then. I want to say that it went hard, but that doesn't even begin to describe it. I had the feeling I was looking, not at a woman, but at an animal. If you've seen the dispassionate expression on a cat's face when it goes for the kill or a lizard swallowing a live insect, you'll know what I mean. She had the alien eyes of a goat in that moment and the stillness of a snake. She spoke with no feeling at all.

"If you fail — or are only partially successful — the job pays nothing. Partial success is of no use to me. You bring me all the material — original and any copies — and it pays twenty thousand pounds, sterling."

I raised an eyebrow at her. "Twenty grand?" That was thirty-five thousand bucks.

"Naturally, I will cover all your expenses."

Outside, the rain had slowed to a wet tapping. "Expenses?" I frowned. "What expenses?"

She reached into her snakeskin handbag and pulled out a surprisingly large manila envelope. From that she extracted a Virgin Atlantic ticket and a smaller, white envelope that smelled like cash and was reassuringly fat. She handed me the ticket.

"That is a flight to New York. It departs tonight. I'd like you to be on it. You will be there for twelve hours and return with the material. I suggest you do your sleeping on the plane. All the instructions are here." She pulled an A4 sheet of paper from the manila envelope and handed me that too, along with a locker key. I put the key in my pocket and slipped the A4 in with the ticket to look at later. She said, "Go to Left Luggage at Heathrow Airport. The key fits a locker. Collect the attaché case from there. It contains fifty thousand dollars. That's the payoff." She held up the white packet. "This is two-and-a-half thousand dollars in small and medium bills. It should more than cover your needs. If there is any over, consider it a tip."

She knew — and so did I — that I was going to New York. I took the reassuringly fat envelope and peered in. By the rack of the eye it was two-and-a-half grand. I slipped it into my pocket.

"How can I contact you when I'm done?"

"You can't. Noddy will arrange it."

I raised an eyebrow at him. That was my line and he knew it, but he looked away, keeping busy washing glasses that were already clean. "All right, Catherine," I said, "you have a deal."

I left Noddy's Diner with a sour feeling in my belly that my brain couldn't identify. I was mad at Noddy for being stupid, but I couldn't place my finger on exactly what he'd done that was stupid. I drove back slow through Notting Hill to Church Street, enjoying the drizzle and the squeak of the wipers on the windshield, watching hunched people under windswept umbrellas dodge each other blindly through wet crowds. I let my thoughts range free among them. They covered just about everything you could imagine except why I had a sour feeling in my belly and exactly how Noddy had been stupid. In the end I decided Catherine Howard was as fascinating as hell and twice as hot, but she was also twice as much trouble, and it made me mad that Noddy couldn't see that. I could, but he couldn't.

That was what I told myself.

I parked and went up to my apartment. I had a duplex on the fifth and sixth floors. Most people didn't know about the fifth, which I used as a den for work and storage. I used the sixth to live in, and that was where people usually found me—if I wanted to be found. I went up there now to prepare an overnight bag. There was a light winking on my phone, telling me there was a message. I listened to it while I cracked a beer and scrambled some eggs. The message was from Russell.

Me and Russell went back a long way. I left LA when I was still in my teens because a film producer, his Italian wife and her Italian family were looking for me, and I wasn't too keen they should find me. In fact, I decided I should move to the farthest place I could find on the planet where they spoke a language similar to my own. I couldn't handle the eternal barbecues in Australia, so I wound up in London and badly in need of bread, as my last job had paid less than I'd hoped. So I'd done some work for some 'gentlemen south of the river' — a cute English term for gangsters. What I didn't realize at the time was that the job included taking the fall for one of those gentlemen. I did six months inside and six months' community service.

That was how I met Russell. He was a mathematician by trade, but he was one of the good guys and did voluntary work on the Community Service Program. I could never understand it, but I guess he thought he saw potential in me, because he took me on as a special project and promised me he would get me on to the straight and narrow path.

I haven't got to the straight and narrow path yet. There always seems to be too much interesting stuff happening on the wide and wending one. But we'd become friends, and I figured I owed him, if only for everything he'd taught me about correctly calculating the odds. His message said, "Liam, it's Russell. I need your help. Well, not me really… It's the nephew of a friend of mine. His uncle's rather unexpectedly dead and…well, it's all a little complicated. I told him you might be able to help him out. Perhaps you could give me a call."

Everybody wanted Liam today. That's the trouble with being useful. I made a mental note to call him when I got back. I ate my eggs, drank my beer, then packed a bag and headed out for Heathrow.

Home of Erotic Romance

Sign up for our newsletter and find out about all our romance book releases, eBook sales and promotions, sneak peeks and FREE romance books!

# About the Author

International, award-winning author David M. Salkin has been entertaining readers since 2005. His brand of thrillers includes military-espionage, horror and crime. Salkin has appeared around the country, including three times as a panelist at New York City's Thrillerfest and also at Books in the Basin, in Midland and Odessa, Texas. Dave enjoys speaking to book clubs and groups about writing, and has appeared on television, radio, and various print media.

David served as an elected official in Freehold Township for twenty-five years (Mayor, Deputy Mayor and Township Committeeman) and was inducted into the New Jersey Elected Officials Hall of Fame in 2019. He is a 1988 graduate of Rutgers College with a BA in English Literature. When not working or writing, Dave prefers to be Scuba diving or traveling. He's a Master Diver, as well as a pretty good chef and wine aficionado. David speaks three languages fluently – English, sarcasm and profanity.

David is an associate member of the Philip A Reynolds Detachment of the Marine Corps League, and board member of the Veterans Community Alliance.

David loves to hear from readers. You can find his contact information, website details and author profile page at https://www.totallybound.com

CPSIA information can be obtained
at www.ICGtesting.com
Printed in the USA
BVHW030949140521
607265BV00007B/212

9 781839 439759